Sheryl

FEELS LIKE HOME

A Haven Cove Novel

Sara Curto

For Justin, Nolan and Abby for being my home.

CONTENTS

Welcome to Haven Cove.

First, thank you for picking up Alice's story. I hope you love it.

I invite you to start receiving your own Love Notes from Haven Cove. A monthly newsletter to inspire your own story of reinvention plus updates on my upcoming novels, exclusive content and my monthly reading recommendations.

To get updates and to receive the Love Note please sign up here: www.saracurto.ca/author.

I'm thrilled to introduce you to this magical world, Sara Curto

SARACURTO

Feels Like Home

a Haven Cove novel

1

ONE

Alice hated the weekend. The long stretches of time with nothing to do made her restless. No social plans reminded her that she had no family or friends which brought on an unwelcome sense of loneliness.

Today was Saturday and Alice was determined to sleep in, especially after the week she just had. She had gone to sleep with dreams of a luxurious morning in bed, waking up around 9:00am and then bringing a coffee and a book to bed. She pictured herself having a long stroll along the beach before hitting up town's main street. Lunch at the diner, a coffee at the café, and finally perusing the shops. It was going to be magnificent.

Unfortunately, Alice's body did not get the memo and woke up at its usual time of 5:30am. After an hour of tossing and turning and trying to fall back asleep, Alice gave up. *It's not a problem*, she thought to herself, *I'll make a coffee and come back to bed. I can easily spend hours here.*

With a coffee, instant, in one hand and the latest bestselling thriller in the other, Alice rested back onto her pillows and began reading. She sighed in content, sure that hours had passed, as she looked at her watch.

Her eyebrows shot up when she saw 7:02am.

With a shake of her head, she grabbed her phone to confirm and saw that, in fact, her watch had been right. She'd been relaxing for only fifteen minutes. With her phone in her hands, she could feel the itch to check her work email. *No work today*, she scolded herself throwing the phone away from her as she got out of bed to get ready for the day.

After a record-breaking ten-minute shower, Alice put her black hair in a ponytail and threw on a pair of shorts and a t-shirt. Heading into the kitchen, Alice was determined to attempt a homemade breakfast. Toast with jam, though she had google, "does jam really expire?" Alice was ready for part two of her day of relaxation.

Alice lived in Haven Cove, a small town of about five thousand people, situated right on the Atlantic Ocean, about an hour from Boston. With a mile long beach and a Main Street to rival any Hallmark movie, Haven Cove was a popular tourist town during the summer.

The summer season was ending and although tourists were still coming, the town was more relaxed while the streets became a bit quieter again. Exactly why Alice moved here.

Two years ago, just after Alice got promoted to her current role as Senior Associate, her loneliness became too much to handle. Long days in the office and nights alone in a city condo left her desperate for a slower pace. When her real estate agent, Raven, brought Alice in their car through the small downtown with a bookstore, a small café, a diner and some high-end souvenir shops, and then past the beach, down a quaint street to Alice's house, she knew it was her house before it was actually hers.

With yellow wooden siding and a bright blue door it was the perfect little bungalow, updated on the inside with a modern kitchen and big bright windows. Alice could instantly picture herself here. Waking up in the cozy bedroom. Walking downtown to grab coffee with friends. Strolling hand in hand with a special gentleman down the beach as the sun rose. Hosting a book club in the beautiful kitchen, filled with the laughter of the people in the community.

She bought it on the spot, excited not only for the house but for the community.

Unfortunately for Alice, it hadn't been that simple. Making friends as an adult was hard. Never mind the fact that's she was shy, hardly ever there and really afraid. What if they ignored her, or hated her, or wanted to run her from town?

She hadn't lost hope, though. She knew one day she would have the courage and the time to actually try to make some friends. One day. Maybe even today.

* * *

Her walk along the beach that she was certain would take her hours, did not. She had planned on taking her time, even sitting to watch the waves kiss the sand. Yes, it was windy, but the real problem was Alice. She felt silly sitting there amongst the early bird families setting up for the day. She wanted to try meditating, but the more Alice tried to clear her mind, the more thoughts would come rushing in, desperate for attention. Her pale legs twitched in annoyance while her bottom slowly dampened until she finally scrapped her walk.

This is not a problem, she assured herself. *I could really go for a proper coffee anyways, especially since its way too early to have lunch.*

The door jingled as Alice walked into the Happiness Café, the local coffee shop. Like most Saturdays, the small café was packed. As Alice waited in line, she plotted out her next move. In the back of the café, there was a lovely fire place with couches to one side, a place to lose yourself in a book. There was also a bar across the window with stools facing the street, front row to people watching.

Alice was chastising herself for not bringing her book when she noticed *him* waiting for his order. She could reach out and touch him that was how close she was. He was the man she looked out for every day while her train passed the beach on her commute to work.

He stood there checking his phone while she drank him in. His brown hair curling around his ears, his Adam's apple bobbing as he swallowed. Suddenly, he looked around him and stopped when he saw her. His eyes startled Alice. She'd only seen them a few times over the years, on the very rare instances they've run into each other, but every time they made her catch her breath. They were a startling blue framed by gloriously long eyelashes. As she gazed into them, she noticed them crinkling as the man smiled at her.

I should say something to him, she told herself, *but what? Something about the coffee? But what would I even say? The weather? No, that's ridiculous. Hello, that's what I'll say!*

As she went to open her mouth, stepping out of line a bit, she was interrupted by a voice calling out, "Colin, here's your latte and Danish. I've also slipped in a little something for Atticus."

The man, Colin, looked away from her to grab his order. "I'm going to blame you when Dr. Spence complains about his weight, Raya." Before he turned to leave, he looked back at Alice, shyly saying, "hi."

"Oh, hi," Alice stammered awkwardly.

"Hi," he said again.

Alice's cheeks reddened and not knowing what to say next, she quickly swiveled around. Embarrassment was not a strong enough word. By the time she was ready to peek at him again, he was already outside, undoing his dog's leash from a pole.

She distracted herself from her humiliating performance by watching the owner of the café. Effervescent was the word that came to mind. Raya Gupta was a tall, vibrant brown woman who sparkled and floated as she talked to customers, took their money and got them food. She was confident in a way that Alice always dreamed of being.

From the little that she knew, purely gathered from eavesdropping while picking up coffee every few months, Raya took over the café five years ago after working in it. It had been owned by a couple for eons before they retired down to Florida.

It was rare to see Raya without a full smile. She truly was lightness personified.

"Buttercup," Raya said happily.

Alice had just walked up to the counter to place her order but looked behind her when Raya said that, assuming she was talking to someone else but there was only a gentleman looking at his phone. She turned back, gesturing to herself. "Me?"

"Sorry, that's my nickname for you!"

"You have a nickname for me?"

"Yep! Buttercup, that's what Anya, my daughter, and I have always called your cottage."

"You know my cottage?"

"Of course, everyone remembers when you bought it. A year ago, right?"

"Two."

"What?"

"Two years ago, I bought it."

"Has it really been that long? Wow, I've been dying to see the inside. I heard the old owners gutted it."

"I guess so. It's really lovely."

"We don't see much of you around here. Do you work in the city or something?"

A clearing throat behind Alice disrupted the conversation. "Raya, stop badgering the lady and get her order. I need my caffeine fix before Aqua fit."

A little old lady was poking her head around the gentleman. Her voice not befitting her tiny stature.

"Yes Dottie," Raya answered while rolling her eyes at Alice, "what'll you have, Buttercup?"

Alice placed her order and went to stand by the counter. She was delighted to have talked to Raya. A real human conversation with someone who lived here. She picked apart the conversation and grew mortified at her awkwardness. She was glad to collect her goodies from the other worker and leave so she could avoid any further humiliation. As she opened the door, she heard from behind her, "don't be a stranger Buttercup." A beaming Raya waving at her.

* * *

Utter failure. That's how Alice felt about herself when, by eleven, she was back in her little cottage. She went to the bookstore but couldn't justify buying a book when she had an entire shelf of them at home that she hadn't even touched.

She meandered through the rest of the little shops, decided against eating at the diner and even tried on some clothes at the vintage clothing store before deciding that she had nowhere to wear cool clothes since she lived in suits.

Alice walked down the street to the Haven Cove Community Center. She knew from her brief visits and from the local newspaper that it was the heart of the community. It had everything a small town might need, a library filled with lovely books and even lovelier librarians. A pool to splash the day away at. Courses to learn and try new things. And then all the events– the Fall Festival, the lighting of the Christmas tree, the Valentine's dance, the summer kickoff event.

Whenever Alice walked in, a mix of peace and cheerfulness wash over her. Today, she perused the bulletin board with all the upcoming events. There was a list of all the fall courses, one of them called Find Your Dream Jo, piqued her interest until she reminded herself that she had a brilliant career, even if it meant she had to work all the time. There were at least a dozen intriguing looking courses; website design, quilting, creative writing, nutrition. Maybe that's what she needed, a new hobby. She took a picture of the schedule for later.

She watched as people walked through the center, laughing with friends or walking solo, but with a purpose. Swimmers filled the pool, despite it being a gorgeous day. The librarian was reading to a group of young kids. The locals chatted away with the community center employees about the upcoming Fall Festival. It was lovely.

Until the realization that she was an outsider looking in hit her like a ton of bricks. It was such a shock to the system that it winded her. She quickly left and made her way home. She didn't always feel like this. In fact, growing up, she was part of a family and even a friend group.

Her parents were only children that moved across

the country from where they grew up. When her grandparents were still alive, they saw them only a few times a year. It was just the three of them, and they were so close. They did everything together. Until that day ten years ago.

Alice had just finished university, graduating top of her class. She was in the final round of interviews with a handful of the top consulting firms in the country. In fact, she was out at lunch with friends, celebrating her final interview with White & Dunn, when she got the call.

"Is this Alice Miller?" a gruff voice sounded over the phone.

"Yes, who is this?"

"Alice, my name is Officer Michael Reilly. Are you the daughter of Christopher and Kristina Miller?"

It was as if Alice's body knew exactly what was coming and she slumped to the ground. Her friends surrounded her and took her to the hospital. They stayed with her, concerned about the glazed look in her eyes, until slowly her brain caught up with the facts.

Car Accident. Drunk Driver. Dead. Both of her parents gone.

Everything had changed that day for Alice Miller. She'd changed.

The grief, anguish and loneliness from that day and all the days since crashed over her suddenly. So, she did what she always did. Switched into autopilot and got ready for work.

It was not until she was on the train that she allowed herself to think of it again. This was why she hated the weekends. Without work to distract her, she remembered what life was like before.

I wasn't always this useless, she reminisced to herself. She'd had friends. In fact, she was Class President in high school, the center of a close-knit group of friends in university. She was sure of herself. Confident even, but something shifted in Alice the day her parents died. It untethered her. She went from being part of a unit to alone. She had to learn how to do everything for herself.

There was only one place where Alice felt some semblance of belonging. Work. And she clung to it like a life raft. Maybe one day she'd find her home again. Not today though.

TWO

"**B**EEP! BEEP! BEEP!"

Alice blearily turned over to snooze her alarm before lying on her back and gazing up at the ceiling. On the weekend, she was up before her normal alarm, but today she struggled to muster the enthusiasm to get out of bed.

This week was what Alice had been working towards for the past ten years, a coveted Partner role. With the promotion announcement this week she had hoped to relax and rejuvenate all weekend but she ended up working late at the office on Saturday after that debacle of a morning. She stayed home yesterday though, in her home office working, but at least not at the office.

Alice tried to avoid looking in the mirror too often. She didn't need the visual reminder of how hard she was working. Today though, she paused as she brushed her teeth to take in the dark circles under her hazel eyes, and her swallow looking skin. Initially, she would wear makeup to mask the signs of exhaustion, but as time went on, makeup proved ineffective in concealing it, prompting her to abandon the practice. With a sigh, Alice pulled her limp, drab black hair into a ponytail. Growing up, her hair was thick and shiny, but she was long overdue for a haircut.

Unfortunately, Alice had taken too long getting ready, so she rushed to catch the train, squeezing through the doors just before they closed. She allowed the briefest of sighs before she powered up to the second floor of the commuter train to grab her normal seat.

Alice got herself set up by the window, took a sip of her to-go instant coffee and looked hungrily out the window as it passed the seaside town.

The beach came into view, the water lapped at the shore calmly. Birds dove into the water to catch their morning breakfast. Alice's heart sank when the beach appeared to be empty. *There they are,* Alice thought to herself in relief as she spotted finally them.

The dog ran to scare away the seagulls dotting the sand. The man, Colin, slowly walked behind him. As the sun crested the horizon, they became silhouetted against its golden light. Suddenly, Colin turned towards the train and raised his hand in a wave. Alice knew he was just waving at the train, but it felt like he was directing it at her. That's the only explanation she could think of for tentatively raising her hand in return before the train curved away.

Alice watched the glimpses of downtown through the trees and houses. She saw the "Happiness Café," sign turn on. She could imagine the smell of the coffee beans as they roasted, the sound of the milk-frother as it steamed and the taste of the perfectly bitter coffee. It was a stark contrast to her quick and easy instant.

Then the train turned away from the town and just like that the best part of Alice's day was done. She slumped in sadness as the anxiety of the big week ahead began to ramp up. It was exhausting being on the partner track at one of the leading consulting firms in the country. It meant Alice woke up with the sun, heading to work before most people in Haven Cove were even awake and then home late at night, the town fast asleep as she stumbled through her cottage straight to bed.

Alice dedicated her weekends to work. Many weeks spent traveling. She was exhausted, but was sure it would be worth it because once she made partner things had to quiet down. That she would finally have time to live her life.

Until then, the morning glimpse of the town slowly waking up would have to do.

* * *

"Good morning, Alice," Alice's Executive Assistant, Miranda, said briskly as she followed Alice into the large office. "You have a full day today."

Alice's blood pressure rose as Miranda walked her through the day's agenda. Meeting after meeting and urgent request after urgent request filled the day. Alice grabbed the hazelnut latte Miranda had ready for her as she took her seat.

Alice's desk groaned under the weight of folders Miranda had laid out on top of all the other paperwork Alice had to complete. *Just one more day,* thought Alice.

"Just one more day, Alice," Miranda said mirroring Alice's thoughts. "Why don't you take a moment to settle in and drink that coffee of yours? I'll make sure all the paperwork is in order and brief you on the way over."

The morning rushed by in a blur of meetings with other partners, Alice attempting to persuade her teams to take more initiative, and struggling to keep the clients' expectations in check. Alice had worked at White & Dunn, one of the top consulting companies in the country since she graduated ten years ago.

While it was challenging keeping up with the hectic pace, Alice knew all the hours and effort would be worth it as she closed in on what she'd been working for all these years–partnership.

Joining White & Dunn had been a unique choice for Alice, considering her degree was in Environmental Science, but Alice had joined to make a difference in the world by working on environmental and sustainability projects for some of the world's biggest organizations. She now project managed global programs, handled budgets in the millions and led hundreds of people.

It was very fulfilling. Most of the time.

"Earth to Alice," an arrogant voice said, interrupting Alice's thoughts, "you reminiscing about how I killed it in the meeting with Solar Corp?"

Alice looked up to see the reflection of Dustin Richards in her office window. Turning around, she replied, "you did well, but why were you in the meeting, anyway? Solar Corp is my client, Dustin."

"Perkins wanted me in there and I don't question

the big guy, but if you want to, go ahead." He strode in and plopped himself down in the guest chair as if he owned the place.

The one downside of White & Dunn was the culture. It was highly competitive and it sometimes felt more like a fraternity than a workplace. The Partners were all men except for one woman, which was why Alice was so hell-bent on getting this promotion. She had stiff competition though, which meant a lot of one-upmanship, backhanded compliments flying around and even some throwing their peers under the bus.

The Senior Associates, what Dustin and Alice were, all had their specialties. Alice's was sustainability and energy-efficiency, Dustin was Oil & Gas. This was why he shouldn't have been at her client's meeting, though she guessed he was trying to diversify his portfolio so it would look good on his partnership resume.

Dustin was a classic frat boy, born connected and had coasted to success because he knew everyone and instinctively knew how to make himself look better than he was. His parents were even friends with Edmund White, the founder.

Pretty much the exact opposite of Alice's upbringing. Her parents were high school sweethearts, married right out of college before having her. They were teachers, and while they had little money, it never seemed to matter. They didn't want Alice to take this job and it pained her that the last conversation they had was about how they wanted more for her than a fancy title and big paycheck.

"Perkins suggested you catch me up on the Solar Corp initiatives as soon as possible so that I can support you," continued Dustin haughtily.

Alice's hackles rose, the initiatives were all going better than expected, why would Alice need support from another Senior Associate? She tried to hide it, not wanting to show a kink in her armor to her competition. "Has Solar Corp approved the cost of you joining the team?"

"I believe we aren't billing them my hours unless we need to. I guess Perkins hasn't included you in the long-term plan?" Dustin asked flippantly.

Flabbergasted, Alice studied Dustin's face. The number one rule of consulting was to bill the clients. To approve a senior associate to work on a project without billing the client was unheard of. It didn't seem to bother Dustin, which worried Alice. "No, not yet. I'll make sure Perkins and I discuss this in our next meeting." Alice wanted to take the Solar Corp file and run, but she knew she had to swallow her pride and look like a team player. "Did you want me to run through it with you now?"

Dustin immediately jumped up. "Me? I need this information as soon as possible, but unfortunately, I have a charity thing tonight. I'll send up a junior around 6:00pm. Thanks Alice, you're a doll."

It was so typical. Dustin would be out schmoozing his way to the top while getting other people like Alice and the junior to do his work. Alice steeled herself. She didn't need him or anyone to excel. Her ticket to that promotion was her hard work and integrity.

"Miranda?"

"Yes, Alice?"

"It looks like another late night. Can you order my usual from Salvo's?"

"May I be honest with you, Alice?" she said in an abnormally motherly tone.

"I guess it depends on what you're going to say," Alice joked.

Miranda closed the door and then sat on the edge of the chair facing Alice. "I'm worried about you."

"Me? You're worried about me? Why?"

"You seem a tad bit overworked. I mean, when was the last time you did anything for fun?"

"On Saturday, I hung out with some friends at a coffee shop," Alice stretched the truth. She went to a coffee shop, and she talked to two people. It wasn't a complete lie.

"Not for long, because I know you worked all weekend. Again."

"It's a big week. I'm not leaving anything up to chance."

"I get that," Miranda leaned back in her chair, "I really do, but it must be lonely. Have you dated anyone since Henry?"

Miranda was referring to Alice's ex-boyfriend. If you could even call him that, he also worked at White & Dunn, and honestly, it was more a relationship of convenience than anything else. He got transferred last year, and it just fizzled out, the two never even breaking up officially. "You know how busy I've been. I haven't had time to meet anyone else. Dating takes a lot of energy, energy that I just don't have."

"That's the other thing. You've lost your luster. You seem so drained all the time."

"I'm just a little tired. The partner announcement is tomorrow, and once I get it things can slow down. I'll maybe even take that vacation I canceled last year."

"And the year before. In fact, I don't think you've ever taken a vacation day or even a sick day in my three years with you. That's not healthy, Alice."

Alice was desperate to snapped at Miranda in defense, but swallowed down her anger. "I do think I'll need a vacation soon. Right now, I can't afford to look weak at all while the decisions are being made."

"Let me help then. This thing with Dustin seems off. Let me help by investigating and getting the inside scoop on it, so you can be prepared.

Alice thought this through. It would be nice to share some of this stress with Miranda, but what if Dustin found out? She didn't want him to think that she was scared. She could do this without Miranda's help. "That's okay, I'll be fine without it."

"Alice," Miranda whispered. "I only want what's best for you. You're too good for this place. Is this all worth it? You don't seem happy."

"You sound like my mother," Alice said absentmindedly.

"Your mother agrees?" Miranda asked, curiously.

Miranda didn't know about Alice's parents. In fact, no one knew except for HR and the senior team. "Honestly, my mom never wanted me to take the job."

Miranda must have noticed how Alice slumped

in her chair as she sat there, silently watching her, patiently waiting for Alice to continue. Alice thought again of how nice it would be to truly let Miranda in on her life, to let her help. It was pointless, though. She would just leave anyway, like everyone else. Alice hardened and layered more bricks on her walls.

"I don't have time to worry about this now. I have less than a day and then I'll know that all the sacrifices I've made these past ten years would have been for a reason. Partnership. That's my only focus right now. So please order my usual from Salvo's and then you can go home."

"Yes, of course, Alice," Miranda reverted to her brisk manner, but as she headed to her desk, Alice caught her look of concern as she picked up the phone.

* * *

"You are my sunshine, my only sunshine…" a quiet voice sang in Alice's ear as a hand lovingly caressed her face. She opened her eyes to a room bathed in golden light from the morning sun and her mother lying in bed beside her.

"Mama."

"I'm here, my sweet girl, always and forever."

"Mama," Alice sobbed out loud as she woke up from her recurring dream. *Not tonight, this can't be happening tonight*, Alice thought.

Since that fateful day that took her parents' lives, Alice has had this recurring dream. While she was asleep, it was peaceful and sweet, but as soon as she woke up, it felt like a nightmare. A stark reminder of what she had lost. That she was all alone. That there was no one coming.

The panic swelled in earnest now, like it did every time she had this dream. A balloon in her chest getting bigger and bigger, threatening to take over her whole body.

Tomorrow was the biggest day of her career. For what, though? She had no one to share the big news with, no one to celebrate her, no one who cared. Alice yearned to have someone to call.

She shook those thoughts away. She didn't need anyone. Having people in her life meant she had people who could leave her life.

She was better off alone. She had her career and in a few brief hours she'll make Partner. All the sacrifices she had made will be worth it.

THREE

"We have a very exciting announcement this morning," Perkins said from the head of the boardroom. As soon as Alice walked in, Miranda had hurriedly told her that this last-minute department meeting had been called. She arrived just as it was starting to find everyone crammed into the room, so she promptly secured a spot in the back.

"As some of you may know, Farley Oil & Gas has been looking to expand and diversify across the energy sector by acquiring an alternative energy organization," Perkins continued, a smug look on his face. "Dustin Richards and I have been working hard on finding the right organization, and this past weekend, we recently closed the deal."

A murmur of excitement and curiosity rippled through the room. A sense of foreboding washed over Alice.

"Dustin has shown incredible commitment and forward-thinking these past few months and all of his, our, hard work paid off this weekend."

There. Right there. That was the moment Alice knew she didn't make partner. She wanted to crumble to the ground, but she stood taller and straighter.

"Farley Oil & Gas acquired Solar Corp as of yesterday evening. They are doing an entire takeover of the organization and merging their teams. Essentially, we'll be handling the closing and restructuring of Solar Corp's product line, locations and employees. This is a deal that's made White & Dunn millions of dollars with millions more to come."

As the room buzzed in excited conversation, Alice caught the eyes of her team and saw that they, too, were concerned and fearful.

"I'd like to officially congratulate Dustin for all of his hard work on closing this deal," he began clapping. "Today really is going to be a day full of celebrations for him."

People left the meeting room after the applause quieted down. Perkins looked throughout the boardroom until he noticed Alice. "Alice, can you meet me in my office in ten minutes?"

The last thing she wanted was to meet with Perkins, instead she desperately wanted to run to the bathroom, no home actually, so she could have a massive cry. A Hail Mary by Dustin that was actually caught, causing her to lose the game she should've won. Now she's going to have to be strong and understanding while Perkins let her down gently and assigned her to the M&A team.

She had been so excited to get away from reporting directly into Perkins, but now it was going to be worse. She would report to Dustin. Maybe she would quit. How could she stay under these circumstances?

Despite the circumstances, she had to stay. 'Closing

and restructuring of Solar Corp's product line' meant dismantling the company, and she refused to let that happen. Solar Corp would have changed the entire energy sector, though she supposed that's why Farley bought them up. Not diversification but annihilation of their competition.

❄ ❄ ❄

"Come in," Perkins said when Alice knocked on his door. She walked in and was surprised that Perkins wasn't alone. Debra from Human Resources was sitting beside him at the small table in his office.

This couldn't be good. Alice quickly scanned through the past few weeks to see if she did something wrong or made a mistake. She came up empty-handed. It must be something, though. Maybe it was to discuss someone on her team. Alice was certain it had to be that because she struggled to think what else it could be.

"What exciting news today," Alice said to butter Perkins up. "I'm so impressed you and Dustin could close such an enormous deal and keep it a secret."

"Well, yes, thank you. Please sit," Perkins instructed, obviously not wanting to engage in conversation. Debra sat there with a strained smile on her face.

Alice took a seat, suddenly nervous and quickly wiped her hands on her skirt before placing them on the table, hoping it was a show of confidence.

"I won't beat around the bush here, Alice. Farley doesn't want to bring over anyone from our Solar Corp team. We have fully resourced all our teams here in Energy with Senior Associates. Which is why I've made the tough decision to eliminate your role here. You've been loyal these past ten years. I thank you for that, but you're no longer needed."

He said that last part as he got out of his chair and walked to the door. Right before he left the room, he turned to her. "Debra will handle the rest. Goodbye Alice."

Growing up, Alice didn't have cable television. Her parents said it was because they didn't believe in it, though she suspected it was more about the cost. What they had was a shelf full of DVDs to watch, including her dad's favorite growing up, Charlie Brown.

She hated the classroom scenes. As an overachiever herself, it bothered her that the teacher's voice was only a "wah wah". She wanted to know what the teacher said. She couldn't understand why it was like that.

Today she understood. That sometimes you simply didn't want to hear what someone was saying. "Wah wah" was all Alice heard coming from Debra's mouth. She had completely zoned out.

Did this just happen? She asked herself, as Debra thrust an envelope into her hands and looked at it in confusion. The feel of something tangible brought her back to Perkins' office and to actual words that Debra said, "Alice? If you have no questions, I'll have Miranda and security escort you out."

Alice walked in a stupor to the door. Outside of it was Miranda with watery eyes and Chuck, the security guard. Alice looked at Debra. "I can't go to my office?"

"I've explained this already Alice," Debra said exasperated, "we'll have your office packed up and sent home. You'll have to leave the building immediately."

Alice was confused. She'd only ever been loyal and trustworthy so why were they treating her like a common criminal? "I don't understand?"

"Miranda?" Debra asked the Executive Assistant, "can you take it from here?"

"It's okay, Alice." Miranda said in her calm and caring voice as she cupped Alice's elbow to guide her towards the elevator.

"What's happening?"

"Perkins came by your office ten minutes ago, told me you're being let go and to pack a box of your key things. Chuck has it now."

Alice looked at Chuck and noticed that he was, in fact, carrying a box. She also noticed all the people watching them. Many with shock on their faces. Pairs and groups gathered together to whisper their guesses.

An awkward elevator ride with Miranda soothingly telling her it would be okay, that Alice would finally get that vacation she had been needing. That maybe she would even have time to do all the things she had been wanting to do.

"I've been wanting partnership, Miranda. Not to lose my job."

"I know dear. You're strong though. You'll bounce back before you know it."

Alice rolled her eyes and looked at Chuck. He stood

in the elevator's corner, obviously very uncomfortable.

"Miranda, I don't need your platitudes. I need answers. What happened?"

The elevator door pinged open. Miranda guided Alice out into the lobby. "I'm not sure, but I can find out for you. I'll help in any way I can."

Alice didn't need her help. She could figure this out herself. She remembered how just this morning her thoughts of no one being there to help her and how suffocating that was. Now though? She was glad.

No one to call to tell this news to. No one to disappoint.

The next thing Alice knew, she was on the front stoop of the building. Miranda looped her laptop bag and purse onto Alice's shoulders, and Chuck placed the box in her hands.

Miranda gave her a quick side hug before she headed back inside, leaving Alice alone outside the building.

Alice squared her shoulders and walked towards the train station as she thought, *No one is coming, but you don't need them.*

FOUR

A lice suddenly found herself getting off the train back in Haven Cove. She struggled to remember how she got there, her mind foggy and disjointed from the unusual daytime train ride. It was barely noon which left her disoriented, as if not familiar with the surroundings.

It was the last week of August and the air of summer coming to an end was all around her. The town was alive with the bustle of tourists. Parents tiredly walking behind their children as they made their way down to the beach. The vacation houses getting ready for their owners to move back in as a large chunk of the town decided to cash in on the summer crowds and escape them all at once.

The colorful gingerbread cottages that lined the streets of Haven Cove usually brought a smile to Alice's face, but not today. Today they seemed to mock her. Each carefully painted facade felt like a jeer at her unemployed stated. As she turned onto her street, her yellow house seemed to laugh the loudest. It's warm color a stark contrast to her gloomy mood.

Her life was supposed to be different here. Better. She had assumed that living here would make her happy. It hadn't.

This was even more obvious when she walked into her house and she noticed how empty it felt. The air inside was stale and a thin layer of dust covered every surface. There was nothing on the walls, no personal touches to suggest a life being lived. The couch looked as if no one had ever sat on it, its cushions stiff and uninviting. The only sign of life in the kitchen was the jar of instant coffee and a pack of protein bars on the counter.

This is embarrassing Alice, she scolded herself. *It's time to get your shit together.*

She dropped her box of shame in the office, not sure how to feel that it was the one room that looked lived in. In her bedroom, she looked for some clothes to lounge in before she gave up and put on her pajamas. They felt like a small comfort, the softness of the fabric a tiny relief against the harshness of reality.

She headed to the kitchen remembering some cleaning products that Raven gave when her when she first moved in as part of a welcome package. With a determined sigh, she started scrubbing. As she worked, she tried to make herself feel hopeful by remembering why she had been so excited to move here. The promise of a fresh start, the allure of community and connection of small-town life and the hope of finding a place to belong.

Tears hit the surface of the counter as she wiped, those dreams felt distant now. Simply moving here hadn't been enough to pull her from her work. Being on the partner track required everything from her and still it wasn't enough. Which meant that now she was left witih no career, no friends and nowhere to belong.

By the time Alice was done, the sun was setting,casting a warm, golden glow through the now-clean windows. She was bone-tired from all the physical work, her muscles aching in a way that felt oddly satisfying. She couldn't stomach another protein bar, so she grabbed a bottle of red wine and promised herself that she would get proper food tomorrow. She flopped down on the couch, the cushions now more welcoming after all that hard work.

She flicked on the TV. There were so many shows and movies that she had been desperate to watch if only she had the time. Now was the time, she guessed, but her "To Watch" list had grown to such epic proportions that she soon gave up trying to choose one from overwhelm.

Instead, Alice ended up on her laptop to update her resume. It may not be the best idea, considering she was halfway through a bottle of wine, but she didn't want to waste a moment. She could edit it tomorrow.

By the time 9:00pm rolled around, Alice had drunk the entire bottle of wine and her resume was done. She could already feel the expansion of time without the pull of her never-ending To Do list. Though her brain and body hadn't quite caught up, occasionally jerking with a "don't I..." or an "oh no..." before remembering she had nothing to do. The sensation was odd and unsettling with its mix of liberation and loss.

Eventually, she gave up and climbed the stairs to bed. The house was quiet, the only sound the creaking of the wodden steps beneath her feet. She paused at the top, looking back down at the darkened living room blow, feeling a strange sense of detachment. Tomorrow she could figure things out. She had to. With a deep breath, she turned and headed to her bedroom, the promise of sleep a small comfort against the vast unknown of her future.

FIVE

Alice struggled to open her swollen eyes as she woke up. Her throat was like sandpaper. She groaned when she saw 5:10am on the clock.

She wasn't all that surprised. This was her wake-up time every morning, after all. To throw on clothes, grab a protein bar and instant coffee before rushing out the door for her train.

She pulled the covers over her head, her bottom lip trembling, fighting another wave of tears, as her brain assaulted her with memories of the day before.

Perkins' face as he looked across the table at her. The quick, "you're no longer needed" before striding out the room as if he didn't just take her career and future and rip it to shreds.

Yesterday morning she was sure she would wake up today as White & Dunn's newest partner. She never expected to be waking up unemployed. Everything she worked for these past ten years. She gave up nights, weekends, her life. All for nothing. They cast her aside like she was trash.

Alice remembered high school and her first heartbreak when her boyfriend dumped her for a cheerleader. She felt the same way. Like she had wasted her time, but more devastatingly like she was worthless and nothing more than something to be cast aside.

Her mom had made it all better. She knew something was up when Alice ran straight to her room without looking at her. She came up, gently knocked on her door before opening it with a whisper, "Aw, honey." Her voice was full of love and concern as she climbed right into bed with Alice. They both called in sick the next day to eat chips, pizza, cake and ice cream while they watched revenge movies. Her mom got her through it.

What I wouldn't do to hear that knock and her voice. How can I get through this without her? Alice thought as her chest tightened and tears pricked at her eyes.

"Nope, not doing that," Alice said aloud as she jumped out of bed, sending a cascade of used tissues all over the floor. Alice worked hard to keep memories of her parents buried deep. If she didn't have work anymore, she would have to find something else.

A relaxing weekday morning, as if Alice was on vacation, not unemployed. Alice had been dreaming of this for the past couple of years. Today was the perfect time to do it. It would be better than Saturday because she wouldn't have thoughts of work distracting her.

She would walk on the beach. Grab a coffee at the Café. Head to the bookstore or library, maybe even both.

Alice pictured herself talking to people, for real this time. She got excited. This could be the start of that new chapter in her life. She looked at the clock again, realizing that if she left soon, she might even see the dog and the man on the beach.

With her head titled to one side, Alice looked critically at what she was wearing. Jeans and a blue tank top that she'd had since college left her wishing that she had more casual clothes. As she brushed her long black hair out, she felt goose pimples on her arms while thinking about actually being on the beach this morning instead of watching it from her train. That brought her back to *who* she might run into on the beach.

Alice didn't know what it was exactly about the man, Colin, that had him circling her thoughts more than she'd like to admit. Sure, he was drop dead gorgeous with those ice-blue eyes, chiseled jawline and eyelashes that went on for days. It was more than that, though. With a sort of quiet confidence he strolled around town, and you could tell he was at peace with himself. Everything about her life was go-go-go, whereas he slowly meandered down the beach tossing sticks for his dog. His life seemed so relaxing in comparison to hers. She had spent the last couple of years yearning to start her mornings that serenely instead of rushing to her train to get into work.

The constant rush and stress had taken a toll on her physical well-being. She often woke up with a knot in her stomach, her heart racing, and a persistent headache. Her days were hectic and barely left her room to take a full breath.

It meant that in the mornings as she passed him and his dog on the beach she clung to a sliver of that peace and it had made her day that little bit more enjoyable. While she was fascinated by him, it was also the life he represented. Hopefully today, she'll get to meet him and grab more than just a sliver of peace.

* * *

A kaleidoscope of butterflies took up residence in Alice's stomach as she made her way down to the beach. What if he wasn't there today? Or worse, what if he was? He probably would be. She saw them most weekday mornings from the train.

As Alice pictured running into him, her brain kicked into overdrive with questions. Did she talk to him? Imagine if he spoke to her? What would she say? Would the dog hate her? How would she introduce herself?

The salty air hit her nose, and she heard the waves crashing against the shore and almost turned around to head back home. She saw the first signs of burnt orange sky as it lightened up the dark blue of the water. Then she felt the physical pull of the beach and all her nerves faded away.

She walked through the tall grasses and stepped onto the sand. There were a few people out walking, but otherwise the summer crowds had not descended yet. She made a beeline to where the water hit the shore. It was almost high tide, which meant that the water was about as high as it would get. The spray from the waves splashed her face, as if welcoming her.

She took a deep breath and watched as the sun inched its way higher and higher. Slowly, the sunlight illuminated the water, allowing her to count the fishing boats that were already out and watch the birds dance in the sky. That coveted, deep sense of peace washed over her.

The sound of a dog's bark awoke her from her trance. Alice turned towards it to see the golden retriever barreling toward her. Her body instinctively dropped to her knees and she began petting it.

"Oh hello," Alice said quietly to it. The dog nuzzled into her and excitedly licked her hands and face before knocking Alice backwards onto the sand.

"Atticus, stop that at once," a stern voice shouted. She looked up, the dog now fully in her lap, panting happily, and saw Colin rushing towards them. Alice had never seen a man as gorgeous as he was. A few inches taller than her, with dark brown hair that was adorably windswept, wearing lightweight jogging pants and a red t-shirt that showed off his toned arms. Sand flew behind him as he ran towards them with the leash in his hands.

He grabbed Atticus by the collar and attached the leash to it, quietly admonishing the dog. "Come here, you rascal." He turned those ice-blue eyes towards Alice. "Oh my, I am so sorry. He really is friendly, and he usually steers clear of the other people and I'm sorry, here let me help you up," he blurted out, clumsily. He reached out his hand to help Alice up.

As Alice slipped her hand into his, she sensed the warmth of his skin as he pulled her to her feet. They held hands for a second and he brushed his thumb over the pad of her thumb, sending a shockwave of electricity up her arm. She jerked her head up in surprise to see the same wide-eyed astonishment reflected at her.

"It's okay," Alice laughed, brushing sand from her legs, "he is so cute and lovely."

"You're really too kind. He was being overly rambunctious and over-friendly, especially for this early in the morning." Atticus had now moved on from Alice and was desperately trying to get free of the leash so he could run off.

"You can let him go. I think there are some birds he needs to scare off. I'm okay really."

"If you're sure," he said as he unleashed Atticus, who immediately dashed off.

The two of them stood there watching the dog live his best dog life for a few minutes before the panic swelled in Alice again. Was it her turn to talk next? What did she say? Or did she leave? Maybe he wanted to spend the morning alone. Probably, she should head home.

"I guess I should..." Alice started, just as he said.

"I've never seen you at the beach..."

"Oh, do you need to leave?" he asked.

Just as Alice replied, "well normally I'm heading into work." This was not going well.

He laughed, "let's start again. Hi, I'm Colin. That's Atticus, my crazy dog. I've seen you around town, but never down here before."

Alice was a little surprised he even remembered her, causing her to pause for longer than was normal. Her body wanted to run, but she just rambled, "I'm Alice. Nice to meet you, Colin. I'm usually working, I'm a bit of a workaholic. Honestly, the only real time I get on the beach is the occasional weekend, but I get to see it from the train," she paused as she gestured to the train that was passing by.

Her train. She squinted into the window of the train car she normally she sat in, curious if someone had taken her seat. It was pointless. All she could see was the sun's reflection. She sighed. It was weird to actually be on the beach instead of dreaming about it while on that train.

That blip of understanding was the only excuse she had for what she came out of her mouth, "and you, too. You and Atticus, I mean. Walking on the beach, I watch you every day as the train goes by." She wished she could swallow those words maybe as the sand swallowed her; they made her sound like an obsessive creep. "I mean, watch you as a curious passenger, not some weird stalker type person..." she trailed off, mortified, looking at anything but his face.

"I've always wondered who was on that train this early in the morning."

"Just people like me, who work all the time and have no life." Alice wanted to die. Why couldn't she stop talking? "But I got fired yesterday, so I guess that won't be me for a while," she laughed awkwardly. It was like she forgot how to be a human and have normal conversations with people. He must be desperate to get as far away from her as possible. Curiosity got the best of her and she peaked at him.

There was no judgement on his kind face, only a look of concern as he said, "I'm sorry to hear that. It must've been a shock."

"You can say that again." Alice couldn't take

standing in one spot anymore worried that her mouth wouldn't stay shut, so she turned and began walking slowly towards Atticus. She felt Colin fall into step beside her. The sun completely rose out of the water, revealing the details of the beach and warming the side of her face.

"I work for myself, which is why I'm not on that train with you but trying to get all of Atticus' energy out of him before sitting at my computer all day, not that you asked or maybe were even wondering." He ran his hand through his hair, seemingly just as self-conscious as she was.

"I did actually. Wonder, I mean. Really, I've thought about it an embarrassing number of times." Now she really *sounded* like she stalked him. She quickly changed tactics, hoping to distract him from her inability to stop humiliating herself. "That must be amazing working for yourself. What kind of work?"

"Boring stuff. Website design, some marketing and copy work. It's great having control of my schedule, but it can be a bit feast or famine, you know?"

She didn't know. It was a feast all the time for her.

"Anyway, what are you going to do with your first day of freedom, Alice?"

"Enjoy the town with nothing hanging over my head. Any recommendations?"

As he talked Alice through some stores and the people she may meet along the way, Alice was reveling because she had just spent the morning walking with the dog and the man on the beach. Mentally, she checked the box in her head. Despite embarrassing herself constantly, it was incredible.

Greeting the sun by walking on the beach with them was as peaceful as she had imagined it would be. It was a delight to her senses with the smell of the salty air, the sound of the water lapping the shore, the birds chirping and the view of the medley of colors as the sun woke up for another day.

They reached the end of the beach and the path that led to downtown. The two looked at each other with a smile. "I'm going to head back now. I need to get to that desk of mine. You have an amazing day, Alice."

"I will. Thank you for letting me crash your morning walk."

"I actually think Atticus crashed yours," he joked. He took a step away from downtown before turning back towards her. "We're here every morning. You're welcome to join us anytime. It would be nice to have someone who can respond to me with more than barks. I mean, if you'd like to."

"I'd like that." A chill ran down Alice's entire body as his face broke out into a grin, showing off a tiny dimple on his cheek. With a nod, Colin and Atticus turned to walk back home.   As Alice walked towards the main street of Haven Cove, a sense of eagerness of what could come filled her. Maybe this new chapter of her life would star more than just her. That maybe letting people in wasn't as scary as she expected.

SIX

The bell above the door of Happiness Café jingled as Alice walked through it. It was much quieter compared to the weekend, which meant that she could really look around and take it in. Straight to the back was a stone fireplace with plush brown leather couches and chairs. A little girl eating breakfast while reading a book, a backpack beside her occupied one of the chairs.

An older couple sat at one of the small tables dotting the café, both reading the paper while munching on a muffin and sipping their coffees. The other tables were ready and waiting for customers to relax in them. She looked over at the large slab of dark wood that was the coffee bar to see the owner behind it taking orders from the people patiently waiting in line.

Alice marveled at the big smile that always seemed to be on her face. Her wavy brown hair swept up into a messy bun, bouncing around as she laughed while frothing some milk. She looked up at the sound of the bell notice Alice.

"Buttercup?" she said in surprise. "What are you doing here? It's not the weekend? Plus, you were just here on Saturday, usually it's months between visits."

Alice could only blink back in response. She didn't

41

even know this woman. How did she know how often she came here? She opened her mouth to say something but couldn't think of anything, so closed it again.

"I've scared you, haven't I? I do that sometimes."

"Sometimes," called out the older gentlemen, affectionately. "Try it's her M.O. Terrify people with all the scoop she hides in that brain of hers."

Alice looked back and forth between them, not sure what she was supposed to do. Was she meant to contribute?

The partner to the gentleman stood up and approached Alice. "I'm sorry, dear, for these heathens. My name is Mary Schmidt, that's my husband Martin over there. It's lovely to meet you after all this time."

"Oh, hello. It's nice to meet you as well."

"And you are," Mary prompted.

"Oh, yes. Alice. I'm Alice."

"What a lovely name."

"Thanks," Alice awkwardly replied, turning to see Raya preparing an order while Mary pulled her over to meet Martin officially.

Alice hadn't interacted with people outside a professional setting in years and was feeling very overwhelmed. She tried to think back to earlier times when it was second nature, but her brain was short-circuiting and was no help at all. Luckily, Martin's curiosity saved her.

"Here, take a seat while you wait," Martin kicked out the chair beside him.

Alice obeyed. "Thanks," she said, again. She placed her hands in her lap, unsure of what she should say.

"We don't see too much of you around town," Martin stated.

"No, I commute to the city and work quite a lot."

"I was glad to never need that train," he continued, "worked for the town, you see. Was the Town Manager before I retired."

"Retired. Pah," Mary laughed. "Alice, he just retired from getting paid. He runs the Recreation Committee, a volunteer position that takes up all his time."

"I do get to have these morning coffees with you though, dear," he placated his wife, putting a hand affectionately atop of hers.

"That you do, and I love them." Mary looked lovingly at her husband, "and I'm not complaining too much. At least you're not under my feet all day!"

The two of them laughed while Alice watched in awe. Mary tapped her on the arm. "I think your drink is ready, dear."

Her drink? She hadn't ordered one, right? Confused, she said goodbye to the two of them and approached the coffee bar. Raya was there holding a cup up. "Hazelnut Latte, right?"

"That's right. How did you know?"

"You order the same thing every time, silly," she chuckled, as if that answered her question.

Alice climbed onto a stool and admired the rose designed in the frothed milk before taking a sip of the coffee and moaning in delight. No one made a better cup of coffee than Raya.

"Alice is your name!" Raya exlaimed. "I've been guessing. I've not been close at all, Stephanie, Jessica, Kathryn, Adrienne. Oh, that one starts with an A, not too far off."

"Umm," Alice muttered, confused that this woman would take the time to brainstorm her name. She was surpised that she wasn't that freaked out, in fact it felt quite nice.

"Mom," said the little girl who suddenly appeared at Alice's elbow. "You're terrifying her with your crazy. Hi Alice, my name is Anya. I'm ten, almost eleven, years old, but very mature for my age. That's Raya, my mom. She's thirty-five years old, but very immature for her age."

Raya stuck her tongue out at her daughter, causing both of them to laugh. Raya handed over a lunch bag. "Here's your lunch, Ms. Annie. It's time to leave. You don't want to be late for camp, my lovely daughter, light of my life."

Anya rolled her eyes, grabbed the bag and stood on her tiptoes, titling her face to accept a quick kiss goodbye on her cheek, before waving to the patrons and rushing out through the doors.

Raya looked at Alice as she made her way back behind the counter. "Alice. You're here. On a Tuesday."

"I am," Alice responded. She debated elaborating but decided against it.

"Seriously though, is everything okay? Like I said, you're never here during the week. You don't have to tell me. I know it's none of my business but..." she rested her chin in her hands as she leaned on the counter.

Alice didn't know what to say and desperately wanted to avoid another spell of verbal diarrhea that inflicted her on the beach with Colin, so she answered with a half-truth, "all good. Just not working today."

"Well, it's my lucky day then that you're here, and it's not too busy. Tell me everything."

"Everything?"

"I've been waiting for two whole years to have an actual conversation with you, so yep. Pretty much everything. Where were you born? What's your middle name? What do you do that takes you away from us? Your hair looks amazing today, how did you get it so shiny? You know just the basics."

Alice's mouth dropped open. People noticed her? Especially someone like Raya, who probably had loads of friends with her gregarious and bubbly personality. "You've wanted to meet me?"

"Of course, haven't you wanted to meet people? Well, maybe you don't since you've haven't actually met anyone."

"How do you know that?"

"It's a small town. We know everything," she said mischievously.

"She wishes," called out Martin.

"You see," she whispered, motioning Alice to come closer. "The walls have ears and eyes."

"I have wanted to meet people," Alice said in response to Raya's question. "My work is pretty hectic, though. It hasn't given me much time to do much of anything."

The bell above the door jingled. Raya looked up to see who entered and immediately began an order. "Well, you must be pretty important." She was barely looking at what her hands were doing as she continued to stare intently at Alice.

"I guess. I work at White & Dunn?"

"Never heard of them. Are they a law firm or something?"

"Or something. They're a consulting firm."

"Consulting? Do they just notice what's going wrong and tell people how to fix it?"

Alice laughed, "essentially actually. We work with companies to help them achieve their strategic growth plans, even to make those plans. We're a mix of fixer, executor, seeker, everything really."

"Sounds impressive. And they're in the city?"

"Right downtown."

Raya paused, holding up a finger at Alice. "Hold that thought." She turned to ring in the order of the new customer while handing them their drink.

Cleaning up as she walked back over, Raya continued her line of questioning. "That must mean you have to commute. That sucks."

"It wasn't so bad."

"Wasn't?"

"Wasn't," Alice replied dejectedly. "I actually got laid off yesterday."

"That's great!"

"What?"

"Oh, I mean, that's horrible for you. They're idiots for laying someone as important as you off."

"You don't even know me."

"I know enough that you're amazing. At least the version I've created of you in my head."

"You've thought of me?"

"Way too much. I'm a divorced single mother in a small town where it's either old fogies or young families. It's slim pickings out there for friends! It's lonely."

"You want to be friends with me?" Alice asked in disbelief.

"Yes, with a capital YES. Unless I've embarrassed you or turned you off. I do that sometimes. I know and remember too much. According to my ex-husband, I was 'too familiar, too quick.'"

"No," Alice responded and then noticed Raya's face fall. "No, you haven't turned me off. Yes, to being friends. Though I bet I'm nothing compared to the version of me you've invented, you'll probably be running for the hills before you know it."

Alice paused. She couldn't believe this was happening. She'd been so afraid of meeting new people, but was it really as easy as this? Was this a trap?

She had to ask. "This isn't a trick, is it? Some 'new girl' hazing ritual that I'm being put through?"

"What do you mean?"

"I walk in here on a Tuesday and suddenly I have a

new friend? It seems too easy."

"Easy? It feels like *'finally!'* To me. I've been impatiently waiting for you to come in on a day that's quiet. I've been too shy to say much of anything. The look of abject terror on your face when I called you Buttercup on Saturday made me think I had scared you off for good."

Alice couldn't remember a better morning than this one. Taste testing Raya's delicious pastries, sampling some of her latte inventions and having a normal conversation with Raya. She had been nervous that she had lost her ability to carry on a conversation about something that didn't have to do with work, but Raya was so warm and friendly that Alice felt right at home. Raya, with her infectious enthusiasm, introduced Alice to the locals, who warmly welcomed her to the town. She couldn't remember a time where she laughed so hard as Raya shared stories about every customer. The morning was a glimpse of what life in Haven Cove, with its meaningful and genuine human connections, could look like. Alice couldn't help but feel a sense of excitement about what the future could hold.

SEVEN

If only the blissful hope of yesterday carried through. Alice woke up with a headache, feeling as if she had a hangover again, but this time it was from the shame of vulnerability rather than alcohol. She had spent hours analyzing her conversations with Colin and Raya, wincing with embarrassment at how awkward she was. It didn't help that the disgrace of being let go hit Alice like a ton of bricks.

No, like a Mack truck, Alice corrected her inner monologue. It was all she could do to move from her bed to her couch, where she preceded to spend the morning making her way through a bag of chips, a box of tissues and a season of Love Island, as per Raya's insistence.

She had briefly considered heading down to the beach and then over to the café, but had dismissed it immediately. Years of only participating in professional conversations left Alice unsure and awkward, second guessing every word that she had uttered the morning before. She didn't think she could show her face again. Thoughts of Colin and Raya sharing stories about the weird woman living in the Buttercup cottage swirled in her head.

It was hard enough when she had a job, but now

that she had this enormous gaping hole in her life, what would she talk about? How could she meet people when she had no clue how to explain her work situation when they invariably asked her "now what is it you do?" Yesterday showed that she either spewed too much information or completely clammed up.

Once the season was done, she mustered the energy for a shower. Showers were truly magical things. It was amazing how it cleansed the body and the soul. Alice came out feeling like a new person. So much so that she decided it was a great time to practice explaining the lay off in the mirror afterwards.

"I'm in between jobs," she said to her reflection. Blech.

"I'm a *very important person* with a *very important job* that I just don't have anymore." Nope.

"I was fired." Next.

"My boss was an asshole and didn't like me since I was a woman, so he fired me." Too angry.

"I don't know what I do anymore. I don't even know who I am anymore. Who am I without a job?" This must've hit too close to home, as Alice noticed the tears leaking from her reflection's eyes before she felt the wetness on her cheeks.

She was desperate to put on her grubby pajamas and go straight back to bed, but instead got dressed and went into her home office. The only room in her house that she had fully set up. She happily remembered when she bought her desk and situated it in front of the window. It faced the ocean and though it wasn't ocean front by any means, you could just see the sparkling water in between the roofs of the houses.

Alice had pictured herself up here, gazing out the window while she solved the world's problems. She hoped to work from home a few days a month, or would stop going into the office on the weekend. It didn't happen, though. She only worked in there on Sundays, and really only because she was too embarrassed to go into the office since that practically shouted that she didn't have family obligations or a life to keep her busy on a Sunday. When she was in here, she would get so engrossed in work she barely looked out the window.

She turned her computer on and checked her personal email, the one she barely used anymore, but now her only one. Besides the usual email subscriptions, there were actual emails in there.

She saw one from Linda, the only other female partner. With a flicker of hope maybe Linda had good news for her, she quickly opened it but deflated,

Alice,

I wanted to reach out personally. Perkins created a strong business case for the elimination of you and a few key members of your team. While I hoped I could've made a home for you on my team, it was just not possible. If you ever need a reference, I would be happy to provide one.

Take Care,

Linda

Alice clenched her fists in anger. Linda should've been more supportive of her. She knew there were spots she could've filled on the Partner's team. Even another department or office she could have worked for.

Alice was sure it was the fact that she was a woman. That company was a bunch of misogynistic, stuck in the Middle Ages twats. If she was a man, she bet they would've moved her to a different team, heck, even a different office like they did Aaron.

Aaron, her ex, had his entire department shut down on the East Coast and they didn't fire him. They moved him to the Chicago office. Why her? Maybe it had nothing to do with her being a woman. Maybe she simply wasn't good at her job.

Feeling extra sorry for herself, Alice continued to check her emails and found multiple ones from Miranda, the most recent ones with ALL CAPS subject lines like, "OPEN THIS" and "URGENT READ IMMEDIATELY". She clicked on one sent just a few minutes ago.

Alice, answer your bloody phone…

Alice remembered she threw her phone in the box with all her office stuff and tossed the box in here on Monday. She rifled through it and found her dead phone. She found her charger and plugged it in and, while waiting, went back to her email.

…you only have a few more days to sign back that resignation letter. If you don't, you'll lose your severance package.

What letter? Alice had a faint memory of an envelope being thrust into her hands and Debra from Human Resources going over something in the meeting.

As soon as her phone had enough power, Alice turned it on. She jumped when it immediately began to vibrate and beep with all the notifications.

Many were from Miranda. And then there were the ones from her team.

I'm so sorry...

Heard the news, am completely shocked...

I got laid off too. Can we talk?

What happened?...

The phone ringing in her hands startled her; the face lighting up with MIRANDA.

"Hello?" Alice turned on the speakerphone and placed it on her desk as she rifled through her box, looking for the envelope.

"Oh thank the lord, it's about time you picked up this phone."

"I forgot about it; it was dead."

"Never mind that. Have you even looked at the letter, Alice?"

All Alice could find were papers. Pausing, she wondered if she had even put the envelope in the box. Did she put it somewhere else? "I'm just looking for it now. I'm sorry I've been feeling a little..." her voice broke.

"I know, hon, it's been a complete shock over here. The situation has completely dumbfounded people here. If they could let *you* go, then no one is safe. But this is important," she continued. "You have until next Tuesday to sign back the letter or you risk losing your severance."

"What day is it today?"

"Thursday."

"Okay, I'll find it and sign it today." Alice stepped away from the box, thinking she had time.

"No!" Miranda whisper screamed into the phone, "don't sign it back yet. I've heard through the grapevine that they're expecting you to ask for more."

"Oh," Alice said in response.

"What you need is a lawyer."

"A lawyer?"

"Yes, I can find you one?"

Alice thought this through. It would make her life easier to have Miranda find her a lawyer. But she didn't like the idea of waiting on Miranda to do it, especially since time was of the essence. Besides, wouldn't it be weird if Miranda helped her with this?

"I don't know. It isn't a conflict of interest for you to do this?"

"Alice, I can help you. Please let me help you. It's the least I can do."

Something occurred to Alice, "wait a second. You didn't get laid off too, did you?" Normally the assistant followed the Senior Associate, so wouldn't that mean that Miranda got laid off too?

"Um, no I didn't. I've been reassigned." Miranda said dejectedly.

"Reassigned? To who?"

There was a pause on the other end.

"Miranda, to who?"

"Dustin." Miranda admitted with a guilty sigh.

"Apparently, they've moved his old EA. They made some excuse for continuity with Solar Corp."

It was as if Alice had been punched. Miranda was now working for the person who ruined her career. "Wow," she said.

"I know, it's the worst. He's the worst. That's why I want to make sure you get a good severance. I feel so guilty about it all."

Alice took a deep breath, swallowing her hurt. She should've expected this. She couldn't count on anyone. "You know what Miranda, it's fine. I don't need your help with a lawyer, I'll find my own. In fact, I think it's best we don't stay in touch. Thanks for everything."

"Alice..."

She never heard what Miranda was going to say. Alice hung up.

EIGHT

The next morning was better. Kind of. Alice woke up angry, which she reasoned was probably better than waking up miserable. She had another pounding headache and her jaw was sore from clenching. In fact, she could see nail marks on the palms of her hands. She must've been clenching her fists in her sleep.

As soon as she hung up on Miranda, Alice had found the termination letter that Miranda had been talking about. Alice didn't want to admit it, but her ex-Executive Assistant was right. Bare minimum severance. Alice was stunned, though she couldn't understand why she had expected them to treat her better during the layoff than they had during her employment.

It sent her into a spiral. The betrayal and the obvious lack of care. That she gave White & Dunn everything and they tossed her aside like rubbish.

She had to find a lawyer. Today. The problem was Alice had no idea where to look. All the lawyers she knew either worked for White & Dunn or were their clients. She had spent the rest of yesterday googling lawyers but ended up more confused than ever. She even reached out to some of her team that got laid off too but hadn't gotten any names yet.

Thinking about her team reminded Alice of all the texts and emails she got from her supposed peers and colleagues. Honestly, she had expected more indignant responses, emails of support and solidarity. Instead, it was as if they had come upon a large car accident and pulled over to find out more and watch her get dragged from the wreckage. Just another reminder that they were not her friends, only her team members and other people she worked with. *Ex-team members and people she had worked with*, she corrected herself.

A wave of loneliness so powerful swept over Alice that she had to sit down. She sat there in a daze as the realization that all her energy building relationships had essentially been wasted, that they only saw her as someone they worked for, not someone they really cared about.

All at once all her anger and motivation drained from her and Alice was overtaken by the need to disappear. She laid down on the couch and pulled a blanket over her head as she curled into a fetal position.

* * *

KNOCK KNOCK, "Hello?! Alice?!"

Alice must've dozed off as someone shouting at the door startled her awake.

KNOCK KNOCK, "Alice! It's me Raya, open up!"

"Raya?" Why would Raya be here? Alice could feel her swollen eyes, her bedhead and was too embarrassed to open the door. Maybe if she was quiet, Raya would eventually give up.

"Alice, open up! If you don't, I'm going to call the fire department to break down your door. Your car is here and you're not around town, so I know you're in there!"

In defeat, Alice went to open the door. As soon as she opened it, Raya took one look at her and pulled her into a hug. "Dear Alice, I thought you might be a little sad. It's okay. Let it all out."

Alice resisted and tried to wriggle out of Raya's clutches. "I'm okay, I really am."

Raya must have worked out, for she was stronger than Alice would have thought, as she had a vice-like grip on her. Her hands caressed the ends of Alice's dark brown hair and she whispered in her ear, "you don't seem like it. It's really okay to let it all out. It'll feel so much better."

Alice debated it. It would feel nice to just lean into Raya's arms and have a good cry. Their friendship was still so new, if you could even call it a friendship. In Alice's experience, friends got sick of sadness and tears pretty quickly. What if she let it all out and it ended up just scaring her one chance at a friend away? She gave up fighting the hug.

Raya began rubbing Alice's back. "It's okay. I'm here now. I'll take care of you."

Alice couldn't fight the tears anymore. She'd longed to hear those words for years, and as soon as Raya uttered them, Alice felt the tidal wave of emotion release from her. She sobbed in this practical stranger's arms while standing in the open doorway.

Eventually, Alice cried out all of her tears and disentangled herself from Raya's embrace. "Oh god, I'm so sorry. How embarrassing. Look at your sweater, it's soaked through. I'm such a mess."

"Of course, you're a mess." Raya swept Alice into the house and guided her back onto her couch. "Now you sit here and let me take care of you."

Alice immediately stood up to protest the help, but Raya gently pushed her back down and tsked at her. "You're not great at letting others care for you, are you, Alice?"

It was difficult to sit there. Alice's legs twitched as she watched Raya bound into the kitchen. She realized she hadn't really had anyone looking out for her for a really long time and it was more difficult than she expected to let someone do it.

Raya was a tornado of energy, bouncing into the kitchen, opening drawers and cupboards. "Instant, really Alice? Okay then, tea it is," she said, grabbing a dusty box of tea. She brought over two mugs and a box of cookies that she brought herself and sat down beside Alice.

"Tell me everything."

"There isn't much to tell. I worked for a company for ten years, sacrificed so much so that I could become a partner. And the day I was supposed to get the promotion, I got laid off instead."

"Bugger, that's messed up." Raya, for once, was speechless.

"Right? What do I do now? I'll have to start over."

"As someone who did have to start over, it was the

hardest thing I ever did. Moving here with Anya as a baby, taking a job in the café and then buying it once the owners retired. There were many nights I thought it would never get better. But you know what?"

Alice hadn't known about the struggle Raya went through. She looked at her and saw this blissfully happy woman and had assumed that she hadn't had to work for it. "What?" Alice asked, rapt with attention.

"I was not in a good relationship with my ex, which meant that the lowest of the lows of starting over were still better than the highs with him. Starting over was the best decision I ever made."

"But you got to make that decision. It was made for me." Alice rushed to continued, "not to even compare, it feels silly honestly. You started over with a baby. The only person I need to worry about is myself."

"It could suck for me AND for you. Life isn't a competition."

Raya picked up the empty mugs and cookie box and brought them into the kitchen. "Go get dressed and I'll make you something more substantial to eat than cookies. Then we'll make a plan."

"What about the café?"

"Hector and Susan are there. On Friday mornings, the 'New Moms Corner' from the community center take over. They can handle it."

"But why? Why are you here?"

"We're friends now, right? Please say we are. I've been desperate for a real true-blue friend," Raya pleaded.

SARACURTO

Alice wasn't used to someone wanting to be her friend. Were they friends? This past hour, she had sobbed, gotten her tears and snot all over Raya's sweater. She complained about her work, even implying that her situation was just as bad as Raya's. Why wasn't Raya running for the hills?

"You still want to be friends with me?"

Raya paused her wiping down the counter to look at Alice. "Maybe they were right."

"Who?"

"Red & Finished."

"Who?"

"You know, your company?"

"White & Dunn?"

"Yes, exactly what I said. I think that maybe they're right."

"Right about what?"

"Maybe you aren't as smart as you appear. I want to be your friend. I've embarrassingly told you until I'm blue in the face. While I guess it would be red in the face from the mortification of practically begging for a friend. I show up on a Friday. You ruin my best sweater with your tears. I try to take care of you. And you're questioning it all? Silly."

Alice got teary during Raya's tirade. "Thank You," was the only response that seemed right.

"You're welcome. I am the best, aren't I? Now scoot. We have a plan to make."

61

NINE

"Thomas!" Raya shouted.

It was a couple of hours later as the two were back lounging on the couch. Alice couldn't remember being more content at home. Raya was serious about taking care of her. She had made the two of them lunch, the most delicious omelet Alice had ever had. Then Alice watched as Raya cleaned up the kitchen from the breakfast counter. Alice had tried to help, but Raya flat out refused.

They had made their way back over to the couch and were finishing the cookies that Raya had brought as Alice told her she needed to find a lawyer and quick. When suddenly Raya shouted a name in her face.

"Who's Thomas? Is he a lawyer?"

"He's the Head of the Community Center. He has a more official title than that but I'm not sure exactly what it is, but he essentially runs the place."

"Oh," Alice replied disappointedly. She needed a lawyer, not someone who set up pickleball games for a living.

"But he *was* a lawyer, a big city lawyer who gave it all up for the community center."

Well, that was an interesting turn, though if he gave

it all up, would he even be able to help?

Raya answered Alice's unspoken question. "I know he can help because he helped Colin years ago when he was laid off!"

Alice couldn't help the little shiver that ran down her spine at the mentioning of Colin. *Focus,* she scolded herself. "Do you think he would help me? He doesn't even know me."

"Of course! Thomas helps everyone, that's just who he is."

Alice found it hard to believe that someone she didn't know would help her. It made no sense. She said as much to Raya.

"I keep forgetting that even though you've lived here for two years, you haven't exactly *lived* here, if you know what I mean. You're used to the city where people are really just looking out for themselves, where there is no community. Haven Cove is nothing like that. Here, we take care of one another. We care about our neighbors and their wellbeing. We do what it takes to make sure everyone has what they need. Thomas, more than anyone, feels it is his personal responsibility to take care of everyone here in the town."

Alice sighed, "I know. It's why I wanted to live here. I feel like a fraud though. I've lived here for two years and have done nothing to become part of this community. It's horrible to start off by depending on someone going out of their way for me, you know?"

"You'll just have to give back then."

Alice could get behind that. Giving back to the community as payback for the help Thomas would give her. She grabbed her notebook and opened up to her To Do list. "Lawyer, check." Alice checked the box next to "lawyer" and created a new item "talk to Thomas today".

"You like To Do lists?"

"I love them. They help me be really efficient and keep me on track."

"Hmm," Raya furrowed her brow in obvious concentration.

"What?"

"I have an idea..." she trailed off. Her fingers moving in the air as the idea took shape in her head.

"Okay," Alice said tentatively, wondering what the idea could be and what it would entail.

"At the café the other day, you mentioned that you've been wanting to do more things in your life, right?"

"Yes..."

"And just now, you were saying you're not really a part of this community yet, but I'm assuming you want to be right?

"Right."

"The only thing that stopped you the last couple of years was that you didn't have the time, right?"

"Right."

"Okay, this is good. So good. You should write a To Do list!"

"I am writing a To Do list."

"Have you ever seen that movie the Bucket

List?" Raya asked, seemingly changing the subject completely.

Alice knew the name sounded familiar and then remembered watching it with her parents. They had actually gone to the movie theater since her dad loved Jack Nicholson. "The movie about two old guys who write a list of things they want to do before they die?"

"That's the one!"

Alice remembered coming home from that night and her dad immediately wrote out his own bucket list. Along with the typical things like "see the Eiffel Tower" and "sky dive," he had also included "walk my Alice down the aisle" and "retire early" on his list. He did sky dive, but he thought he had plenty of time to finish the list. He didn't realize he only had five years.

"I don't want to sky dive," Alice mumbled quietly.

"No, not like that kind of bucket list. More of 'become part of Haven Cove bucket list' or something like that. The title needs to be workshopped."

Alice considered the idea. "The thing is Raya, I'll be really busy looking for a new job. I don't know how much time I'll have."

"I knew you would say that, okay hear me out." Raya turned in her seat to face Alice. "You've lived here for two years and have done almost nothing, right? On Wednesday, you were lit up talking and meeting with the townsfolk, your eyes brightening when people mentioned the different activities and such that they were doing. I know we're barely friends, but I think you want more than a job taking up your life."

Did she? Alice had only known work for so long that

it was hard to picture spending time on hobbies and such. But she had moved here for a reason and that was to have a life that was more than work. "I think I do," Alice agreed quietly.

"I get you need to find a new job, but maybe you could look for a new job AND do a Haven Cove Adventures List? Title tbd."

Alice knew she needed something to focus on other than her future. Raya was right. She had been putting off getting more involved with the community, finding friends, and having fun. It was possible to make it work.

"Okay, let's do it," Alice said.

"Yes!" Raya jumped into Alice's lap in her excitement. "This is going to be amazing. And yes, I know I'm way too invested in this and in you, considering I really just met you, but I am."

"Thank God you are. I would've probably continued to be miserable if it weren't for you," Alice turned to a new page in her journal and wrote at the top; "Alice's List of Adventures."

"Ooh, I like that name."

"Okay, what should I put on this list?" Alice asked. She chewed on her pen as she came up with ideas of things she wanted to try.

"Kiss someone," Raya giggled, "that should go at the top."

Alice blushed. Colin was the first person that popped into her head. While she was ready to let Raya in, she wasn't ready to tell her friend about the crush she had on him. "I was thinking more like 'sign up for course at Community Center.'"

"That's a good one, but I saw you go all googly eyed over a certain gentleman last weekend."

Alice stared intently at the page, biting her lip to stop herself from smiling. "Fine, I'll write 'kiss someone down,' but no names!"

Raya put her hands up in defeat.

"This house needs work," Raya said delicately. "This looks like a sparse Airbnb, actually worse because at least those are typically decorated nicely. It looks like no one actually lives here."

Alice took in her living room with only a couch, TV and coffee table, the empty dining room and the empty walls and knew that Raya had a point. So, she added that to the list.

"I want to read more. My bookshelves are full of books, but I never get the time or have the energy to actually read them. I want to read a book a week."

"That's perfect because we need some actual community things on this list and I was going to suggest that you join our book club. It meets next Wednesday."

A book club? Alice wasn't so sure about that. The thought of being in a room full of local women made her knees tremble. She reminded herself that was kind of the point. With a deep breath and a smile, she added it to the list.

Over the next hour, Alice and Raya brainstormed. Raya's ideas got grander and grander as the time went on; "A Safari!" "Get married!" "Open a store next to the café!" but they ended up creating a list that had Alice a mix of nauseous and invigorated, which Raya insisted meant it was the best list.

Alice couldn't wait to get started.

Alice's List of Adventures

- Sign up for Course at the Community Center
- Kiss Someone
- Make house look like a home
- Read a book a week
- Join Bookclub
- Go for drinks
- Dance with someone at Harvest Dance
- Take an exercise class
- Have a party
- Swim in the ocean

TEN

Alice walked nervously into the community center with her termination letter safely tucked into her purse. She had tried to call ahead but wasn't able to get Thomas on the phone, so she mustered up the courage and came down, hoping to catch him before he went home for the weekend.

The sun shone through the glass roof, causing the main lobby to glow. Alice made her way past the pool with its swimmers travelling up and down the length of the pool looking like a well-oiled machine. She passed a group of children all lined up in pairs, holding hands with sticky faces and big eyes looking around them as they walked towards the library, Alice assumed for a Story-time.

"Hi, I can help you," greeted a young woman with a friendly smile once Alice had approached the reception desk.

"Hello, I'm actually looking for Thomas? I was wondering if he was in by chance?"

"I can certainly check for you. Who shall I say is here for him?"

"Oh, I don't think he'll know me, but it's Alice Miller."

"I'll call his office," the woman said, picking up the phone. As she waited for him to answer, she asked, "you live in the yellow cottage right?"

Alice smiled. It was true what Raya pointed out, that in a small town, you could not go unnoticed. Everyone knew of her, even if they didn't know her. Yet.

"He'll see you. Head down that hallway there, his is the last office on the right."

As Alice walked down the hall, her nerves intensified with each step. She was sure he would think she was crazy. She didn't even know him and suddenly she was going to ask him to do this big favor for her? Her body screamed at her to turn around but with the excitement of her both her To Do lists fresh on her mind, she proceeded down to his office.

As she stressed about whether to knock or push the door ajar, it opened to reveal a distinguished looking gentleman with dark skin, darker eyes and salt and pepper hair.

"You must be Alice. Come in and have a seat."

Although his office was small and utilitarian, with a plain, clean desk and a couple of plastic chairs, it was also very warm and welcoming. The walls were full of pictures showcasing the town at the many events that the community center held. Alice sat down in a chair and preceded to fidget with the envelope in her hand, unsure if she should start or wait for him. She was grateful that Thomas spoke first.

"It's so nice to meet you, Alice. Raya called to alert me that you would be coming. She mentioned something about, and I quote 'some evil company was trying to take advantage of our Alice and could you defend her'," Thomas chuckled, "She's a firecracker, that one. Now why don't you tell me what she means and how I can help you?"

Alice explained the situation to Thomas and that Raya remembered Thomas helping Colin when she was at a loss for where to find a lawyer.

"Have you met Colin then?"

"Only once, really, at the beach. The other day, actually."

"He and Atticus love that beach. Now why don't I look at that letter of yours?"

"Yes, I've also brought along my most recent employment contract from when I got promoted a couple of years ago. I wasn't sure exactly what you needed. Honestly, I'm just glad I had a little ink left in my printer," Alice was rambling now. "When you have a job, there are so many little things that you become so used to that I've had to completely rethink. Like printing things."

Alice kept her mouth shut once Thomas starting reading through the documents, a pair of reading glass perched on the edge of his nose. He took his time, making notes on a yellow notepad beside him.

"Okay Alice, I've got good news. I can help you. I don't want to make any promises, but I think doubling this package is very reasonable to expect."

"Double? Are you sure? That would be amazing."

"I think I can get them around. Lucky for you, I spent years on the other side fighting for the corporations, which means I know all their tricks.

While I've retired from being a lawyer, I've kept my license active and am always willing to help someone from the town, like you, when they need it."

Delighted that he included her as part of Haven Cove, his kindness also blew her away. "You're a godsend. How does payment work?"

"Payment? I don't want payment, don't need it."

"I have to pay. You'll be securing me a lot of money. I must pay you."

"When it comes to those who require my services and insist on compensation, my usual suggestion is to make a donation to the Community Center, as it is always in need."

"Of course, I'll definitely do that."

"I will notify White & Dunn today that we are working on a response to extend our deadline. Nevertheless, I will forward it to you on Monday. How does that arrangement sound?"

"Like the best news I could've hoped for." Gratitude flooded Alice. At White & Dunn, no one ever did things out of the goodness of their heart. Bill, bill, bill was the motto. If you so much as thought of a client in the shower, you were to bill them those thirty seconds.

She gathered her things, but Thomas interrupted her. "Great. Now before you go, Alice, I'm curious. What will you do next?"

"Honestly? I don't know. I may want to go to another consulting firm or maybe with a client in the Alternative Energy sector. Though I am also wondering if I should consider doing something else."

Alice did not know where that came from. She hadn't wondered about a new career at all. She had been assuming that she would go right back into the same type of work. But as soon as she said the words, she knew them to be true. That it would be interesting to see if there was something else out there for her.

"As someone who walked away from a similar career, you'll be surprised to know how many skills you have that will be very useful in another field."

"Hmm, I hadn't really thought about that. I might want to think about a new career. I don't know where I would even get started."

"Well, there is a course here."

"Yes, I saw that this past weekend, something about Dream Jobs?"

"Yes, Find Your Dream Job. It's facilitated by a local Career Coach, Claire Hudson. It starts next week and goes every Tuesday afternoon for twelve weeks. You should register."

Twelve weeks? That was a long time to sit on the sidelines. It may even be a waste of time, too. She was sure she'd probably just end up in a similar role. It was something she was great at. Plus, she'd heard about the leadership coaches at White & Dunn that were for the partners. They asked a lot of questions. She hated being asked questions she didn't know the answer to. Honestly, she didn't know if she needed any help. There must be companies out there that wanted to hire her.

Though thinking about it, she had rushed into a career in consulting. Plus, she did put a course on "Alice's List of Adventures," it could be an easy way to check that box plus she was sure it could be helpful in her job search and it would be a bonus if anything else came out of it.

"You're right, I should sign up for that." Alice got up from her seat. "I will, right now, actually." She thrust her hand out across the desk. "Thomas, I don't think I can express just how grateful I am. You have been way more help than I could've ever hoped for."

Thomas' eyes crinkled as he shook her hand. "Welcome to the community, Alice."

ELEVEN

Alice's eyes fluttered open as she slowly awoke to the sounds of the birds chirping outside her window. She remained still in her bed as it dawned on her that it was Tuesday. It was crazy to think that exactly one week ago she struggled to wake up. The exhaustion and nervousness she felt about the announcement happening that day seemed like years ago.

So much had happened in just seven days. She got laid off. She met a new friend. She signed up for a course. She wrote a list of adventures for her to complete. Alice could never have expected this being her reality.

As she laid there, feeling the warmth of her sheets under her, she tried to identify that feeling she woke up with. She wasn't bone-tired. In fact, she was completely rested.

But there was a buzzing restlessness that she felt as well. She wasn't used to doing nothing and too much time alone let idle thoughts take up more room than she wanted. As she fell asleep last night, Alice decided that today was going to be her Day One. The start of something new.

She knew exactly how she wanted to start, greeting

the sun as it rose over the water. Throwing on some clothes, and grabbing a blanket, she headed down to the beach.

Inhaling the salty air, she sighed contently as her feet sank into the sand. The sky was just beginning to lighten, and she had the beach to herself. All the tourists were officially gone for the season. Alice approached the shore, laid out the blanket, and sat in silence, taking it all in.

It was still almost pitch black, but the waves reflected the sky as it lightened. It turned purple, then pink and peach. She breathed deeply as she was overcome with a sense of peace. It wasn't a familiar feeling. Her fingers sat quietly on her lap, not itching for her phone. Her mind focused on the beauty in front of her instead of a never ending To Do list.

Just as the sun peeped out over the water, she heard the sound she didn't realize she was waiting for. The sound of paws and boots as they made their way across the sand. She looked up with a smile just as Atticus bounded onto the blanket, spraying sand all over her.

"Atticus! Not again." Colin yelled, exasperated.

Alice laughed, "it's okay! Honestly, it's nice that someone is this excited to see me."

"He certainly seems to be quite enamored with you. He spent the rest of last week running up and down the beach as if he was looking for someone. I guess all it took was one walk for him to fall head over heels in love with you." Colin paused, the tips of his ears reddening. He hurried over, stretching his arm out to help her up.

It was as if the two had an unspoken agreement

that Alice would walk with them. They each grabbed an end of the blanket to fold it up. As they came together to gather the end pieces, their fingers grazed and a warm buzzing ran through her fingers, right up to her shoulder. As she looked at him, she couldn't help but think that his eyes were the type that people wrote love songs about.

Atticus began jumping up at them, as if jealous that they would ignore him for even a second. Alice watched as Colin calmed his dog down. "There, there, boy. We didn't forget you." He picked up a stick and threw it down the beach for the golden retriever.

They steered closer to the water and looked for the shells that were left behind by the tide. Alice picked one up that looked like a curled into itself, a perfect pink specimen. The sand under her feet, the shell in her hand, the man walking beside her. "I love it here," she sighed.

"Me too, moved here for this very beach," Colin said, pausing to admire the watercolor splashes of color that the sun painted in the sky. Alice's life was spent rushing all day long, but she was learning from this thoughtful man that sometimes the best thing to do was to stop and smell the roses.

"I did too. When did you move here?"

"About the same time as Raya, ten years ago. I'm the navy-blue house with a light blue door."

All the houses in Haven Cove were painted in vibrant or Easter egg colors. Gingerbread houses were the name. Every house was different. Which was why that description made complete sense and Alice immediately knew which house was his. It was only a block away from her house. "That's a big house for just the two of you."

"It could be. Actually, I didn't have Atticus when I bought the house. Got him six years ago."

Alice was an expert in leaving things unsaid and she could tell he was purposefully not providing any more detail. She desperately wanted to know, but decided not to pry any further. "Raya mentioned Thomas helped you when you got laid off, so you lived here before you got laid off too?"

"We...I did." Alice's ears perked up at the quick change of pronouns. "Thomas was a massive help. Even though I was already planning to leave, I was shocked when they pulled me in and told me my job was eliminated.

"It's so cold and heartless, isn't it?"

"Yes, you would think they could come up with a better way of doing it. Though it ended up helping me. They essentially paid me to launch my business, which was an idea I had been toying with. It sucked, but it really was the best thing that could've happened to me."

"I'm hoping for the same. I go through waves of emotion honestly. From feeling like my life as I know it is over to a sort of cautious optimism."

"You don't wish you were on that train right now?"

Alice hadn't even noticed, but her normal train snaked past the beach. She had been enjoying this walk so much, she couldn't imagine not being here right now. She looked at the train as it brought all its prisoners downtown for a day toiling at the office and knew that for today, she did not want to be on it. "And miss out on this walk? No way."

They had reached the end of the beach, Alice looked back to see the sun fully above the water. It was going to be a beautiful day.

"I'm really glad you came again, Alice," Colin said. "I was afraid that my awkwardness last week scared you off. Once you get to know me, you'll realize that I'm actually normal, but I'm terrible at making first impressions."

Alice looked at him in shock before blurting out, "your awkwardness? What about my blathering mouth? I was nervous you would go straight to the police station to report me for stalking."

Colin threw his head back in laughter and Alice joined in, relieved that she wasn't the only one who wasn't confident talking to new people. "I'd never report you, Alice. Then who would Atticus trample every day?"

Alice knew it was time to go, but she didn't want this walk to end.

"I'm heading to Raya's for a coffee? Um, did you want to join me?" Colin asked nervously.

Alice bit her lip to hide her excitement. "I thought you would never ask."

* * *

The bell above the door signalled their arrival at the café. Raya and Anya on either side of the bar, Raya getting a hot chocolate and Anya perched on the stool with a muffin and a yogurt parfait. They both looked over at the pair and broke into wide, matching grins.

"Good morning, you two," Raya exclaimed joyfully.

"Colin!" shouted Anya, "It's my first day of school! Fifth grade! Wait a second, where's Atticus?"

"We dropped him off at the house. Sorry Miss A," he said ruffling her hair before changing the subject, "you must be excited about school though."

While he chatted with Anya, Raya looked at Alice and raised her eyebrows suggestively, mouthing "we?" Alice gave a little shake of her head but couldn't help the smile on her face. She liked the sound of "we".

"You're Alice, right?" Anya asked.

"You got it, and you're Anya. Ten, almost eleven years old. And much more mature than your mother. Do I have that right?"

"You do," she said seriously, "I'm in the fifth grade. I'm a dancer. My best friends are Abby and Olivia and my favorite color is mauve."

"Mauve? Interesting."

"Yes, it's a mature color," she said in a serious tone. "It's pale purple, a little red. I want to paint my bedroom walls it."

"Problem is, last week your favorite color was blush. I'm afraid to paint your room, only to have you change your mind *again*."

"Oh Mother," Anya said, rolling her eyes.

"Oh Annie," Raya said right back. "Now eat your breakfast and let Colin and Alice grab their own."

After getting their coffees, the pair settled on the cozy chairs beside the stone fireplace. A small rush of people came in for their coffees, many of them stopping to meet Alice and say 'Hi' to Colin before taking their coffees to go.

Mary and Martin came over to greet the two. Mary told Alice about the upcoming Fall Festival, but she found it difficult to concentrate, as she couldn't stop sneaking glances at Colin as he laughed and joked with Martin. Her heart fluttered when his eyes lit up with excitement, and she knew she would give anything to bask in the glow of being with him as long as possible.

Eventually, Mary and Martin went to their usual table with the newspaper and Alice got to have Colin all to herself. She watched him intently, savoring every detail as he told a story about Atticus. When he took a sip of his black coffee, Alice found she longed to be the rim of the coffee cup that got to touch his lips.

Luckily for her sanity, Raya joined them once there was a lull, and she had Anya on her way to school. Raya collapsed on one of the plush chairs. "Sheesh, sometimes these early mornings are tough on an old gal,"

"Old? You don't look at day over sixty," Colin joked.

Raya snapped her dishtowel at him. "Hush you."

Alice watched the two old friends in awe, both of them so open and comfortable with each other. It had been a long time since Alice had felt so relaxed around anyone that it almost felt weird to be witnessing it. Though she supposed she had been witnessing it all morning. If Alice was going to be a part of Haven Cove, then she realized she must work on becoming a part of people's lives and allowing them to be part of hers. While she was sure she'd feel like a fish out of water, she knew she at least wanted to try.

Colin took one last sip of his coffee before hopping up. "Well ladies, I must be off. I have a client's newsletter to write."

"Thanks for the walk this morning," Alice said.

"It was my pleasure. I mean Atticus' and my pleasure." He ran his hand through his hair, grimacing at himself. "Anyway, will I see you down there tomorrow?"

Alice didn't have to think too long. "That sounds like a plan."

Colin walked towards the door, and Alice couldn't help but notice the way his jeans fit his backside perfectly. Her cheeks flushed when she saw Raya looking at her, her mouth agape.

"What. Was. That?"

"What?"

"*That*" Raya waved her hands between the door and Alice.

"Raya, I obviously don't know what *that* you're talking about."

"The two of you, the chemistry, the googly eyes, the..." she trailed off in a loss of words. "Just like I said, you already have the 'kiss someone' person chosen."

Before Alice could say anything though, Raya looked at her watch. "Shoot, it's almost 10!" She rushed back behind the counter, "come over here and sit. Keep me company before the Stitch & Bitch group come in and takes over the café. I need to get stuff ready for them."

Alice watched Raya make a fresh pot of coffee, get the pastries topped off, and got the espresso machine ready. Raya was a master of multi-tasking, continuing to pepper Alice with questions about Thomas and her morning.

"It feels good?"

"Being in here with you?"

"No, well okay yes, but more your first official week of freedom?"

"It hasn't been as hard as I expected, but it's hard to miss being in the office when you get to watch the sunrise on the beach and then hang out here with you."

"You're right, I'm way better than a career." Raya stuck her tongue out at Alice as she filled up the metal jugs with a variety of milks.

"Especially since you introduced me to Thomas, he's been such a help. Oh, and he recommended I sign up for a course! Which means I get to check something off my Adventures list."

"That's my girl." Raya raised her hand for a high five. "Which course?"

"Find Your Dream Job? With a Career Coach. Claire, I think her name is."

"Yes, Claire is *amazing*. She lives a couple of towns over. I've heard fantastic things about that course. People come from all over to take it."

"Honestly I'm a little nervous about it."

"What do *you* have to be nervous about? You're a

hotshot city professional."

"Yeah right, I never really thought about my career and what I wanted for it. I took this job right out of university because everyone said I would be crazy not to. Except my parents, they didn't want me to take it."

"No? Why's that?"

As soon as Alice had said that, she wanted to take it back. She didn't tell anyone about her parents, and her friendship with Raya was so new. She understood that, in theory, you told friends things about yourselves, especially important facts like being an orphan. In reality, it felt like exposing a gaping wound.

"Oh, you know parents, they have this idealized vision of what you can do. I think they just wanted more for me than a consulting job."

"They must be a little relieved that you got laid off then."

This was exactly why she regretted bringing her parents up. How was one supposed to tell other people that not only were both of her parents dead, but that a drunk driver also killed them?

Maybe it was time, though. Alice had already sobbed all over her last week and Raya didn't run away. In fact, she took care of Alice and even shared about her divorce. She went to say something, but then fear overwhelmed her. This friendship was very new, and this wasn't just some baggage, this was heavy stuff. In her experience, it was too heavy for most people. All people. Everyone who knew hadn't stuck around.

Lucky for her, before she had to lie, the bell on the door jingled and a large group of women with a smattering of men came donning a variety of knitted wear in a multitude of colors and carrying large bags trailing yarn. *Saved by the Stitch & Bitch Group,* she thought to herself.

"I'll take this as my cue to head home. Thanks Raya for everything."

"See you tomorrow?"

"You bet."

* * *

As she walked home, taking the long way along the beach again, she tried to push her parents out of her mind by focusing on the afternoon. She should find out from Thomas about White & Dunn's reply to her severance request, and she had the course starting up.

Remembering that her parents had wanted more for her made her really uncomfortable. Although she wasn't completely convinced that she needed a dream job, she was looking forward to the course. It was sure to be the distraction she did in fact need. This week she'd thought of her parents more than she had this past year, and she didn't like it one bit. Hopefully, this course would help keep her mind off of them.

TWELVE

"Come in Alice," Thomas welcomed her into his office. As she took a seat, she smoothed her dress pants under her. She hadn't been sure what she to wear to the Find Your Dream Job course, but figured since she really only had suits or her one pair of jeans that business wear would have to do.

"Hi Thomas, I got your message and figured I would pop by before the course today."

"I'm glad. I much prefer delivering good news in person."

Alice's breath caught in her throat. She had hoped for good news, but after the treatment that White & Dunn had given her, she was sure that they wouldn't budge on the horrible severance package. "Good news," she got out.

Thomas folded his hands on his desk. His face broke into a grin so wide that his white teeth popped against his dark skin. "Yes, they have fully agreed to our requests, no push back at all. Makes me wonder if we should've asked for more."

Alice leant back in her chair, feeling relieved as tears threatened to sting her eyes, and a massive weight lifted off her shoulders. "One year of pay, wow."

"Yes, now I pushed back on one thing that I didn't run by you, and they've accepted. I hope that is okay."

Alice waited with bated breath. She knew that there had to be something. "Of course. What was it?"

"They wanted the severance to end once you secured a new position and then pay you only 50% of what the remained. To be honest, that is fairly standard, but I negotiated 75%." Thomas winked at her.

"That's amazing Thomas. This eases so much stress," Alice said, shaking her head in disbelief.

Thomas picked up the revised contract and passed it to her to review. He sat silently as she looked through it. Just as she was about to pick up a pen to sign, Thomas interrupted her. "Before you sign, can I be candid, Alice?"

"Of course you can."

"I think that they're nervous about a wrongful dismissal suit. Perhaps they didn't go about the layoff in the most professional way?"

Alice nodded. "It was different from normal. This wasn't the first time that a client purchased another client. Sometimes we even lose a client. In those cases, they transfer those impacted to another team or office. They even transferred a few people from my team. Everyone but me and a couple of my closest team members."

Alice paused, thinking about the situation and how unexpected it was. In her ten years, she couldn't remember anyone being let go unless they were poor performers. "Honestly, my boss always treated me differently. I've had this inkling it was because I was a woman. I still think that, but I think he also got rid of the people that would pushback on this merger."

Thomas rested his chin on his fingers. "I had my suspicions. If you wanted, we could pursue a wrongful dismissal suit. Though I have to warn you it would take a lot of time and effort and, most unfortunately, it could tarnish your reputation."

Alice considered this. It would be glorious to see Perkins go down for how he treated her, not just recently, but across her entire time working for him. What would be the point though? "Truthfully, Thomas, I want to put the whole thing behind me. I want to focus on what my future could be."

"That's what I thought. Which means all you need to do is sign the new termination agreement and you'll get to start this next chapter."

Alice couldn't stop gushing over how helpful and amazing Thomas was as she made the termination official. "You really have made this horrible situation so much better for me, Thomas. I don't think I can ever fully repay you."

Thomas walked her out into the atrium. "You can repay me by coming to the Fall Festival. Plus, I don't want you to be a stranger. Stop in and visit me. I want to hear about where life is taking you because of this."

❊ ❊ ❊

Alice still couldn't believe her luck as she settled into

the course room, getting all of her supplies laid out in front of her on the table. A fresh notebook, pen and highlighter, thanks to the stationary section at one store downtown, and her personality assessment results, as outlined in her instructions email from Claire. She sat there nervously as some other students made small talk with the Career Coach.

Claire stood at the front of the room wearing jeans, blundstone boots, a t-shirt and suit jacket. Her blond hair fell to her shoulders, her blue eyes warm and friendly. it was obvious she loved what she did as she laughed with some students. Alice had a feeling she was going to be a brilliant teacher.

"Okay, let's get started," Claire said with a clap of her hands. "If anyone needs any of the handouts for this class, I have extra up here, along with some pens."

Claire took it easy on them this first class, outlining what they would learn over the twelve weeks and the challenges that they could expect to face. She emphasized that frustration, confusion and a desire to throw it all away was normal, that there will be times that the class will hate her.

The class laughed at that. Alice thought that maybe the others would want to throw in the towel, but she was an excellent and devoted student. She knew she would never give up.

Claire then talked them through their personality assessment results. "Who has heard of the Myers Briggs Type Indicator, or MBTI before this class?"

A couple of hands raised, and each individual provided their thoughts.

"We use it here because it is the gold standard of personality assessments in the career world as it helps us determine not only what careers would be a good fit but, more importantly, the type of environment you should work in."

Claire walked around the room as she taught, gesticulating with her hands to get her points across. "Anyone want to volunteer their type and I'll walk you through what it means to you?"

Alice looked around at the nervous faces, but no hands shot up. Despite feeling vulnerable, Alice raised her hand, wanting to show that she was a keen student.

"Alice?" the instructor read her name tag. "What did you get?"

"ENFJ."

"Aw the ENFJ. The most introverted of our extroverts. You love to be with people, crave it even, but you also need alone time."

"Sounds about right," Alice agreed as she remembered growing up. She loved being busy as a bee on Saturdays with all the social activities. Then on Sundays she went to her beloved library by herself, doing homework and reading.

"The most important thing for an ENFJ career is that it has an impact, usually on people. What is it you do or did?"

Alice explained how her job actually had very little impact on people but that she still enjoyed it.

"We can enjoy something, but it does not fulfill us. Like we can enjoy an apple, but if we'd really been craving ice cream, it doesn't fulfill that need, right?"

Alice thought about it. She agreed with Claire, as she always had the feeling that her job was missing something that she couldn't quite identify. Though a large part of her adamantly refused to believe that this was true.

Claire made her way to the table up front and leaned against it. She looked at Alice as if she could see the battle going on inside her head. "You probably ended up chasing promotions to fulfill the need, only to be confused because that desire never went away?"

Alice's stomach dropped. How did Claire know? Especially when Alice didn't even know until just now.

"I can tell by your face that I nailed it. It happens. All the time. You aren't the first and most certainly won't be the last, chasing mountains we don't care about."

The class sat quietly while Alice processed all this. *Is that what this partnership goal was?* Alice wondered, *did I use it to distract me from not being happy?* She looked up at Claire, who was watching her with a caring look, waiting for permission to continue. Alice nodded to give her assent.

"ENFJs are natural collaborators and leaders. They desire a team that is as dedicated to the goal as they are. Their strong sense of commitment to their team and their impact inspires others around them."

Thinking about the people she worked with; collaborative was *not* the word she would use to describe it. "I worked in a highly competitive, dog eat dog company."

"How did that make you feel about your work?"

"Confused. Frustrated. Lonely. Like I was the only

one who actually cared about my client because I wasn't in it for the money or accolades."

"How did that impact your work? I'm thinking specifically about problem solving, coming up with solutions, things like that."

"I worked hard and was great at my job. Solving problems or coming up with solutions was easy."

"Let me back up here, how did it compare to other times in your life, when you had a more collaborative and purposeful environment?"

Alice tried to remember a time where that was the case. Maybe university? But then her parents were alive, and she was a completely different person. "It's honestly really hard to remember. I was at my company for ten years and that was my only proper job."

"No problem. The thing is, I believe we can be successful anywhere. It's more a difference of how hard or easy it is to find that success. When we work in an environment that isn't suited to our personality type, like yours, then we have to hustle or white knuckle our way to success."

Alice nodded in agreement. She had to work so much harder than some others. She looked around to find others nodding along too, rapt with attention.

"When we get to work in an environment that aligns with our personality type, it all becomes so much easier. We're more creative, more relaxed, more... everything. We don't have to white knuckle it anymore. Success just happens naturally."

"That's why it's so important for us to know this personality type, so that we can find work that suits the purpose you're made for and the environment that allows you to be the most successful you've ever been without having to hustle. That's true fulfillment. The best part? It also leads to a deep sense of true happiness."

It was like Alice's eyes were open in a way they hadn't been before. Filled with a newfound energy, she listened closely as Claire explained some of the other types that people had in the class and the environment that suited them.

On her walk home, she thought back over the years. The constant feeling of running on a treadmill uphill, working so hard to get nowhere. The deep sense of loneliness. She thought she had turned into an introvert and a loner, but she was now realizing that maybe spending so much time alone actually exhausted her.

Alice had thrived in university. Getting straight A's was easy. Alice had assumed it was her being a good overachiever, but after hearing Claire talk, it's hard not to see that she had to do a lot of group projects and that she really loved being a part of a team, all working towards something. She also had an active social life with large groups of friends and was constantly on the go.

It's difficult to really look back because that was before. And this was after. Losing your parents can change you. But maybe they didn't change this part of her.

Alice had been so energized this past week, and she had figured it was the lack of work and a commute. While she was sure that was some of it, she had a feeling that spending time with Raya and Colin and meeting new people from the town were also big factors. She felt more alive and connected. The thought of returning to her solitary lifestyle filled her with a deep sense of dread. She refused to go back to that isolation. She couldn't.

THIRTEEN

Tonight was Alice's first book club and she was nervous. She didn't know why she was so scared, she had met some of the women over the past couple of days and had even read the book, the latest Lisa Jewell thriller, which she ripped through over the weekend.

Unfortunately, her brain was *not* getting the message. Instead, it told her all the reasons she should be really nervous.

You'll be showing up by yourself.

Everyone has known each other for years.

You're an interloper.

It was working. She was way more nervous than excited. She spent an exorbitant amount of time getting ready hoping if she looked perfect, then she'd at least feel better. On her bed was a pile the size of Everest of all the discarded clothes she chose not to wear. Her closet overflowed with business wear and she did not have enough normal clothes. In the end, she chose her jeans that she'd worn practically daily since they were her only pair and one of her dressy work blouses in a deep red that really popped against her pearly white skin and black hair.

Unfortunately, her hands were shaking so much that she ruined her makeup and didn't have time to redo it. She washed her face and ran out the door, make-up free. The last thing she wanted to be was late.

She was late. Only by a couple of minutes, but still the café packed with all twenty members of the book club and when the bell announced her arrival, the murmur of talking stopped and she sensed all forty eyes bore into her.

"Alice! You made it," Raya called out, and rushed over to greet her. "Come in, come in. Everyone, this is Alice. She lives in the yellow cottage and has finally become my best friend, so now she must do everything I do."

This caused a smattering of laughter and a bunch of hellos.

"Hi Alice," said Mary with a warm and welcoming smile on her face. "I brought in nametags for all of us to wear since we didn't want to overwhelm you with a bunch of names. We're all so happy you're here and we don't want to scare you off!"

"Yes, we've been so curious about you," cried a voice that belonged to a woman in her fifties with short reddish grey hair and a knitted sweater with a sloth reading a book on it. Alice could see that this woman's name was "Cat" based on the nametag on that gorgeous sweater.

"Come, I've saved you a seat," said a bold voice and a papery hand guided Alice to a chair beside the owner. In the seat was an older lady with a face that showed off just how happy a life she'd had and a perfectly set purple hair do. "I'm Dottie, and I'll take care of you while Raya buzzes around taking care of everyone else."

Alice took the chair gratefully, gathered her book, notebook and a pen and then sat like a prim student with her hands folded on her lap, ready for the discussion.

"It isn't a serious book club, dear," Dottie said playfully, gesturing to Alice's posture and set up. "Like all book clubs, it's more about the occasion than the book."

"We won't talk about the book?" Alice asked, concerned. She had only mentally prepared herself for book talk, but as she looked around the room, she saw the groups of women chatting away, not seeming to be in any rush to get started.

Dottie patted Alice's hand. "We'll talk about it, but we'll also talk about everything else."

Alice nodded along with Dottie, trying to convince herself that she could handle this. She was thinking through all the things that they might discuss when Dottie interrupted her thoughts,

"I suppose you're used to things being pretty serious from that city job that let you go."

lice's eyes widened in surprise. "What? You heard about that?"

"It's a small town, dear, and you have fascinated us these past two years. You bought the old Henschel cottage."

"I thought I bought it from a Campbell?"

"Yes, but the Henschel's originally built it, but anyway you moved in and we rarely saw you. Back and forth to the city, early mornings, late nights, weekends too. The few times we did if someone said 'hello'," she chuckled, "the look on your face was priceless. Like a deer in headlights. I'm glad you've started saying hello back."

Alice was getting used to this, not comfortable, but used to people knowing so much about her. It made her feel exposed, but she could also see how it was really a testament to how close they were as a community.

"How long have you lived here, Dottie?"

"My whole life. I was born in my cottage, actually. When my parents passed, my Eddie and I moved in with our three little ones. Eddie's joined my parents now, and my three littles have grown and moved away with grand-littles of their own."

"Wow. Did they move far?"

"Most of them. All but one of my grandkids have dispersed across the globe, it seems. Just my Poppy, she couldn't come tonight. She's youngest granddaughter and lives here in Haven Cove. Her parents, my daughter and her husband live in a town not too far from here. It allows me to see them about once a week without them getting into my business too much," she said with a wink.

Raya dropped a cup of tea on the table next to Dottie and gave Alice a glass of red before spinning on her heel, clapping her hands. "Okay everyone, let's get started."

They really only talked about the book for half an hour, and only that long because of an intense competition between a few of the ladies on who figured out that last jaw-dropping twist first, before it became more of a mix and mingle, as Dottie promised.

While Alice had been nervous, she decided to just relax. This wasn't a test. She didn't have to be perfect. No one was going to nitpick her. She just got curious and met as many people as she could.

Alice found out more about Dottie's escapades. She was on her third boyfriend this year, met entirely online! She met the woman with the Sloth sweater, Cat, who tried to convince Alice that all she needed in her life was a good pair of knitting needles and the Stitch n Bitch. Before talking with a couple in their twenties (both named Jen) who were local artists. She had so many conversations that she lost track.

She stayed with Raya as the book club members finally began trickling back home, helping her friend clear up the debris, loading the dishwasher with the cups and plates before they both crashed into the couch together.

Raya put her arm around Alice's shoulders, bringing her into a side hug. "I'm exhausted. I can't believe I have to get up in six hours only to come right back here. If it wasn't for Anya back home, I would just sleep right on this couch."

"Who's watching her, anyway?"

"My mom, the ever-interfering Indian woman who so disapproves of my lifestyle, but does it in an annoyingly supportive way. Like, 'you wouldn't even need me, *beti,* if you stayed with Krish.' But she comes, and she cleans, fills my fridge and freezer and loves Annie with all her heart, so I can't complain. Too much."

From what Raya had told Alice of her marriage, it wasn't even a healthy one, never mind happy. "How did you meet your ex, by the way? Wait, you don't have to answer that."

Raya waved her hand at Alice. "Of course I'll answer it. Our parents arranged it but a more modern day arranged. They discussed our 'suitability' and set us up on a first date. We weren't forced together or anything. We could decide not to get married, but back then I really didn't want to let my parents down. So, while I never really loved him, when he proposed, in front of our whole families no less, I said yes."

"How long were you married?"

"I left him when Anya was only two years old. It was really hard. No one in my family had ever gotten divorced. My parents at first did not accept it, so I had no one to go to."

"That's so brave Ray."

"It didn't feel brave. It felt like it was the only choice I had. Krish is a holy name, but the man was far from it. He drinks a lot, parties hard. Had at least one side piece. I just looked at my baby girl and wanted her to be proud of me, and how could she be if I wasn't proud of me?"

Alice reached for Raya's hand. "She must be so proud of you now."

"Well, as much as any ten, almost eleven-year-old is of their mother. She's a great kid. Unfortunately, she doesn't get to see her father as much as she wants. He sees her as a mini-me and reminds him of how much I embarrassed him by leaving him. My parents eventually came around, not wanting to lose me and

Anya over it, and while they don't really understand the choice I made, they at least provide all the support they can. Even when it comes with a continuous diatribe of snide remarks about my life."

Alice sat there, looking at her friend with admiration. She risked giving up everything to build a new life for herself and Anya. In a way, it was like Alice. Raya went from having a family to not having one at all. By choice, yes and with a daughter, but still. Raya didn't let that stop her from going after what she wanted. She became a part of this community to build a new life and a new family. Even welcome some of her family back in. Alice wished she could have a smidge of Raya's courage.

Raya laughed, breaking up the somber atmosphere. "Enough about me though. Did you have fun?"

"It was terrific. Everyone was great. I finally read a book. I was really nervous but I'm glad I came. Though a little weirded out by how much everyone knew about me and I must've heard, 'we've been just so *fascinated* by you' at least a hundred times."

"That's life in a small town. We all know each other's business and you were so mysterious for so long. Though, I'm sure some were quite disappointed to learn you weren't a spy, as that was the leading wager."

"That's three things done on my list, the course, the book and the book club."

"How does it feel to be making headway on that?"

"It feels wonderful, like I'm living my life by design instead of just doing the same things day in and day out that I didn't even enjoy."

"Okay, what's next? *Kiss someone?* You and Colin are spending a lot of time together," Raya turned to look at Alice, who buried her face in her hands, "but we can talk about that another time."

Alice appreciated this. She definitely had feelings for Colin, but doesn't really know what it all meant. Colin had been someone to daydream about, and now that he was becoming a reality with their daily walks on the beach, it was a lot scarier.

"Besides, I have something not on the list. Anya's birthday party," Raya offered.

"I think I've heard Anya mention her upcoming birthday once, or maybe a hundred of times."

"To say she's excited would be an understatement. You can to come to her party, it's on Saturday. I'm actually going to close the café and everything. You can meet my whole crazy family then!"

"I don't know," Alice replied. She barely knew Raya and Anya. Wouldn't it be weird if she went to a family event? She hadn't gone to a party, never mind a birthday party, in years.

Raya turned in her seat to look at Alice sternly, "and why not?"

Alice went to speak before Raya stopped her. "On second thought, I don't want to hear your excuses. You're my friend and my *whole* family is going to be there. They love to come so that they can all talk about how wrong I was to leave my husband. That way, I can become the cautionary tale of what happens if you get divorced. I need you there."

Alice raised her hands in defeat. "Okay, okay! I'll come."

"Good," Raya slowly moved to get up, "now you're going to have to pull me up. My body has given up on me and I must get home."

FOURTEEN

As Alice fell asleep on Friday night, she had a moment of disbelief at how drastically her life had changed is such a short time. The days working at White & Dunn all blurred and blended together, nothing much distinguishing them. Sleep. Eat. Work. She never considered that life could ever be any different. While she desperately craved more for her life, she was also terrified of what that could mean. More relationships that could be taken from her. Heartbreak. Anguish. Loneliness.

It was why she stayed in that autopilot setting for so long. It was scary shaking things up. Isn't it interesting sometimes how, even when you refuse to change, it doesn't protect you from things actually changing? You could have your plans, but the universe can have others. Like the shock of losing your job instead of getting a promotion.

That jolt had forced Alice off autopilot, and she had done more in the last two weeks than she had the last two years. Today was a week of walks on the beach with Colin. Her new morning routine. After the walk, they headed to Raya's for a coffee. Some days Colin sat with her while others he ran off to get started on work. In the afternoons, she focused on job searching and coursework.

That week they had done a bunch of exercises that Claire called "self-discovery exercises" which really were a bunch of hard to answer questions like "what did you love about your last job?" and "what do you want to be remembered for?" It honestly hurt her brain trying to come up with answers. Claire had warned them that these questions were tough, to "break their brain" so she said.

Their homework was to reflect and add to what they started in class, and to do lots of monotonous tasks like cooking, cleaning, and walking while they thought it through.

Alice did not know how this was going to help, but she was open to giving it a shot.

* * *

Every other day this week, Alice had woken up excited about the day ahead. Which was why it was unsettling when she woke up with a mood to match the weather. Dark and stormy. She didn't quite understand why. She was looking forward to Anya's birthday, but it had also brought on some unwelcome memories.

When Alice turned eleven, her parents planned a bunch of celebrations. It was the first time that she and her two best friends got to go to the movies *alone*, well, kind of alone. Her dad sat a few rows back from them. They saw the "Bodyguard" and they gasped and cried and cheered with big buckets of popcorn and sickly sweet sodas.

Then there was her present, a weekend in New York City. The three of them walking around Central Park, spending hours at the Museum of Natural History and watching "The Phantom of the Opera" on Broadway.

Her favorite was her actual birthday though. Her parents would decorate her kitchen chair with balloons and streamers and would make her a stack of chocolate chip pancakes with crispy bacon. They'd sing her happy birthday then and again before cake after their pizza dinner. They would finish the day by climbing on their couch together to watch the "Sound of Music", all three hours of it. Even if it was a school night.

Her twenty-third birthday was the last they celebrated all together, but not completely because she blew off the "Sound of Music" to go out dancing and partying with her friends. What she wouldn't give to go back in time and decline the invitation and instead watch all three hours of the movie safely snuggled in between in her two parents.

Since then, she had avoided celebrating not only her birthday but most others as well, since it was just a reminder of what she didn't have anymore. Which was probably why she felt so off this morning. Anya's would be the first birthday she had celebrated in ten years.

She was determined to celebrate Anya's birthday today and to not break down while she did it. With a deep inhale, Alice grounded herself and stuffed all that pain and sadness down before climbing out of bed to get ready.

❋ ❋ ❋

Alice walked down the street, listening to the sound of raindrops hitting her umbrella, as she made her way to Anya's big birthday party. She had tried to perk up but found it difficult to be excited. Trying to shake her pent -up emotions off sent raindrops from her umbrella flying everywhere.

"Whoa," a voice chuckled from behind her. "Have you been spending too much time with Atticus?"

Alice glanced over her shoulder to see Colin and could feel herself immediately relax, happy to arrive with someone.

He looked as handsome as ever, in black jeans, a red Henley and boots. His blue eyes sparkled as he smiled, showing off the hint of scruff on his face.

"Sorry," she said, "I haven't been to a party in an embarrassingly long time, just a little nervous."

"What do you have to be nervous about? Everyone loves you," he insisted.

They didn't even make it up the walkway before the birthday girl pulled the door open herself.

"Alice! You're here!" she exclaimed as she rushed out into the rain to give Alice a hug.

Her heart ached at this expression of affection. "Of course I am, sweet girl. How would I give you your special present if I didn't come?" Alice handed the birthday girl the gift she had painstakingly picked out.

"What about me kiddo, aren't you happy I came?" asked Colin with a look of mock annoyance.

"Thank you for coming, Mr. Delaney," the birthday

girl said, suddenly the picture of manners before she grabbed his present and ran off back into the house, narrowly avoiding her mother.

"Alice, Colin, welcome to the madhouse," laughed Raya. "Colin, the beer is in the kitchen. Go grab us some, please." Raya shooed him off before grabbing Alice's hand.

"I want to introduce you to everyone," she pulled Alice into the living room, "I've been wanting a best friend my whole life and I want to show you off."

Alice's face hurt from smiling so much as she met Raya's massive family, including her parents, all her aunties and cousins. It was amazing all these people could fit in her small house. Raya rushed into the kitchen to get things ready and left Alice with her mother, Satya.

"It's a shame that the weather is not cooperating today," said Satya with a faint Indian accent, "normally we would be outside and now we're all crammed in here."

Alice just nodded in agreement. It was obvious where Raya's strength came from. Raya's mother was a formidable woman. She was shorter, wearing a bright blue and gold sari, but spoke in a way that commanded the attention and obedience of others.

"So you're Raya's new friend," she said, looking at Alice appraisingly.

Alice could feel her back straighten, suddenly desperate to get this woman's approval. "Yes, I am. Ma'am."

"What do you do?"

"I'm in consulting."

"That pays really well, doesn't it?"

"Well, I guess. I did just get laid off, though."

Satya's eyes narrowed at Alice. "Why? Because you're no good at your job?"

Alice's heart caught in her throat. "Um, I don't think so. Another company bought my client out, so they eliminated most of my team."

"You had your own team?" Now Satya looked impressed.

It was like Alice was under the third degree as she nodded assent.

"That's good. You'll find a new job soon, I think," the woman said. "What about your parents? Your family and your relationship with them are important for me to know about. It tells me what type of person my daughter has called a friend."

Alice froze. What did being orphaned at twenty-three with absolutely no family show? That she was surely unworthy of being her daughter's friend?

"Don't be so nosy Auntie Satya," interrupted one of the many cousins. She pulled Alice away from Raya's mother and onto the couch beside her.

"Alice, I want to hear everything about you. I'm Priya, since you probably don't remember. What do you do? How long have you lived here? Tell me all of Ray's secrets," she said conspiratorially.

"I worked for one of the big consulting firms, but right now I do not know what it is I do," Alice laughed, slightly embarrassed, "I've lived here for a couple of years and actually one good thing about getting laid off is I finally get to see things. And not telling you any of Ray's secrets."

"Damn, thought I would trick you into giving me all the goss. She is the only one in our family to get a divorce and so technically, we aren't really supposed to talk about it. Which means, of course, we all do constantly. So I'm dying to know if she's lonely or dating or any of it." She looked at Alice imploringly.

Alice only nodded in response. She was proud of Raya for having the courage for putting her and Anya's needs first.

"Fine." Priya said disappointed. "At least tell me all about that hottie."

Alice followed her gaze to Colin, standing in the doorway between the living room and dining room.

Priya leaned closer to Alice. "I think he's trying to call you over."

She was right. Alice saw Colin hold two beers and was tilting one towards her.

Alice said goodbye as she squeezed her way through the crowd to Colin.

"You looked like you needed saving from the cousins. They can be *ruthless*."

"I did, you're a lifesaver." Alice took a sip of the ice-cold beer, gazing around the two rooms overflowing with people. "This is really overwhelming."

Colin cupped her elbow. "Let's go help Raya then." His breath tickled her neck, sending a shiver down her spine. He led Alice through the crowd to the kitchen where Raya was at the counter, frantically filling up serving platters.

"How can we help Raya?" Colin asked.

"Thank goddess you're here," she said hurriedly. "Colin, can you fill up the cooler with drinks? They're in the garage. Alice, I need you here."

"At your service," Colin saluted before heading into the garage.

Alice stepped up to the counter and unloaded a box of samosas onto a plastic orange platter.

"Why is no one in here?" Alice asked in confusion, there's almost no room to move in the other rooms and yet it was empty in the kitchen.

"They know if you're in the kitchen, you have to help," she explained. "But I'm fine with it. My mom always has to nitpick what I'm doing, and I want to show them I can do this all on my own, even if I don't know if I can."

"You can Raya, you're amazing. You own your own café, you're a great mom to Anya and do so much for the community," Alice told her, wishing Raya could see herself as Alice saw her.

The two of them worked away in comfortable silence. The counter and kitchen table slowly filled up with platters of curry, naan, pizza, and tandoori.

Alice was shocked how quickly the party passed. They ate, watched Anya open a multitude of presents (she screamed, "Alice, how did you know!" when she opened the watercolor kit Alice had bought), and sang "Happy Birthday".

Once everyone finished eating the chocolate birthday cake, they started leaving in droves. Alice went to leave with Colin but Raya stopped her, begging Alice to stay and have a glass of wine with her.

"Happiest of birthdays, little one," Colin said softly before hugging Anya, then Raya. He turned to Alice. "I'll see you tomorrow morning, then?"

"Wouldn't miss it."

He wrapped his arms around her, Alice's arms instinctively went around his waist like they belonged there. She wanted to bury her face in his neck as she filled her nose with the smell of the woods and the sea, a perfect combination. With one extra squeeze, he let her go. His eyes crinkled with a smile as he looked at her. "Atticus and I can't wait."

"That chemistry," Raya practically shouted as she sank into her couch with a large glass of red wine after the two had cleaned the kitchen and got a tired birthday girl in front of a movie, snuggled up in Raya's bed.

"I know, I know. Damn he's, well, hot." Alice giggled. "Gosh what I wouldn't do to …" in the distance she heard the train horn shaking her out of the fantasy. The weight of the day settled on her, leaving her exhausted. The constant questions about her work and the reminder of just how alone she was in the world.

"What? Don't leave me hanging!" Raya squealed.

Alice sighed. "My life is an absolute mess right now. I don't have a job. I don't even know who I am anymore. I can't fall in love or begin dating. Maybe once I have my life figured out, but until then, friends. That will have to be enough."

Raya sat up, her face filled with concern. "Are you okay, Alice?"

Alice fantasized about opening up to Raya, but her friend had had enough to deal with today. She didn't need to support her, so she forced a smile, "I am, I truly am. Today was so wonderful. Thank you so much for inviting me. You put on the best birthday party for Anya. "

"Wonderful in your eyes. To my mother? 'Aw Beti, the samosas are store-bought, your house so small, wouldn't it be so much easier with a husband...' and all I can say is 'yes Mummy-ji, thank you for your advice'. I love her, but moms are just tough to deal with, right?"

Alice didn't know what to say, so she said nothing. She yearned to have a mom to complain about.

FIFTEEN

Alice walked into her house after a busy morning of desperately trying to finish her homework before her third class that afternoon. She had sat curled up on one of the chairs by the fire at Happiness Café with a coffee and notebook. The café was so cozy and warm, it kind of felt like being in a living room with limitless drinks and pastries.

Which was why it was so glaringly obvious how empty her house was of not just personality but even furniture. Like with most things, Alice had wanted to buy furniture and decorate the house but struggled with it. When she first bought the cottage, she had tried to go shopping but was overwhelmed with all the choices. She didn't really know what she wanted and didn't have anyone to help. Which meant that she ended up moving her old condo furnishings here. That may have been fine if her house wasn't twice as big.

It looked practically empty, but also cold. Alice needed to fix this fast. Especially since it would also get her a checkmark on her Adventures list.

She quickly sent Raya an SOS text.

Help! I need to buy furniture and decorate the house. I need your expertise!

She saw three dots appear before disappearing then almost dropped her phone when it began ringing in her hand. "Hey Ray," she answered.

Raya jumped right into the conversation as if they had just been talking. "I'm no expert with this stuff. Now I know what you're going to say, 'but Raya the café is so nice, your house is so nice too, you must be a master interior decorator' and trust me what I wouldn't give to say that is true, but it's not. Honestly, a few years ago, this café was old and outdated, and I didn't have any money to get all new stuff. It was Colin who helped me. He knows all these amazing places and can get a great deal. You should ask him!"

Alice immediately grew suspicious. "Are you sure you're not just trying to throw us together?"

"Who me? Yes, obviously I want you together, but that's not what I'm doing, *in this instance*. His ex was some sort of interior designer or photographer or something who used to work with a lot of the stores. They all hired Colin to do website design and stuff like that. Plus, I guess her 'eye for design' rubbed off on him because he picked out pretty much everything. You should see his house."

The two hung up the phone so Raya could feed the descending mob of pickballers that had just walked in. Alice thought about Raya's assertion that it was Colin who could help her. She honestly didn't know whether to believe her, though it felt like an incredibly elaborate story for even Raya to concoct.

Colin and Alice's relationship had so far been confined to their daily walks and he occasionally stayed for a coffee at the café after, but not always. She was a little nervous about asking him for a favor and taking them off the beach. What if it changed things? Or he didn't want to help? Would it make things awkward?

Maybe she could do it on her own? She had more time now without her job. She could research things on Pinterest and then go out shopping. Though it would be nice to have help, and if she was being really honest with herself, it would also be nice to spend more time with him. At least she'd have until tomorrow to decide what to do.

* * *

This week's class was a doozy. They were brainstorming career ideas for themselves, and Claire was relentless. She wanted them to think of this like a normal brainstorming session where no idea was a bad idea, nothing was too silly or stupid. They weren't even supposed to worry about if the career was possible or how they would do it.

If at any point in time in their life something excited or interested them, they wrote it down because apparently there was a lot to learn from them. Alice was struggling to see what she could learn from her desire to be a lifeguard when she was five. She wasn't the only one questioning, a woman asked, "and what exactly does me wanting to be Wonder Woman mean?"

Claire smiled at her, "how amazing would that be? I would love to have my own invisible jet and lasso of truth!" The group laughed along with her before she continued, "but why did you want to be Wonder

Woman?"

"To be strong and invincible, to fight the bad guys."

"You wanted a life and career that would have you solving problems with your strength, internal and external. To stand up for the people who couldn't stand up for themselves. To protect them, and to make a positive difference in their lives. Save their lives even."

"When you put it like that," the woman joked. "I guess I can see where you're coming from."

The class ended with Claire asking the students to add to their lists, "I want you to spend some time fantasizing career ideas, think about what life could look like working in those roles and of course why you'd want to. Watch TV, movies, read books, talk to people, open your eyes to the variety of career options out there."

Alice hung back to talk with Claire. She was really struggling with getting over five things on her list and wanted to know just how long she was supposed to do this.

"Honestly, there isn't a timeline. I still constantly fantasize about fun career options. Just this week I thought about being a pet therapist, a personal shopper and a forest ranger. Though a good list of at least fifteen to twenty different careers is probably the answer you want."

"I only have five, and there's nothing else that makes sense."

"Alice, I encourage you to throw out the fact that it should make sense. If I was doing this list, a pet therapist would go down, although I'm highly allergic to most animals. I care less about the actual career, *right now,* then I do the why. And the more open you are to possibility, the more you'll see and recognize it as it makes it way towards you."

Alice was an overachieving straight-A student, and right now it was like she was failing.

Claire continued, "Alice, there is no perfect here. Though I can see that you're an overachiever and want to do this exactly right, but there isn't a generalized definition of right, just right for you. This is the hard part of the process and it will take us a couple of weeks to work through all this information. Which is *good,* no rushed decisions. Now go have an amazing week and have so much fun fantasizing about all the exciting things you could do for work!"

* * *

Alice walked through the community center, absorbing all the activity and happy faces around her. There was a lineup of really young children all holding hands with two daycare workers sandwiching the line. There was a group of older gentlemen sitting at the tables playing chess and eating from Happiness Café boxes bursting with pastries, all laughing and spewing crumbs everywhere as they enjoyed their time together. The gym brought noises of cheers, and bounces and swacks as a few teams played an intense game of pickleball.

The impact of Claire's words must've sunk in as Alice began fantasizing about working here at the community center, the heart of this small community. Thoughts of planning, organizing and managing things like the daycare and the courses to help not only this community but those other towns surrounding Haven Cove ran through her head. To have a hub where people socialized and laughed. A place where people could stay active and in touch. To help bring smiles to people's faces. She turned in her spot, taking it all in, completely lost to the fantasy.

Then she shook her head and lectured herself, *don't be silly*. Working here wasn't an option, it made absolutely no sense. She decided she wouldn't even write it down, as she already knew she would cross it off her list.

"Alice?"

She startled, shaking her head to come back to earth, to notice a beaming Colin standing in front of her with two kids by his side.

"Colin! What are you doing here?"

"I teach an after-school creative writing course here on Tuesdays."

Alice had known that he did some writing for his work, but did not know that he also taught. She loved learning more and more about this man. "Oh wow, that's amazing."

"We enjoy it, don't we, Nolan and Abby?"

Alice looked at the two children flanking Colin's side. They both looked about Anya's age.

"We love it. We're making a graphic novel right now," Nolan mentioned excitedly.

"Hey," said Abby questioningly. "You're Ms. Raya's best friend, right?"

Alice's cheeks warmed at the realization that people knew her as Raya's friend. "I am, yes. Hmm Abby, does that make you Anya's best friend?"

"Yep," she said proudly.

Colin patted the two on their backs. "Well, you two head into the classroom. We still have a few minutes before class starts. I'll be right in."

They watched as the kids gave a quick wave before rushing into the room. Alice turned back to Colin, desperate to know more about his course. "You teach creative writing?"

"I teach creative writing," he parroted back to her.

"That's amazing. I have so many questions." Alice paused, thinking about where to start first. "For how long? Why creative writing? Why students? Do you also teach adults? Are you writing a novel or something?"

"Whoa, whoa, whoa," Colin said, putting his hands up to slow Alice down. He paused, rubbing his finger against his lips. "Three years now. It was my major, if you can believe it. I love working with kids. Occasionally I do adults classes. And no, I'm not writing a novel."

Alice opened her mouth to ask more, but Colin stopped her. "Enough about me. You had your own course today, right?"

"Yes, get this. Our *homework* is to spend the week fantasizing and daydreaming about fun careers," Alice said, rolling her eyes.

"That actually sounds quite fun."

"It depends on your definition of fun."

"Is that what you were just doing? Spinning in a circle in the middle of the center?"

Alice reddened at getting caught being so lost in her thoughts. "I was. Just thinking about how cool it would be to work here and get to give back to the community."

"The coolest. Thomas apparently really revitalized this place. I heard that before he took it over. It was just an under-used building with a pool and library, and even then, they were struggling. Then he came along, pitched his Executive Director role and the rest, as they say, is history."

Hearing this, Alice knew she was justified in not even writing that idea down. Thomas was the perfect Executive Director, and he wasn't going anywhere. It would be a waste of her time focusing on something that was impossible.

They walked towards his classroom when she remembered the furniture, and before she could talk herself out of it she spat out, "okay I'm going to ask a favor but you can totally say no. You see, my house is a barren landscape–it doesn't even feel like a hotel. I need furniture and I need décor, and Raya told me you were the person to ask."

"That explains the text she sent me: *take Alice to that store you took me.* Talk about cryptic," he jokingly told her. "Of course, I know all the places. This may be too last minute, but my day tomorrow is actually pretty light. Shall we go then?"

"Yes, that would be great if it isn't too much of an

imposition?"

"Honestly, not at all. I love this stuff actually. I should do some measurements. Maybe I can swing by after our walk tomorrow morning? Then we can head out shortly after that? I'll drive, since your tiny car won't be able to bring anything home."

"Okay." Alice said happily. Impressed that it all came together so easily. "That sounds amazing."

They had an awkward moment at the door to his classroom. The two stood there looking goofily at each other, not knowing how to say goodbye. Did they hug? Shake hands? Should she just turn around and leave? Eventually, Colin went to give her a fist bump as she went to do a high five. They laughed as she cupped her hand around his fist.

SIXTEEN

Alice was rushing around the cottage, trying to not only have it look presentable but also make herself ready for Colin. She skipped out on coffee today and raced home after their walk on the beach to give herself enough time.

The doorbell rang just as she swiped some mascara on her lashes. She opened the door and couldn't help glowing at the man in front of her. His ocean eyes met hers and they crinkled as he returned the smile. She fought the desire to pull him into a hug so she could bury her nose in his neck. *Pull yourself together. He's only here to measure. It's not a date,* she lectured herself.

Alice moved aside to let him in. "I'm warning you, the house is devoid of any charm and desperately needs furniture."

"Yes, I think you've mentioned that, only about ten times. Just this morning." Colin winked at her.

"Haha," she laughed. "I didn't really notice for so long, but once you see it, you can't unsee it. Know what I mean?"

They walked room by room, Colin taking some pictures and whipping out a measuring tape to measure out walls, room sizes, and even certain areas.

Alice was a little discombobulated watching him in each room. He wasn't a tall man, only a couple of inches taller than her, but his presence filled each room. She would lead them into a cold, empty room and then turn around to find that his presence immediately made the room feel warm and bright.

She was glad to climb into his SUV to start their journey.

"I want to make sure you love your house, Alice, which means I'm going to need to find out more about what you want your house to be like in order for me to help you."

Alice didn't love personal questions as they always seemed to lead to talk of families. She knew it was only a matter of time before it came up. "Okay, what does that entail?"

"I'll just ask you some questions. Like colors, what ones do you love?"

"Well, red is my favorite, especially to wear, but I think for walls and furniture I like greyish colors."

"Not browns like Happiness Café?"

"I love the browns there because they match the brick walls and the bar, but yeah, not for my home."

"Dark or light?"

"I think I'll paint my walls light grey, but I think dark? Honestly not sure."

"I think seeing some pieces will help. Pops of color, like maybe red throw pillows or art work, blankets, that sort of thing?"

"Red definitely. Maybe navy? You seem to wear navy

all the time." Alice tugged on the sleeve of Colin's cashmere sweater to prove her point. "I think I like it."

A twinge of redness tinted Colin's cheeks as he cleared his throat, "red and navy it is. How do you want your house to feel?"

"Like someone actually lives in it," joked Alice, causing Colin to laugh. Alice thought about it, wanting to give a more serious answer, but was stumped. How *did* she want the house to feel? Obviously like a home, but what did that even mean?

Alice furrowed her eyebrows. She didn't want to waste Colin's time. "Okay, I'm not sure. I think I'm just going to say a bunch of stuff. Is that okay?"

With a turn of his head, Colin looked reassuringly at her. "Hey that's perfect. Stream of consciousness is the best."

"This is all probably going to sound silly. I want it to feel comfortable and safe, like I'm walking into an embrace. A place I can retreat too so I can recharge, like it's a home, a place to relax. I know my house now looks like I'm a minimalist, but I'm the opposite."

"A maximalist."

"A what?"

"It's a term they use for the opposite of minimalist, a maximalist. A person who likes stuff."

"That's me. I don't like sharp corners and edges. Instead, I want furniture that's cozy and soft. I want people to walk in and think, 'someone happy lives here, they bake here, they host friends over, they have movie nights.' I want a place that I belong to."

Alice turned to him. She had just shared a piece of herself that she usually kept hidden. "Did any of that make sense?"

"More than you know," he replied in a huskier than normal voice. "I want to give that to you. Everything."

"I'm glad that you understood some of it. It's not like I gave you a straightforward answer, like I want an L-shaped couch and a bookshelf."

"The exact pieces matter a lot less than the feeling they evoke. The feeling is what matters. And what you described sounds like heaven."

Heaven was shopping with Colin. Every store they visited welcomed him warmly, with the owners happy to see him and eager to help. She did get an L-shaped couch in dark grey (with red and navy throw pillows), a new wall unit, a coffee table and lamps for her living room. She decided to turn her small den that had been sitting empty into a library, so she bought a whole wall worth of bookshelves, an arched floor lamp, and she couldn't help herself from buying an emerald green velvet chair.

At a local houseware store, she bought new dish towels, bath towels, blankets, pillows, placemats, and an embarrassing amount of décor like candles, picture frames and the like.

Colin suggested they head to some small local galleries to find pieces for her walls, but her stomach grumbled, signaling a need to stop for lunch.

They found a pub with an outdoor garden patio where they could enjoy the warm September day. They both ordered the fish and chips with a beer at the bar before taking their pint out to the patio.

"I think that was one hell of a productive morning if you ask me," Colin said, bringing his glass up to cheers with hers.

Alice took a big gulp, quenching her thirst. "You are an absolute gem, Colin. Wow. I would've drowned with all the choices, but somehow you knew exactly what would work for my house and for me. You're really talented at this."

"This was my ex's business. I helped her out a lot as she built it up."

Alice had heard a bit about his ex, and she was dying to know more. "If you don't mind me asking, how long ago did the two of you, you know, part ways?"

"Just over a year after we moved here, she left because she was convinced that being in a small town was going to hinder her success, so she moved back to the city."

"Oh? Did she not want to move out here?"

"Funnily enough, it was her idea. She wanted to slow down. The city was a chokehold on her creativity, her words not mine. I found Haven Cove, but it was exactly what she wanted. Until it wasn't."

Colin said all this while staring into his pint, obviously not entirely at ease talking about it. Alice regretted bringing it up and hoped it wouldn't ruin the mood. "I'm sorry Colin, it's hard to picture a future with someone and then it not happening."

"It is." He said as he lifted his shoulders. He took a sip of his beer and then looked back at her. "What about you Alice? Any big heartbreaks in your past?"

The answer was yes, but not the type of heartbreak he was thinking about. She knew she couldn't avoid telling Colin about her parents forever, but she desperately wanted to get back to the lighthearted mood from before. Instead, she told him about Aaron.

"Embarrassingly no. A few years ago, I dated a co-worker. I realize now it was more a relationship of convenience because we hardly spoke or spent time together. A year into our relationship, he got transferred, but we didn't even break up. We just stopped talking altogether. Last I saw on Facebook, he's married with a kid on the way. Sometimes I think I should just email him out of the blue to plan a date like we used to, 'Roberto's at 7:00pm, mine after?' just to see what his reaction would be."

It worked. Colin visibly relaxed as he threw his head back in laughter. Their food arrived, and they changed subjects completely as they got busy crunching away on the perfectly fried fish.

"Would you ever want to become an interior decorator?" Alice asked Colin.

"God no, I love doing friend's homes but I would hate to do it for a living. Stephanie, my ex, had the patience of an angel with her clients and their constantly changing desires, but not me. No, if I could do anything, I would be a writer."

"Hence the creative writing course."

"Yes, well, I've got my Masters in Creative Writing with the sole purpose of writing a novel."

"Are you writing anything now?"

"Besides website and social media copy? Nope. It's

been years since I wrote more than a few thousand words. I'll have an idea, and then it just fizzles out."

"What would you want to write about?"

"That's part of the problem. I don't know what genre I want to write. But I do have an idea that I've been ruminating on these past couple of weeks."

"Oh, yeah?"

"It's super early. I don't even want to talk about it for fear of jinxing it, but I'm outlining a novel and honestly, I'm more excited about it than I have been about anything else in a long time."

"Well, I can't wait to read it. I mean, if you would be okay with me reading it."

Alice shyly glanced at him to find him gazing at her. They both jumped at the spark of attraction, awkwardly looking away. Overwhelmed, Alice hopped up to run to the bathroom to collect herself.

* * *

"You were right, my car would not have handled a quarter of this stuff," Alice gestured to the full trunk and back seat. The sizeable pieces were all getting delivered, but the SUV was still packed. They had a successful outing at the galleries with a few pieces acquired, including a beautiful painting of a sunrise at their beach. It reminded her of that very first morning, after being laid off, that she sat there. Like the first time she saw her house, she knew it belonged with her as soon as she looked at it. If she was honest to herself, she felt the same way about Colin, too.

"I'm glad to help. In just a few days, your entire house will be transformed."

"My whole life feels transformed."

"For the better, I hope."

"For the way better. It's hard to believe. It was like getting laid off gave me the opportunity to look at my life in the mirror for the first time. And I did not like what I saw."

"And you've done so much with that."

"Of course, I did."

"Not of course. Most people would have looked in the mirror and instead of changing anything, they would rush back into that life they don't like in order to avoid looking in the mirror again. It takes eyes to notice the need to change. It takes courage to make the change. You should be proud of yourself, Alice."

"When you put it like that, I guess I am."

"Any more luck fantasizing about new careers?"

"I briefly considered interior decorating until I remembered that I'm hopeless at it," she joked, watching his face light up as he barked out a surprised laugh.

"In all seriousness, it's harder than you would think, but I'm trying."

"Are you in a rush to find something?"

Alice thought about that. If Colin had asked her a week ago, the answer would have been a resounding yes. Now though? She was actually really enjoying herself. She knew what awaited her in another job like her previous one; lots of hours, a long commute, and no life. She wanted to relish this time as much as possible.

"I have time, especially thanks to Thomas, so I don't want to rush. My career is hectic, to say the least, so I think I just want to take some time to enjoy having a life for once."

"Does your career have to be hectic?"

Alice looked at Colin in surprise. "That's just the way it is. Clients expect someone available 24/7. Renewable energy, my field of expertise, is an international industry, so I'll have to travel."

Colin looked forward, his thumb stroking the steering wheel as he absorbed what she said. "Would you want to do something different? Where you maybe didn't have to work so long or travel or commute? Isn't that why you're taking Claire's course?"

Alice fidgeted in her seat, uncomfortable with this line of questioning. "No. I joined her course to help me find a job," she paused, realizing that wasn't entirely true.

"Maybe. I don't really know," she continued. "I love the idea of finding something that gives me more time. Where I have time to see Raya. Can be a part of the town." She swallowed, steeling herself for what she wanted to say next. "Where I can keep walking on the beach with you and Atticus," she chanced a look at him and saw a hint of a smile appear.

"That would be nice, wouldn't it?" He answered with a quick glance at her.

"The problem is that I don't know if that exists. While I'm not in a rush, I don't know if I'll wait forever to find a magical consulting job that isn't in the city and doesn't require my complete dedication."

Alice noticed Colin slump in disappointment, and her heart broke a little. She really did not want to give up those walks. "Though that won't stop me from at least trying to find it."

SEVENTEEN

Alice couldn't wait to get started on her house once she got back home. Over the next few days, she found a women's shelter who were more than happy to grab her old couch and some other donations, as she turned her cottage into her dream home.

It helped to keep busy. She was used to her job not just taking up a lot of hours, but also mental energy and attention. It was vital to keep the anxiety and sadness at bay.

It was difficult to ignore the rising guilt at her lack of focus on at least trying to find a new job, but was flooded with humiliation and confusion every time she sat down at her computer. She would try to power through it by trying to find job postings, but instead the pain of losing her job would come raining down on her. So, she avoided it.

Especially since she was having a lot of fun with everyone in Haven Cove. Building friendships hadn't been as difficult as she had expected. She had been terrified that would have to bare her soul in order to be friends, but so far, she hadn't had to tell anyone about her parents. Honestly, she was secretly hoping it would never really come up at all.

Alice hung the painting of the sunrise over her bed and was measuring her wall when she had a vision of Colin smiling deeply at her while grabbing her hand. Her pulse quickened in fear at the thought. Her feelings for him were deepening at a rapid rate and that was a problem. While she figured she could keep a friend at arm's length, it would be much more difficult to do the same with a romantic partner.

Never mind the fact that her life was a disaster right now and succumbing to her feelings for him would be a massive mistake. Alice vowed to remain friends with him. *It's for the best,* she decided.

Her heart didn't seem to agree with her head, though. Every thought of Colin brought on butterflies.

❊ ❊ ❊

The smattering of fallen leaves crunched under Alice's feet as she approached the Haven Cove Community Center's front doors. She traveled with a crowd and had to make sure not to trip over the children impatiently weaving amongst all the townspeople so they could enter the Fall Festival's headquarters.

Alice smiled to herself in disbelief that she was actually here. For two years, she would see the signs and the preparations around town and would promise herself that she would go. She never did. Work would pull her away, but also it was scary going by yourself when you didn't know anyone.

Not today. Today she was here. No work to pull her away. Friends to meet up with.

"Alice! You made it!" Anya screeched as she threw herself into Alice's arms to give her a hug. The little girl was dressed in a spandex scarecrow costume with her hair pulled back into a tight bun.

Alice gave the girl a little squeeze, responding, "I wouldn't miss it for the world. Especially your special performance."

Anya practically shouted in a sing-song voice, "it's going to be ah-mazing!"

Alice pretended to look serious and asked, "now remind me, what time exactly is the dance at?"

Her curls bounced as she bobbed in place. "2:30pm. On the *main* stage. I'm so excited I could barf!" She exclaimed before catching sight of her friends, "There's Abby and Olivia, bye! See you later Alice!"

Just like that, she was gone. Alice wondered where Raya was, she knew her friend had closed the café early so that she wouldn't miss her daughter's performance.

Alice didn't have to wonder long as Raya's arm curled around her shoulders.

"Hey there friend," she said.

Warmth filled Alice's heart, being called friend hadn't grown old yet. She hadn't been anyone's friend in a long time. Only coworker, subordinate, manager, and client.

"Have you seen Colin yet?" Raya asked suggestively with a wink as they walked into the festive building.

Alice had confided to Raya about the charged conversation she and Colin had. About how drawn to him she had always been. While she insisted to Raya that now was not the time to start a relationship, what Alice hadn't shared was how scared she was and how she didn't feel ready for something more. Secretly, Alice didn't think her heart could survive getting broken since it hadn't even fully repaired after losing her parents. Which meant that Colin was firmly in the friend zone.

"Raya," Alice said sternly, "friends. We're just friends."

"As you keep claiming." It was obvious that Raya did not agree, but Alice appreciated that she held her tongue. "Well, I hope you see him soon. I have to abandon you since I've got to run and help Annie and her dance team get ready. See you in there?"

Alice was actually glad to be alone right now so that she could take all of this in. The atrium was a vision. Hay bales lined walls decorated with paper fall-colored foliage. There were pumpkins of all shapes, sizes and even colors strewn about the room. Alice loved the autumn sun, especially today as it poured into the room through the glass ceiling, casting a golden glow to everything and everyone in the room.

She went to stand beside a wooden pole with arrows pointed to all the fun activities, community BBQ and performance stages as she observed the buzz of excitement that rippled through the room as people entered and took in the decorated center.

Thomas was standing nearby, waving and talking to people as they entered. She approached him and noticed that while he looked distinguished, like normal, he also looked a little thinner and way more tired than typical. His eyes still sparkled as he saw her, though. "Hello, there Alice. Welcome to the Fall Festival. I believe this is your first time coming. Is that correct?"

"It is. I can't believe I've missed it all these years. This is absolutely magical, Thomas," Alice gushed, gesturing around her.

"Well, I have to admit that this year is a *special* year. I think we've outdone ourselves. I'm hoping it will be an event to remember."

A couple of kids passed them, giving Thomas a high five as they did so. Alice couldn't help but notice that Thomas had emphasized 'special' and wondered what that was about.

Alice looked around, excited to do it all but unsure of where to start. "Thomas, give me your expert advice here. What should I do first? I want to do it all right away and am having trouble picking."

Thomas chuckled, "a big ask, Alice, like picking a favorite child. Let me think, the performances are in the afternoon, the BBQ will not start cooking for another hour. Perhaps the fall maze? It's out back in the field. My team worked all yesterday afternoon assembling the hay bales. It can get quite busy as the day goes on, so you may want to get in before you have all the young children underfoot."

"Excellent suggestion!" Alice responded, clapping her hands together excitedly.

"Will you also be attending the Harvest dance tomorrow evening, Alice?" he asked.

"I wouldn't miss it for the world. Raya even helped me pick out a dress for it. Will you save me a dance,

Thomas?"

"Why, of course I will," he answered in surprise. A wistful look crossed his face. "I want this entire weekend to be full of wonderful memories for me and the town."

"Oh?"

"Yes. It's a special year." He said more to himself as he gazed out across the crowd.

"You mentioned that. Forgive my ignorance. Why is this year so special?"

The wistful look became poignant, and he got a faraway look in his eyes before he quickly recovered with a shake and then smiled kindly at Alice and said, "well, you've finally been able to come, haven't you, dear Alice? Now you must get to that maze. You want to beat the rush. I hope you have an excellent day."

Thomas broke off the conversation by turning to a family on his other side.

Alice paused in confusion and concern. What did Thomas mean? There was something about the way he said *special* and that look on his face and in his eyes that left her uneasy. She certainly wasn't falling for that deflection of it being her. She had to remember to ask Raya later.

Alice woke up from her daze when she felt a rough tongue licking her hands, and she looked down to see Colin's golden retriever, Atticus. She kneeled down to pat his ears. "Atticus, you're here! Will you help me through the maze, make sure I don't get lost?"

"Oh, I wouldn't depend on him. He gets me lost in there every year," a deep voice said. Alice glanced up into the crystal blue eyes of Colin. "But good thing I have an excellent sense of direction. I'll make sure you don't get lost."

Alice rose, her hand stroking Atticus' ear. "Well then, Mr. Delaney, I'll put my life in your hands then."

As the two left the building, she looked back at Thomas. He was now by himself watching everyone, a small nostalgic smile on his face as he watched all the radiant smiles of the people of Haven Cove wandering around.

EIGHTEEN

"**W**ho's a good boy?" Martin was cooing lovingly to Atticus as he rubbed the dog's ears. "That's right, you are."

"Hiya Martin," Colin said, interrupted the love fest.

"Colin. Alice." Martin's tone turned ultra serious as he drew his attention away from Atticus. "Are you two doing the maze?"

"Us three," Alice corrected him.

Martin's stern façade broke a bit. "Excuse me, you three."

Martin rubbed his hands together, in obvious anticipation of what he was about to say next. "Okay, the rules. The goal is to get to the center of the maze where you will find the Harvest Cup. Do not take the cup, I repeat, do not take the cup."

"No cup," Colin replied in mock seriousness back.

"The cup stays, but inside the cup you'll find a pile of paper leaves. You may grab *one*, only one each. Humans only. You use the provided markers to write your name on said leaf and then you can pin it up to the walls of the maze. Leave the marker though, do not take them."

"Forgive my husband," came a friendly voice from behind Alice. "He takes this responsibility very seriously."

"Mary, it's serious business. If the cup gets taken, then the whole point is ruined."

"Yes honey, did you talk about if they get lost or hurt?"

"That's not as important, but fine," a disgruntled Martin rushed through a complicated explanation of what to do if they needed help.

"Or we could use our cell phones to call for help," Colin suggested.

"Yes, I guess you could if you had to," grumbled Martin.

Alice and Colin laughed their way into the corn maze as they heard Martin begin his spiel with another group. Colin shook his head, chuckling, "every year it's the same. Martin Schmidt, the protector of the Harvest Cup."

"It's kind of cute how much he cares. I mean, he's retired but devotes so much time back to the community, it's admirable really."

"That's the thing with small towns. We all chip in as much as possible. Mary's the same."

"The both of them are amazing. I love watching them in the mornings at the café. He's like a prickly cactus and she's an ivy plant able to get around those spikes. He gets into a rant and gets all worked up until she swoops in and calms him down effortlessly. #couplegoals."

They got to their first fork in the road and had to decide which way to go. Atticus pulled the leash to the right, Colin looked at Alice with a shrug. "It looks like he knows where to go. Should we follow him?"

Thomas had been right. The maze was practically empty, so there were no people to follow. It meant that they were walking blind but also meant that they got to figure it out themselves. "Lead the way Atticus!"

"My parents are #couplegoals, married forty years. They still hold hands in public, dance in the kitchen and genuinely love spending time together."

Alice's heart rate quickened at the mention of families. She wasn't sure how she should respond. Did she ask more questions? Supply information about her parents? She decided on a simple, "Wow."

"I wish I saw them more. They live in the Midwest, so too far from the ocean for my liking. They moved out there to help my sister with her family when she got divorced."

"Did you grow up close to here?"

"Maine. It's very similar. Winter is way easier down here though. What about you?"

Alice could sense that the topic of her parents was close at hand, she had to deflect the topic off of her. "In the city. Do you miss Maine at all?"

"I miss the Maine of my childhood, but with my parents and sister not living there, it's not the same. I love Haven Cove. It's even better than the town I grew up in. It's where I'd want to settle down and have a family of my own someday."

Alice swallowed as an image of the two of them walking the beach with Atticus and a couple of kids as the sun rose came rushing at her. It brought tears to her eyes. Tears because it was so lovely to be have a family again but also because she didn't quite believe it could happen.

They reached a dead end. Alice was thankful for it as she hoped it was also a dead end for this conversation.

"Atticus, you led us astray!" Alice exclaimed.

"I warned you he gets me lost every year."

They turned around and took the first turn.

"Good thing I'm not in any rush to finish," Colin said.

Alice looked at Colin shyly. Even when her body wanted to run and hide, she did really love to be in his company. "Me neither."

They walked in silence for a few moments. They could hear the excited squeals of kids outside the maze as they played some of the festival games. An announcement came over the speaker system to state that the BBQ was all fired up and the crowd cheered.

"So," Colin cleared his throat nervously, Alice looked over to see him biting his lip. How she wished she was the one biting that lip. "Are you going to the Harvest Dance tomorrow night?"

"Yep. It'll be my first one. I've always wondered about it, honestly it feels like something out of a Hallmark movie. You know, at the end? The newly in-love couple dance as the credits roll, signifying the start of the happy ever after." Alice was blathering on again. "Anyway, I'm excited. Raya helped me buy a dress, especially for it."

Alice turned to Colin and a warmth spread through

her body at the sight of his face. He was looking at her in awe, like she was the most beautiful sunrise he'd seen. "Are you going with Raya and Anya then?" he asked quietly.

"I hadn't thought about that. I don't think so. I guess I could go by myself. Do people show up alone? Probably, this isn't high school, right?" She shut her mouth, desperate to stop the nervous rambling.

"Um, I could pick you up?"

"Yes," Alice said too quickly and loudly, "I mean, that would be lovely. I don't really want to show up by myself. Actually, I would really like to go with you."

"I would like to go with you too."

They had stopped by this point, turning to face each other. The air crackled with electricity around them. Atticus had even sat on the ground between them, looking back and forth at their faces.

Then Alice's promise that she made to herself earlier, that Colin was just a friend, washed over her like a cold shower. She started walking, berating herself for saying yes, but taking a quick peek at Colin, she saw how happy he was. She couldn't take it back now.

Though if she was truly honest with herself, she didn't want to take it back. If they went together, then they would dance together and she really wanted to dance with him.

Her desire was the only explanation she had for what she did next. She grabbed his arm to stop him and looked into his sparkling eyes and asked, "can I make you dinner? I mean, you could come to pick me up early and we can eat? Most of the furniture has shown up, and the house looks amazing. I want you to see it and actually host someone for dinner in it. It feels like that very first person should be you. I wouldn't have been able to do anything about it without you, after all."

"I would love to," Colin bit his lip again before he smiled. Alice had noticed Colin did this when he was particularly pleased. A smile wasn't hard to earn, but that pre-smile lip bite was special and Alice loved it when she caused them.

Suddenly Atticus barked and yanked on Colin's arm, who grabbed Alice's hand as they all took off for some unknown reason. The humans ran desperately, trying to keep up with Atticus, who was relentless in his pursuit of something.

It all became clear when they were pulled into the center of the maze, the Harvest Cup shining atop a pile of hay bales and at the base of those bales, treats. Treats for kids, for grownups and for the pets. Atticus must've sniffed out those dog treats and had gotten hungry.

"Atticus, you did it!" Alice praised the canine.

"Who would've thought?" Colin joked. Colin grabbed the cup, "quick let's get a picture of our success."

Alice pulled out her phone as Colin wrapped his arm around her shoulder, pulling her in close and thrusting the cup in front of them.

It took a few tries and many laughs for them to get both their heads and the cup into frame, especially with Atticus excitedly yipping around them, but they got it.

Later that night, Alice looked at the photo of them.

Their eyes twinkling with laughter, their cheeks so close they were almost touching. Happy. She looked happier than she had in a long time. She felt happier too. She wasn't sure if she was ready for someone like Colin to come into her life, but she also couldn't stop herself from dreaming about what their life could look like. Him loving her, caring for her, supporting her. That's just the way he is.

They had spent the entire day together. Grabbing hot dogs from the community BBQ and eating with some of Colin's friends. Watching a beaming Anya dancing away on stage. When it got especially crowded, Colin's hand tenderly touched the small of her back to keep her close.

She loved the doting way he spoke to Anya, as he congratulated her. The help he was always offering to any townspeople, like getting Dottie's lunch, so she didn't have to navigate the line.

Alice craved to have someone to take care of her, like her parents did for her and each other. The problem was just the idea of it sent her into a state of jitters because it was also really scary. She had gotten so used to not needing anyone since there was no one there. It had become a badge of honor, actually. Never mind the fact that if she let someone in and let them take care of her, it would mean that she would have to open herself up to the heartbreak of them leaving her again.

On the other hand, Alice figured there was no harm in a little daydreaming, so she let herself give in to the fantasy and Colin's laughing ocean eyes as she drifted off to sleep.

NINETEEN

"It's like you actually live here," Raya exclaimed as she and Anya walked into Alice's living room.

"Hilarious," Alice responded.

"Seriously. I didn't want to say anything before, but your house gave off creepy spy slash serial killer vibes before. Like you were just stopping for a short period for your next mission *or next victim*."

"Mom, your imagination is very interesting," Anya said as she hopped onto the couch.

"Annie, you didn't see it before. It was weird. I almost decided that Alice wasn't the best friend I always thought she was, but I risked it anyway."

Alice watched as Raya walked through the downstairs, admiring the cozier living room. "Love this couch, and wow, an actual place to put your drinks on." She stroked the coffee table. "And look, you have artwork. This is gorgeous."

Alice took Raya on a tour of the rest of the house that got a facelift, including her new favorite room, the small library with its walls of books, twinkle lights around the top of the shelves, and a curved reading lamp over the plush emerald green velvet chair.

When they ended back in the kitchen, Raya pulled Alice into a tight hug. "I'm so proud of you. You've come so far."

Alice was surprised at the tears that pricked her eyes at this sentiment, to hear those words from someone she cared about. It was more than she could handle. "Wine," she said as a way of distraction. "I think I'll need some liquid courage for tonight. Though it's not a date, just two friends going to a dance together."

"You're making a person whom you like dinner and then he's taking you to a dance. Excuse me, how does that not sound like a date?"

"No, don't! I get too nervous when I think of it as a date. It's easier for me to think it's not one."

"Fine, if lying to yourself gets you through it, then I guess I can play along."

"Lying is bad, Mom and Alice, you're two adults and you should know better," Anya admonished the two of them, a shocked look on her face.

"Beti, honey," cooed Raya, "when you're older, you'll understand. Now why don't you watch a movie while I help Alice get dressed?"

"Mama, you and Alice need all the help you can get," she said as she pointedly looked them up and down. "I think it's best if I come."

* * *

"Damn, you look stunning," Raya said as Alice stepped

out of the bathroom.

Alice walked over there to the floor-length mirror and examined how she looked. The V-neck highlighted her creamy white neck, the dark red velvet dress hugged her upper body before it flared out to hit her above the knee. She rubbed the soft fabric of the long sleeves as she shivered in anticipation. Her black hair was wavy and hung to her shoulders.

There had been a few mishaps with her makeup, but thankfully Anya had come to the rescue. "TikTok," she explained when questioned. "I can't wait to war make-up and since Mama can't tell the difference between eyeliner and an eyebrow pen, I have to learn from it. Really, both of you should spend more time learning." Alice admired the end result of a perfect smoky eye and dark red lips while Raya tickled Anya behind her.

"I've packed your purse with everything you might need." Raya handed her the small bag. "More lipstick, especially since you still have dinner to eat. Tissues, a mirror, some Advil, and a tenner."

"Is this too much? I don't want to stand out for being overdressed."

"Believe me, you'll fit right in." Raya paused thoughtfully. "Well to be honest, it is a mixed bag. You have the people who show up in jeans and then those who use it as an excuse to wear all their fanciest dresses, I'm talking prom dresses, bridesmaid dresses, you know the type of dress that would sit at the back of your closet collecting dust unless you decide to go all out for a small local community dance?"

"Mama, you're describing yourself. You wear a bridesmaid dress or sari every year."

"They cost an arm and a leg. I've got to get some use out of them! Tonight, I'll be donning a floor length navy dress I wore as a bridesmaid for a friend from university. It even has a tiny train, so don't you worry about being the most dressed up."

"Wasn't that too small for you?" Anya teased.

"Shush you, now head on downstairs." As Anya ran out the door, Raya turned to Alice and whispered, "I had to have it let out, but shh."

* * *

Alice opened the door to Colin, and a quick glance at him in his charcoal grey suit and dark blue shirt left her face matching her dress. She turned to gesture him in, hoping to mask the blush.

Sneaking a look back at him as she led him into the living room she saw a distinct rosiness to his cheeks too. Though she convinced herself the wind caused it.

"Welcome," she said nervously as she motioned to the room.

"Stunning."

"It is. Isn't it? Your help was really priceless..." she trailed off as she caught him looking at her, not at the living room. "Me? Thanks. You look pretty dashing yourself."

She was drawn to him but was so out of practice that she had no clue what to do so she just stood there smiling goofily at him. He stood there with a grin that matched hers. She loved how equally awkward he was.

"Flowers," Colin pushed a bouquet in her hands. "I mean, I picked you up some flowers."

Alice took them and stuck her nose in to smell the bouquet of red, orange, and yellow flowers.

"Thank you, Colin." As she turned to walk into the kitchen, she realized that this was the first bouquet anyone had ever bought for her. She said as much to Colin, adding, "and I've never bought any for myself, either. How embarrassing really. I don't even know what I'm supposed to do with them."

Colin followed her in, "well why don't you grab a vase, or a water jug or tall glass if you don't have one and I'll get them ready."

While Colin trimmed the ends of the flowers, he explained the different types to Alice in his melodic voice, "these are rust colored lilies, bronze daisies, burgundy mini roses, and buttery chrysanthemums."

Their fingers grazed as they put the bouquet in a water jug filled with water, as Alice did not have a vase. The electricity of their touch no longer shocked Alice. She had gotten used to it and, in fact, craved that rush of excitement his touches brought.

She placed the jug in the middle of the dining room table that she'd already set for their dinner. "Why don't you sit and relax? Dinner is almost ready. Can I get you a beer? Wine? I've already opened a bottle of red, is that rude to say? I needed some liquid courage honestly and well Raya and Anya were here to get me ready, not trusting me, I guess, to dress appropriately. In all fairness, they were right. Anya did my makeup, if you can imagine." Every time Alice was with Colin, she couldn't seem to stop herself from rambling. She closed her eyes to show Colin Anya's handiwork, hoping her mouth would close too.

"Wow, Anya did an amazing job. She's a force of an eleven-year-old, that's for certain," he said as he sat down on a barstool at her breakfast bar. "I'll take some wine, if that's what you're having."

They quietly sipped the wine, Colin marveling at how perfectly it matched the color of her dress. Usually when they were together there was something to distract her like the beach, Atticus, other people, but right now it was just him in her kitchen looking gorgeous. She stared hungrily at him, taking in little details, like the way his tongue wet his soft lips, a hint of a beauty mark on his upper lip, and the dusting of chest hair peeking out from his shirt.

She looked up, catching him watching her. "I couldn't do a tie tonight. I tried it, but it was choking me."

"I like the no tie, I was like that with the shapewear Raya was trying to get me to wear, too constrictive."

"Shapewear?"

Alice flushed *again*. The nervousness was really causing a massive disconnect between her brain and her mouth. "You know, the things women wear to smooth all the bumps and stuff under dresses?"

"I like all your bumps and stuff. I mean, not that you have bumps..."

"I have bumps, it's fine. I like them too, well I try to."

Luckily, they were quite literally saved by the bell. The oven timer going off announcing dinner was done. "Plus wearing shapewear makes it difficult to enjoy food, and I didn't slave all day making this lasagna not to enjoy it."

Alice served up the plates while Colin brought their glasses and the salad to the table. They were quiet for the first few bites, except for Colin's noises of appreciation.

"Where did you learn to make lasagna like this?"

"My mother was Italian. One of my earliest memories is of her and my Nonna, who passed away when I was a child, in the kitchen making a proper Bolognese, with big chunks of meat not the ground beef version we eat. Anyway, after my Nonna died, my mom carried on the Italian Sunday tradition of a big pot of soup, sauce and a hunk of meat. She cooked for an army even though it was only the three of us, so we would eat the leftovers for lunch all week."

"Now that sounds idyllic."

"It was. I haven't thought about that in ages. I loved helping her in the kitchen learning all the recipes that her Nonna's Nonna brought over from Italy. Most are in my head, but I have them all written in my mother's hand, packed away somewhere. I should pull it out sometime."

"Do your parents live close by?"

Alice glanced at Colin. She had known that she could only avoid this moment for so long. She wished she could just say a quick no and then change the subject so she could avoid talking about it but also so she could keep Colin at arm's length. Though a growing part of her didn't want to do that anymore. She finally wanted to tell him.

The problem was, she didn't like saying the words out loud. She wasn't exactly sure why. Maybe hearing them from her own voice would make it true, even though nothing could make them not true. It was silly, really.

"No, they, um," Alice stammered, her eyes had travelled down to her hands which were clenched together, her heart beating ferociously in her chest, "died. In a car accident, hit by a drunk driver just over ten years ago."

It was extremely quiet, Alice only hearing the wave of panic that threatened to overtake her when Colin's hand clasped hers, his shirt dragging through the sauce on her plate, his palm shifting as he got up from his chair to come kneel beside her.

She was desperate to fill the silence. "It's not something I've really told anyone before. I don't like talking about it or even thinking about it. I just," her voice cracked, "didn't want to *not* tell you."

"Come here," Colin said, his voice thick with emotion, as he pulled her up into a hug, his arms wound around her waist, drawing her against his chest. As she placed her arms around his neck, his hands rubbed her back. "I can only imagine how hard it is to talk about. Thank you for trusting me enough to share it."

Alice pulled back to look at him. "Thanks for, well, being you, I guess. We should go before I ruin Anya's makeup. I shudder to think her reaction if I show up and her masterpiece is ruined."

Colin pressed his forehead against hers for a moment, his face relaxing as his eyes closed. She breathed him in, before pulling him back into a tight hug, burying her face into his neck, trying to memorize the smell of him, that mix of salty air and trees.

"I'll help you clean up and then let's go," he whispered into her hair.

TWENTY

On the walk to the dance, Colin talked away, pointing out houses and talking about the people who lived in them, but Alice was so nervous she didn't hear a sound.

She was nervous about revealing her parents' death to Colin. It had been so long since she had let anyone in. While her immediate reaction was relief, her fear of him leaving her had only intensified with each step they took. If only she could rewind the evening and take it all back, but she couldn't. Which meant she just wanted to run home, climb into bed and hide under her covers.

She knew Colin could sense the change in her. She was pretty sure that was why he was trying to distract her with inane conversation, but since that obviously wasn't working; he clasped her hand in his. He seemed to sending the message. *I'm right here. I'm not going anywhere*, and her body got it. The agitation calmed down and her breathing became more regular. She felt cared for. She leaned her head on his shoulder. "Thanks," she whispered.

"I've got you," he responded.

They walked into the dance hand-in-hand, and immediately heads turned. Raya did a double take before rushing over. "Look at you two, all cozy. How was dinner?"

"It was delicious, probably one of the best meals I've ever eaten," Colin said as he rubbed his stomach in appreciation.

Raya looked between the two of them, "excuse me? Alice cooked the best meal you've ever eaten? I thought you never cooked, that you subsisted on protein bars?"

"Hey, I take offence to that. I haven't cooked in a really long time, but I used to cook all the time with my mom."

"You're going to have to cook for me now. Show me this hidden talent of yours. But right now, it's time to dance. I love this song."

Alice looked back at Colin with a shrug as Raya pulled her onto the dance floor. Raya jumping up and down to a song, singing at the top of her lungs as the train of her bridesmaid dress whipped around behind her was a sight to see. Alice watched her friend and, not for the first time, wished she had a bit of Raya's "live life out loud" personality.

As the song ended, Raya looped her arm through Alice's as she directed her to the refreshments table. "Phew, I'm not as young as I think I am"

The two both thanked Thomas' Executive Assistant, Hana, for the bottles of water and took a breather. Alice finally got the chance to really look at the gym. It had been utterly transformed.

The corners had displays of hay bales, pumpkins and large containers of rust-colored flowers. The lights were dim, but there were also lanterns dotting the room as centerpieces on the tables. Someone had set up a photo wall with an arch of balloons. There was even a small stage set up with a DJ booth.

They approached the table where Colin sat with a few book club members and their partners. Colin pulled out a seat, patting it as he said, "I've saved you a seat."

Raya plopped down on it. "Thanks, I needed it."

"I think he meant Alice," Anita chuckled. Anita, or Dr. Anita, as the townspeople called her, was a local therapist. She sat with her husband, also a doctor who worked in the hospital a couple of towns over.

"I'm sure he did, but Alice has more stamina than me. She can walk the two extra steps to the empty seat on the other side of Colin. I could not."

Alice took the seat, happy when Colin shifted so that their chairs were touching each other. He grabbed her hand and laced his fingers through it, a question in his eyes. She squeezed back in response.

Their moment was interrupted when Raya exclaimed, "will you look at Dottie? She's magnificent."

Dottie was standing a couple of feet away, surrounded by a group of wrinkled men, all vying for her attention. Dottie was resplendent in a knee length sparkly shift dress, and a feathery headband, all shades of purple to match her hair.

A slow song came on over the speakers and they watched as Dottie picked one gentleman, leading him to the dance floor. The others deflated in defeat before perking up when Dottie called back over her shoulder, "don't worry boys, you'll all get your chance to dance with me tonight."

Raya wolf whistled, causing Dottie to throw a quick wink at the table.

"That woman has more game than I do," Raya said in awe. "I need to get some dating tips from her."

Alice's face was hurting from smiling and laughing so much. She hadn't had this much fun in years. Raya recovered and finally pulled herself away from staring at Dottie, and the three of them danced up a storm. Thomas kept his promise and slow danced with her. As did Martin, who moved her around the dance floor gracefully, confessing that he loved any opportunity to show off his dance skills gained from the ballroom classes that he and Mary regularly took at the Community Center.

Alice was quite popular with people coming up to her in order to introduce themselves. Others pulled her to the photo wall to grab pictures. She knew she would cherish the photograph she took with Raya, Anya, and Colin, all of them making silly faces.

The night was coming to a close and Alice still had not slow danced with Colin. She found him standing by the now empty buffet just as the music cut out.

"Is it over? We didn't even get to dance!" she distressed.

Colin pulled her close to him, "don't worry. It's just a speech."

A portly gentleman, dressed in a too tight tuxedo, grabbed a microphone from the DJ and stood in the middle of the temporary stage. He tapped the microphone, causing a shriek of feedback, "oops sorry everyone!"

"Who's that?" Alice whispered to Colin.

He leaned in close, his breath tickling her ear as he answered, "the mayor, Dean Cummings."

Alice was ashamed that she didn't even know who their mayor was, though in her defense, he was elected before she moved here.

"What a night, what a night," the mayor proclaimed as the crowd cheered. "Before I introduce the man of the hour, I just wanted to say a massive thank you to Thomas Wells and the Haven Cove Community Center staff for putting on another amazing Fall Festival and Harvest Dance!"

Alice clapped and whooped alongside Colin. She listened closely as the mayor talked about how wonderful a community Haven Cove was and how they all looked forward to spending time at the community center whether it was daily, weekly or at these events.

"And now the mastermind behind this incredible night.... Thomas Wells!"

If Alice thought the cheers were loud before, they became deafening. A group of children chanted "Thomas! Thomas!" Tears pricked her eyes at this display of affection. Thomas looked shaky up there, as he was obviously overcome with gratitude and emotion. He stood and waved his hands, gesturing for them to stop.

Dean pulled him into a hug and handed off the microphone to him. Thomas' eyes glistened as he looked out at the crowd still clapping away. "Thank you everyone," he said and immediately everyone quieted down.

"I hope you all had a great time this evening. I love the Harvest Dance and tonight my vision of why we have it truly came to life. Seeing the children dancing alongside our more mature dancers warms my heart. The smiles and memories we make here will hopefully last us a lifetime." He paused, looking out over the crowd with so much love in his eyes. "I know the memories I've made tonight and all the years past will certainly stay with me until my dying day. Thank you, Haven Cove, for tonight and for all the yesterdays. We are such a special community. Thank you."

He paused, dabbing his eyes as the crowd continued to applaud. "It's time for the last dance of the evening, so grab the one you love and head to the dance floor."

The beginning strums to "Still Falling For You" by Ellie Goulding came over the speakers. Colin raised his eyebrows at Alice and held out his hand towards her.

She grabbed it, and he twirled her into him, planting a kiss on her cheek before turning her to face him. She wrapped her arms around his neck, his arms embracing her waist. He was only an inch taller than her so she could look directly into his glorious eyes.

"I could stare into your eyes forever," she couldn't help but say.

"Me too."

"We should get you a mirror then," she joked.

"Haha, you know what I mean. Your eyes twinkle. You see and think so much more than you let on, but your eyes give me a hint of what's going on in that beautiful head of yours."

"Your eyes are the ocean, awe-inspiring and

endless."

They swayed together, Alice resting her head on his shoulder, Colin's arms tightening around her.

"Can I tell you a secret?" He breathed into her ear.

Alice lifted her head to gaze at his soft lips and murmured her assent.

His Adam's apple bobbed as he swallowed nervously. "Raya wasn't the only one who spent these last two years intrigued by you."

Alice's eyebrows raised in surprise. "Oh?"

"I remember the first time I saw you, the day you moved in. I was taking Atticus for a walk. It was such a windy day."

Alice reminisced back to that day, the way the movers struggled to prop the door open against the wind. "It was. I remember being afraid my things would blow away."

"You were helping the movers, directing them from the porch, and your hair was blowing all over the place. You looked up at us as we walked by, and you smiled and gave a little scared but hopeful wave."

Alice scoured her memory for this, but couldn't remember seeing him. Her memories of that day were foggy. She had expected being so full of hope and excitement, but it had brought so many emotions to the surface that she hadn't been expecting. Feelings of grief because she had no one to share that excitement with. She didn't get to celebrate moving into her very first house with her parents. It was a reminder that she wouldn't get to celebrate anything with them again.

"You probably don't even remember, but I knew then that I wanted to meet you. I would get so nervous seeing you around town. You looked like a lost puppy and I desperately wanted to help, but honestly, I just shut down those rare times you showed up. I would go home and get myself all prepared to talk to you, but then I wouldn't see you for months. Then, bam, you would show up unexpectedly and it would happen all over again."

Alice couldn't believe that this was true, that Colin felt the same way she did. "I thought it was just me. I mean, I remember the first time I saw you. It was my first day commuting to work. The train came upon the beach and there were you and Atticus, this peaceful moment that I got to witness. Day after day, I wished I could be on that beach with you two."

"And now you are."

"And now I am."

Their eyes locked on each other as they danced. Alice could feel her heart pick up as the warmth of his hands radiated against her back, and the tickle of his hair on her hands. His jawbone was sharp against the softness of his hair and she wanted to leave a trail of kiss from it down to where his neck met his shirt. Her eyes met his again, the blue almost consumed by his black pupils as he gazed at her as hungry as she felt.

"I really want to kiss you," Colin said as he bit his lip.

"I'm dying to kiss you," Alice replied.

He slid his hand up to her cheek, pulling her closer, his lips tentatively caressing hers. She pushed herself harder into him, his tongue opening her mouth a little.

A fire brighter than she'd ever had before grew as her body awakened as if from a deep slumber. Longing shot through her stomach, and a warmth spread throughout her body. Their kiss deepened in intensity before a whistle interrupted them.

Alice looked to find the women of the book club cheering and clapping as their dancing partners looked on with smirks on their face.

They chuckled, Colin planting a kiss on her forehead. "I think we're going to head out now," he exclaimed to her, but mostly for the others' benefit.

They left the dance as they arrived, hand in hand.

TWENTY-ONE

Alice woke up with a smile on her face, wondering if the night before had been a dream or real. She stroked her lips, swollen from a night of kissing. She stretched, reveling in the memories of her and Colin on her porch.

The sensation of her toes slowly freezing while the rest of her body was hot with desire for this kind, sexy, and smart man. Plunging her hands underneath his coat and tracing the muscles underneath his dress shirt. His hands stroking her face, running through her hair, caressing her back. Their lips not wanting to part except for exploring other areas, her drinking in the salty taste of his neck, shivering while he nibbled at her ears.

She wanted him to come in, but also knew that she did not want to rush this thing with Colin, and eventually he had to go home to Atticus. The promise of seeing each other the next morning was the only concession.

Ping, her phone, showed a new text.

Raya: "DETAILS, I NEED DETAILS!"

Alice went to respond, but three dots showed up, Raya was not done.

R:WAIT!

R:DON'T TELL ME YET!

A: Stop yelling at me, I just woke up.

R: Come by the café around 2pm. It's usually pretty quiet then. Tell me everything then.

A: tell you everything about what?

R: Don't be cheeky with me. Best friends code–tell them EVERYTHING.

R: WAIT A SECOND, HE IS THERE RIGHT NOW?

A: Ask nicely and maybe I'll tell you.

R: You're driving me mad woman.

A: He's not here. I'll see you later.

R: Oh and check off the 'kiss someone' and you can thank me later for adding that to your list. I really like chocolate. Oh, and diamonds.

* * *

Alice practically skipped down to the beach. Waiting for that first hint of pink was torture. She was desperate to see Colin again.

There he was. Standing looking in her direction. The moment he clocked her, his face broke open into a giddy grin, matching the one she could feel on her own face. She picked up her pace, almost at a run, as he did the same.

They crashed into each other, lips finding lips, arms finding purchase on the other's body. It was as if they were being reuniting after ages apart, not just a few hours.

Atticus lost his mind, barking and jumping up on the two of them, confused at this sudden change in behavior. "Hey boy, down," Colin said, his eyes not leaving Alice's, his thumb rubbing her cheek. "Morning," he whispered into her mouth before tenderly kissing her again.

Eventually, they parted and let Atticus loose on the beach. The dog didn't immediately sprint off but licked their hands that were clasped together, but eventually he gave into the temptation of all the seagulls to chase away and the shells left by high tide to smell.

"I want to take you somewhere," Colin said, breaking the contented silence.

"Yeah?"

"Yeah. A place I discovered a few years ago, right after I got laid off, actually."

"Interesting. What kind of place?"

"It's a hike to this lookout point over the ocean. On a clear day you can see for miles in the distance, sometimes even see a pod of whales or dolphins swimming by. It's pretty special."

"Sounds like heaven. I would love to go. When?"

"I'm not working Wednesday. How about then? I can bring a picnic and we'll make a day of it?"

"Perfect, it's a date," she said as she squeezed his hand.

* * *

Alice was embarrassed to admit that she'd never really been on a hike, so she did not know what to wear to her and Colin's date. She was thankful for Instagram and a quick shop at REI to get the gear. It meant she had to miss her Find Your Dream Job class, but she was sure it was well worth it, especially since she didn't do any of the homework.

She had done little in the way of looking for a new job, but she was loving how busy she'd been. She was convinced that being busy suited her. Preparing for her first hike and her first proper date in years took way more time and energy than one would expect.

She examined her look in the mirror, new hiking boots on her feet, a pair of tights with wool socks pulled over the top, a t-shirt and a flannel. Her black hair was braided, topped with a red toque. She figured if she could pass for an outdoorsy influencer, then she would be fine for a hike. Though she now worried she wasn't dressy enough for a date, but with a shake of her head, she forced herself to stop stressing so much.

As soon as she saw Colin, she knew she made the right choice as they looked like they both stepped off their phone screens. His blue toque and flannel complimenting her reds.

"I brought Atticus. I hope that's okay," he asked as they walked down the path to his SUV with an excited dog panting in the back seat.

"It would be weird if you didn't." Colin opened the car door for her but before she got in, she leaned into him, giving him a quick kiss. "Hi," she sighed.

"Hello to you," he breathed, pulling her tight against him. A howl from the backseat interrupted them, as Atticus reminded them of his presence.

The hike was a few hours away but Alice did not complain, since the great music, magnificent views and even greater company made it fly by. Alice sat turned in her seat towards him, their hands clasped over the center console. Colin was making her laugh, describing an especially picky client who changed their mind about their website on the daily.

They arrived at the trailhead's parking lot, surrounded by mammoth trees. You would never know they were close to the ocean but for the faint smell of the sea. Colin handed her a small backpack to carry while he strapped on a much larger one.

"I've got the food and wine, but I've put some bottles of water, a thermos of coffee, and some blankets in your pack."

"This is exciting! Can I tell you something embarrassing?"

As they entered the woods, Alice told Colin about her lack of hiking experience, which shocked him and her intense research sessions on Instagram, which he found hilarious. Alice found her head bobbing up and down to take in the towering trees that surrounded them while checking the rocky terrain below her feet. The last thing she wanted to do was to trip and embarrass herself.

Alice was pleasantly surprised at just how quiet it was, no sounds of human life, just the sounds of the birds and the forest surrounding them. They walked by a babbling brook with the tiniest of waterfalls that soothed the soul.

They came to a steep section of the trail and Alice was actually happy to see signs of human existence with manmade stone stairs leading up the path.

"This is the best part," Colin said in anticipation, grabbing her hand. He wanted to be as close to her as possible, as she had experienced it for the first time.

They walked out of the trees onto a large slab of rock connected with other large slabs. Trees carpeted the view in a spectacular array of fall colors; fiery reds, burnt oranges, and bronzy yellows. And then in the distance the dark blue of the sea, as far as the eye could see. Alice gasped at the beauty of the scene in front of her.

She turned her head to look at Colin beside her to find him watching her. "It's breath-taking, isn't it?" he said softly, not wanting to break the spell that seemed to envelope them.

"I don't even have the words. I want to stay here for hours just taking it all in."

"Good thing I've brought refreshments." Colin leashed Atticus up to prevent him from getting himself into a precarious situation while she laid out a picnic blanket.

As she settled herself, pulling another blanket over her legs, Colin set up a veritable feast for them – red wine, a cutting board with baguette, different cheeses, salamis, grapes and nuts. Atticus wasn't forgotten with transportable food and water bowls.

They sat in comfortable silence, taking in the views as they indulged. After a dessert of cupcakes and coffee from Raya's, they sighed in contentment.

"You good to stay longer?"

"I never want to leave. Besides, I think Atticus isn't ready yet either," she gestured towards the dog, fast asleep beside the blanket.

Colin rubbed his hands together, "I wish I could start a fire up here, but they aren't allowed"

"Oh gosh, I'm hogging the blanket! Come here, let's share," she said, making room for him to snuggle in tight.

"I'll take any excuse to get closer to you," he said, planting a kiss on her shoulder.

Alice laid down on the blanket, Colin propped himself beside her before dropping his mouth down to hers, giving her bottom lip a tug before finally taking her mouth in his. Alice's body warmed with his touch as she traced her hand up his arm to his hair, running her hands through it as she pulled him slightly closer.

Colin groaned into her mouth, "I'm crazy for you Alice Miller," his arm travelling down her body as he pulled her towards him and placing his leg in between hers. The movement freed Alice's arm, so she grasped at his flannel and t-shirt, desperate to feel his skin.

Alice was deliriously happy, but still wanted more, wanted all of Colin. It had been so long that she felt this way that it was like a dam bursting, her desire like water crashing down over her, threatening to pull her under. Colin's hand had moved to the bottom of her t-shirt, playing with the hem. Alice burst with the need for her to feel his hands on her skin. He finally relieved the pressure by trailing his hand up her stomach to the bottom of her bra. His thumb stroked her breast, causing Alice to moan in pleasure.

Alice was not the type to have sex in public, but she was willing to put that all aside right here and now with Colin.

Until they heard voices.

They jumped apart from each other, getting their clothes straightened back out, Colin grabbing the blanket to ensure it covered the bulge in his pants.

Just in time too, as a group of older women made their way onto the rock.

* * *

"The look on your face when the woman asked if you'd ever popped a tent up there!" Alice laughed, the three of them safely back in the car.

It had been agonizing. Alice had wanted to leave as soon as she saw them, but knew they had to wait a moment while Colin collected himself. Especially when one woman dove into a long story about night camping up there, including asking that timely question.

"If only she knew that I'd literally just had," Colin joked, running his hands through his hair

"It was excruciating trying to not burst from laughter, and to take that entire conversation seriously."

"Despite the interrupted ending, did you enjoy your

first hike?"

"Loved it. I'm only sad that it's taken me this long to take one."

"You'll do it again?"

"With the right company, I could probably be persuaded," she said coyly.

"The right company does make it more special. I love that hike. It's my favorite, but I've only ever done it by myself. Having you there made it even more amazing, which I never thought possible."

"You never took Stephanie?"

"Nah, we were on the long road to our ending by the time I found it. I honestly only came across it because I had just been laid off. Suddenly, I was home all the time, and she worked from home, so it became strained to say the least. She was stressed because we had just bought this house and I, inconsiderately, got laid off."

Alice watched his jaw as it tensed. Obviously, this was not a happy period in his life.

"Eventually, I would just tell her I was looking for a job at the library and instead would go out exploring, travelling further until I stumbled across this place. This is where I came up with the idea for what kind of business I wanted to start."

"Really? How did you know that's what you wanted to do?"

"It was a mix of things. I had already been wanting to start something when I got laid off. Though once that happened, I thought I should just find another job, but when I looked at job postings, they only covered a part of what I wanted to do. There wasn't anything that would let me do it all. Plus, I hated commuting and wanted the flexibility to live my life the way I wanted to. Like today, being able to take it off without having to ask someone's permission. I wanted to work from home too. Back then, it was really rare."

"You weren't scared? Going off on your own?"

"I was terrified. Especially about finances with Steph, who was also an entrepreneur."

"I don't think I could do that. Take a risk like that."

"You could. If you wanted. Owning your business isn't for everyone, but I always dreamed of being my own boss, even as a kid, so I knew I had to at least try."

"And it worked."

"It did."

They rode in silence as guilt ate at Alice. She had ignored everything to do with her job search, but she knew she had to do something eventually. She was jealous of Colin. He'd always known that he wanted to own his own business. She had no clue what she wanted. As a kid, she wanted to be a teacher, like her parents.

Alice gazed out the window as she remembered, with a heavy heart, playing teacher with her stuffed animals and parents. They were always up for being her students, and she loved the reversal of roles. Not for the first time since she'd been laid off, she ached to talk to her them. They could have helped her. They knew her better than anyone. Now no one knew her since she had been so terrified of letting anyone in.

She shook off the memories and turned to Colin. He

looked at her with such adoration that she was glad that she had begun to let him in.

"Thanks for sharing this place with me. It's obviously really important to you."

"We've really only known each other for a few weeks, but I knew I had to bring you here with me."

She could definitely picture her life with Colin completely in it. Her heart swelled as she visualized their potential future. A smile blossomed as she watched him drive, his fingers tapping the steering wheel along to the music, as she dreamed about long drives and road trips in years to come.

Out of nowhere, a wave of panic washed over her, her heart racing and hands growing clammy. She glanced out the window to avoid Colin noticing. While the reality of her and Colin was new, her thoughts of him weren't. This was what she had dreamed of every morning as she watched him and Atticus walk down that beach. It's why this relationship, while really new, felt like it had been years. He was already in her life so completely. Her happiness was already so tied up with him.

Tears pricked at her eyes as she fought the urge to jump out of the car. Everything was happening so quickly. Too quickly. This relationship could end and then she would lose him. Not only that though, but if this soured, it wouldn't just be him she lost, but probably the entire community as well.

As she fought to steady her breathing, she recognized things couldn't keep going at this pace. She had to slow things down.

TWENTY-TWO

"**P**ump those arms ladies and gentlemen," cried the Aquafit instructor from the pool deck as Alice, Raya and a group of older women and men marched in place in the pool.

"Tell me again about the part of you almost having sex on the top of a mountain," Raya said breathlessly. "Damn. Either I'm really out of shape or this is much harder than I thought."

"Especially when you see Mary, Beatrice and Dottie all doing this effortlessly," huffed Alice. "I'm really quite embarrassed, actually. The checking things off the bucket list was supposed to improve my confidence, not have it crashing down around me."

Swimming was on Alice's List of Adventures and while it was supposed to be in the ocean, she and Raya decided that a swim in the pool was a start. Unfortunately, the two women didn't check the schedule, which meant that when they showed up for free swim, it was Aquafit instead. They were about to turn around, but Mary caught them first and insisted that they join in.

Aquafit was nothing like Alice had imagined. There was an instructor blaring a mix of upbeat pop and oldies music while standing on the deck demonstrating the moves to a pool full of participants. She was quite shocked because the average age of the participants had to be about 80, but they were a lively bunch. Laughing and working hard.

Alice tentatively dipped a toe in the water, afraid of the coldness, but was surprised at how warm it was. Dottie noticed and laughed. "It's us old fogies. We don't like cold water and we're the pool's best customers, so they jack up the heat to appease us."

The two friends tried to settle themselves in beside Dottie. She was an obvious expert, but she quickly shooed them away. "Don't stand beside me, I've got my eyes on that fine gentleman there," she said pointing obviously to a man covered in liver spots and who seemed to have more hair sticking out of his nose and ears than he did on the top of his head. "He's a hunk and my next victim. Aquafit is the best place to show them my stamina between the sheets, you know.," she said, winking at them.

That was how they ended up in the back behind everyone else, but it worked as it allowed them to keep talking, something Raya was desperate to do since she wouldn't drop the topic of Colin.

"Good thing you don't need to be good at Aquafit when you have a hottie like Colin feeling you up. Tell me about that part again."

"Raya," Alice said sternly.

"Fine, fine. It's just been forever since I've gotten any, and I want to live vicariously through you. You and Colin are the closest I've been to action in years."

"Have you dated anyone since the divorce?"

"Only a date here or there, mostly just an innocent kiss. Only one one-night stand, something I expected to be way more exciting than it actually was, instead it was just mediocre sex and a hangover."

"Why don't you date more then? If you're desperate for it, not that you need anyone."

"It's hard when you have a daughter and a business. My parents watch Annie enough. They don't really approve of dating, unless it's a pre-selected suitor, of course. They aren't used to this idea of dating people that haven't been deeply vetted by the family. And I get it, they've had to come to terms with me breaking tradition and getting the divorce, and I love that support which is why I don't to push it too much by requiring their babysitting so that I can get some action."

"Everyone loves you and Annie. Surely one of the townspeople would babysit. Heck, I'll babysit!"

"I know, I know, but it honestly feels weird getting one of you to babysit. To take the time out of your own busy lives to watch *my* daughter while I'm off on dates."

"You're allowed to have your own needs that exist outside of Anya or your business."

"I get that, in theory, but when it comes down to it, it's much harder than one would think."

"Here's the thing Raya, you're the most incredible person I've ever met. You're so giving and supportive to everyone. Let me babysit for you, once a week, twice a week, heck every night. Go on dates and get yourself laid."

Alice and Raya had been so deep in conversation

that they hadn't noticed that the class was ending. And as luck would have it, the music stopped just as Alice was demanding Raya get laid.

"Hear, hear," Dottie cried, her arm curled through that man she had her eyes on.

* * *

Alice was relaxing at home, excited to have a night to herself. Becoming a larger part of the community, especially her blossoming relationship with Colin and friendship with Raya, was a revelation, but it's also been exhausting. Alice had not talked to this many people about actual things going on in their lives since before her parent's death.

Alice had plans to make herself some Cacio e Pepe, open a bottle of red wine and watch a RomCom. The niggling about her job search just wouldn't go away though. She decided she had to stop avoiding it, and that she should at least check her email. She had taken it off her phone to give her brain a break from being on after all those years, having made the choice that she would only do "work" stuff on her laptop.

As she made her way up to her office with a cup of tea, the guilt overtook her. She had essentially put her future on pause while she gallivanted around town. Plus, she still hadn't done her homework for class. The homework required too much self-reflection. Claire kept encouraging they go back in time, to a time where the world felt like an oyster, where they could literally do anything they wanted. The thing is, her life wasn't the same. Back then, she had support, was loved, and had parents that celebrated her every move. It was not like that anymore.

She couldn't help but remember the last set of conversations she and her parents had about her career. They were disheartened to hear that she had applied to and was considering the role with White & Dunn. They had wanted more for her, not to become some corporate drone. She had tried to explain how much she believed in solar energy and how she wanted to help it become the standard.

"It's not that, honey. That's an admiral goal for sure, for someone else," her dad had said.

"Why them but not me? You aren't making any sense."

"It's nothing about you," her mother said placatingly. "You will be successful no matter what you do, that I know for sure. I only want you to be happy as well. And I can't see you being happy working at a place like that."

"You don't even know what it's like to work for any company, never mind a one of *the* top consulting firms in the country."

"You're right honey, and maybe we're wrong but..."

Alice jumped in, "everyone in my graduating class would kill for an opportunity to work there, and I'm the only one who got an interview. I would be crazy to turn the offer down, if they even offer it to me."

Tears stung her eyes as she walked into the office. This was why she hated this process. Hated not working, in fact. It was bringing up so many memories that she assumed were safely stuffed away.

Alice opened her inbox to see only a few emails had come in. It stung a bit since she was used to her inbox drowning her in constant emails in just a few hours. Five days of not checking and her new emails barely hit double digits.

Then an email jumped out at her. It had the subject line, "New Job Opportunity" from a name she didn't recognize. She opened it, surprised to see it was from a recruiter reaching out for a director level role with an undisclosed solar energy company. They were wondering if she could call them to discuss it further.

Alice's heart pounded in her chest, excitement, gratitude and terror running through her veins. *What should I do?* She thought. In the month since she'd been let go, she had to constantly fight the memories and grief from overtaking her. She had met Raya and Colin. She had done things like the book club, walking on the beach and finally getting to know people.

She imagined that being a member of the community would make her feel like she belonged somewhere, but sometimes it only highlighted her loneliness even more.

She also hadn't anticipated the fear and panic that haunted her. Everyone would eventually notice that she didn't really belong, and she shuddered to think what would happen then if she didn't at least have a job to fall back on.

It was easier to lose yourself to work. She knew what was expected of her. She knew what was going to happen the next day, week, or year even. While work didn't make her feel less lonely, at least she felt safer.

The thing was, she had thought she wanted to explore other options. But did she really? Maybe this kind of director opportunity was, actually, exactly what she wanted. Without wasting another moment, she picked up the phone and called.

TWENTY-THREE

"I've got an interview this afternoon," Alice told Colin on their daily walk on the beach. Atticus bounded up ahead of them.

It was Monday morning, and the two hadn't talked since Friday. Colin had tried to reach out by calling and texting, but Alice ignored him. She had sequestered herself in her house to prepare for the interview. When she saw him this morning, she was ready for his questioning look, but what she wasn't ready for was the look of hurt on his face when he asked about the weekend.

"That's great Alice, what for?"

"A Director role with another Solar Energy company." She picked up the stick Atticus placed at her feet and threw it off in the distance, startling a flock of seagulls. "It's in the city."

"Oh."

Although Alice had been expecting this response, she still snapped, "what?"

"It's just that I thought you wanted something different?" Colin's face became stone, and Alice struggled to decipher what he was feeling.

"Well, yeah, but I also can't wait forever to figure out

what different even looks like," she said defensively.

Colin looked at her curiously. "It hasn't been that long."

"Maybe for you, Colin, but I worked fifty-to-seventy-hour weeks for an entire decade. If I stay off too long, I may lose my edge."

Over on the train tracks, her train came into view. Alice watched it enviously, looking at the people through the windows, on their way into something that gave them purpose. It made her feel like she was a waste of space. She turned to Colin to find him sadly watching her.

"What?" she barked. She was seething. See, this was why she shouldn't get serious about him. He didn't understand.

"Nothing," he replied, walking ahead of her.

"No, it's not nothing." She picked up her pace to catch up with him. Atticus ran up to her, concern etched the dog's face as he looked between the two of them as if sensing the tension.

"Don't you want me to find a job, Colin?"

"Of course, I do. I also want you to be happy."

Alice softened a bit, and tried to lighten the mood by joking, "I'll be happy when I'm busy again. I'm not meant to be a woman of leisure."

It didn't work. Colin humored Alice, his mouth turned up in the tiniest of smile that didn't reach his eyes. "Will you be happy doing a job you're not even sure you want anymore?"

"I won't know until I try it, right?"

"You still have time, Alice. You're right at the beginning of figuring it all out. Why rush to the first job that comes your way?"

"If I get this job, and remember I haven't even interviewed for it never mind got it, I can still figure it all out. It'll be even easier, actually."

Colin looked at her almost pitifully. "How will it be easier?"

"I feel like a waste of space right now. Don't you understand? If I have a job, I won't have time to get lost in all the negativity. I'll only be focusing on the good things, so it'll actually be way easier."

"I believed you wanted a job closer to home, where you wouldn't be spending two hours a day commuting while working fifty plus hours a week."

"In an ideal world, Colin, that would be great, but beggars can't be choosers."

"What happens when you get this job? You lived here for two whole years before we finally had an actual conversation. What about Raya, Anya, all the friends you've made these last months? What happens to us?"

"Nothing, I'm not moving anywhere, just getting a job."

"Okay," he replied disbelievingly, a hint of anger tinging his tone.

"You don't get it Colin."

"Explain it to me, Alice. A week ago, you were determined to take as long as a year to find that perfect role that wouldn't take away from this life you've been creating."

"It's all getting to be too much. I went from years of not being anything to anyone, of having no one in my life. And now, I've gotten everything I've ever wanted. A group of friends, a best friend, even a," she trailed off about to say something she knew she would regret before replacing it with, "you."

Colin grabbed Alice's hand, turning her to grab the other one, looked in her eyes as if searching for something she couldn't pinpoint.

Alice had found the life she'd dreamed about. It was why she moved to Haven Cove. She now understood that saying, "be careful what you wish for" because while it had been amazing having people in her life. It was also scary.

She needed them too much. What happened when they got sick of her or they found someone more worthy, or they just disappeared? The only thing for it was to get a job that filled some holes so that she didn't need them so much.

Alice looked down at her hands in Colins', his thumbs caressed her palms with care. She yanked her hands away, glancing up to catch the shock in his eyes.

"This is *my* future on the line, Colin, not yours. You barely even know me after all. I think I know what's best for me. I didn't tell you for your opinion, only your support."

Alice began hurrying down the beach, rushing to the path to town, wanting this conversation to end.

"If you think that this is what you want, Alice, then I do support you. Okay?"

"Fine. I'm actually going to go straight home. I

need to get ready." Alice said as she turned away from downtown and back towards her cottage.

"Good Luck Alice," Colin called to her back as she rushed away. Putting the leash on Atticus, he walked in the opposite direction.

❋ ❋ ❋

To say Alice bombed the interview would be an understatement.

Getting ready she was distracted by just how seething mad she was at Colin. It didn't help that her old office suits didn't fit right. She had lost some weight and gained some muscle from all of her walking. Which meant the waistband was loose, but the legs were tight and uncomfortable. Her feet seemed to have changed too and her old work heels hurt like hell. In fact, she kind of forgotten how to even walk in them.

It hasn't been that long. How can this feel so weird? Alice thought to herself, worried that she had completely lost her edge.

Alice was late to the train station, just barely catching her train in to the city. The seat was uncomfortable, and she fidgeted, trying to get relax.

As the train meandered past the beach, she couldn't help but scan it to look for Colin and Atticus, but they were long gone. The sun was high in the sky now. She wished they didn't leave their fight like that. She shook her head and scolded herself, *now is not the time to think about Colin.*

After googling "most common interview questions" this weekend, she had scrambled to prepare answers to all of them. Now she grabbed her notes, hoping that the answers would somehow get stuck in her head during this train ride.

It was difficult for Alice to concentrate though, the sounds of the train, the rocking back and forth, and the hard seat under her. It made her feel a little queasy. How did she do this for years? She spent two hours a day on here, working most of that time. She used to tune everything out, but now the images passing by out the window kept calling her name and she found herself gazing out at them.

The conversation with Colin reminded Alice too much of the conversation she had with her parents when they found out about her interview with White & Dunn, the one she was remembering right before she got this interview. She was sure that's why she reacted the way she did. In fact, she could see that she was expecting him to respond to her news like that.

He didn't understand, though, just like they didn't. The corporate world was her home, it was where she belonged. She hated not having a job. She enjoyed going for walks with Colin, hanging out with Raya and checking off items on her adventure list. But, that wasn't real life. It was more like an extended, forced vacation. *Is it though?* A nugget crept through her mind, an idea that she could find something that allowed her to still have all that. *No, I've been loafing about too long,* she answered herself.

She was glad she had gotten this interview; it was a much-needed wake up call in her opinion. It was time to find her way to back to reality. *Why? You still have almost a year to figure things out,* the voice said. In theory, yes, but how was it going to look with this gaping hole on her resume? They would think something was wrong with her if she took the whole time off.

Plus, she didn't have to take this job. *It's just an interview!* She thought. She had to come to it because she hadn't actually interviewed for a job in ages and she needed the practice. *I can say no,* she told herself.

The sound of the train engineer announcing their arrival downtown shook from her internal monologue. Alice quickly grabbed her things, angry with herself for not reading through her notes more. It was weird. Alice's body instinctively knew exactly what to do and where to go in the train station, but her mind felt disconnected, like she didn't quite fit anymore.

It was noisy and smelly, the sounds and smells overwhelming her senses. Her feet ached from her heels. Her heart hurt from the lack of smiles from the people she passed. She got annoyed with herself that she had already turned into a cliched heroine from a romance novel.

The offices of Black Crow Solar were right around the corner from White & Dunn, leaving her on edge, terrified of running into someone from there. At one point, Alice thought she saw Perkins turnaround in front of her, but it wasn't him at all. It would be a nightmare running into him. She could just picture his smug face as he looked her up and down and concluded that he had made the right call. That not only was she not cut out, not for partnership, but for their business all together.

She tried to shake the nerves off, but with every step she took, they grew and grew.

* * *

"So, Alice, the recruiter had excellent things to say about you. Honestly, we're excited at the prospect of hiring someone from White & Dunn, especially from their Energy division," the interviewer said to Alice as they settled themselves into the interviewing room.

The board room was so high up the tower that it actually had views of the bay that led out to the ocean. Alice could see sailboats dotting the water. The thought, *how lucky those people are to be out there and not in here*, fluttered, unwelcome, through her brain.

She looked at the interviewer, who seemed to wait for her to say something. She quickly went through what he had just said, "yes, my experience would be very valuable".

"I would love to know more about your time there. You were there for so long, and you progressed nicely. Can you tell me about that?"

That was not the question Alice was expecting. She didn't know where to start, at the beginning or the end? What did they want to know about her time?

Alice jumped in; it was much harder than she expected talking through her decade of experience at White & Dunn. She rambled and went on too long, but also felt like she wasn't saying much of anything at all. The interviewer's, *what was his name again?*, eyes glazed over and she knew she had lost him. She quickly jumped to Solar Corp and their purchase.

"Okay, that's good. I'm curious, why did you leave White & Dunn after the acquisition?"

"Oh, it wasn't my choice," slipped out before Alice could stop it. Her eyes widened in shock, matching that of the interviewer's. Her palms had gotten so sweaty she was leaving streaks on her pants as she tried to wipe them dry. She rushed on, "well, you see, that makes it sound worse than it was. Apparently, Farley Oil & Gas wanted to make a cultural and strategic pivot as they took over Solar Corp, and the few of us on the original team who were very loyal to the leadership, organization and product line were let go to ease the transition."

"I can see that. The news surrounding the takeover sounds like a nightmare to organizations like ours, however it doesn't hurt that it's taken out one of our competitors. I am still surprised that they laid you off, though."

"You and me both," Alice murmured but not quietly enough as the interviewer definitely heard her.

Alice knew then it was done. The interviewer's whole demeanor changed. Gone was the excitement and interest and instead it became perfunctory, him asking the questions because he was obliged to.

Alice wished she could say that she rose to the occasion, fighting for herself, but her answers got worse and worse. Long rambling messes she knew made little sense and did not answer the questions properly.

By the time they got to the part where she could ask questions, the interviewer was making a point of checking his phone, so she didn't even bother. The sooner she could be done with this, the better.

TWENTY-FOUR

"You are my sunshine, my only sunshine…" a quiet voice sang in Alice's ear as a hand lovingly caressed her face. She opened her eyes to a room full of sunshine and her mother lying in bed beside her.

"Mama."

"I'm here, my sweet girl, always and forever." "I feel so lost, mama."

"Oh darling, you aren't lost. You're exactly where you need to be."

"I am though, I need you and Daddy so much," tears streamed down Alice's face, her mother wiping them away before they hit the pillow. "I miss you both so much."

"We're still here with you, my darling sweet girl," her mother moved her hand from Alice's face to her heart. "Right in here, always and forever,"

Alice awoke, her face damp with tears. She laid there on her back waiting for the sobs to come, but she her heart calmed and a sense of peacefulness settled. The dream was longer than ever before, and it was as if she actually talked with her mother. It was enough to give her the courage to face the day.

Not enough courage to go down to the beach or downtown. She wasn't ready for that. Maybe she would go to Raya's before her class today, but she was not ready to see Colin. Grabbing her phone to check for any updates and she couldn't help but notice that Colin had texted her multiple times. She quickly deleted them without reading a single one. She did not want any of his kind words distracting her.

The morning passed in a blur as Alice tried to keep herself busy, but she couldn't stop herself from constantly refreshing her email to see if there were any updates from the recruiter. She knew she had blown it, but there was this tiniest bit of hope that the interviewer, Tom (she finally remembered his name on the way home), had seen her potential. That he would value her experience more than her abysmal interview. He had to, right?

Just as she was about to make herself some lunch, her phone rang. The recruiter's name popping up on the screen. "Hello?" Alice answered, hopeful.

"Hi Alice, hope you're doing well," the recruiter said in a rush, "I'll cut to the chase here, Black Crow Solar has decided not to move forward, the feedback I had was that now was not the right time to bring someone with your experience onboard, you may be overqualified even, and Tom was concerned you would get bored. However, he wanted me to call you with the feedback, as he wants you to think of them for your move after your next position."

"What do you mean?"

"Tom thinks you'll be a better fit with another organization and then when you're ready to leave that company to come to them."

"You mean Tom wants to hire me eventually, after he's certain I'm a good hire? He doesn't want to take a chance on me and wants to see if someone else will? All because I got let go from White & Dunn?"

"Not at all," the recruiter tried to placate Alice.

"Thanks for the update. At least you called," Alice said. "Goodbye."

Even though Alice knew that this was probably going to happen, it didn't take the sting out of it. The shame of it all spread through her body. She was so embarrassed. What if news of this interview travelled through the industry? It could blackball her, consider her a pariah. Maybe she'd never get a job in Solar Energy again.

It was hard to think about how she did in the interview, but she forced herself to reflect on her performance. It was out of character for her to be so horrible. Normally, she was good at that sort of meeting. Sure, she hadn't interviewed for a job in years, but she had made pitches to clients and won. It couldn't have been her lack of practice.

When Alice was really honest with herself, she could see that she didn't really want to be there, and while a part of her knew that, the larger part just wanted to slot right back into somewhere.

Which left Alice with one glaring reason why she did so horribly in the interview. Colin and the fight she had with him.

All sense of peace and tranquility that she had when she woke up this morning had all but disappeared. In its place was a seething hot rage at Colin, mixed with a cocktail of shame and disappointment. She looked at her phone and there were a few more texts from him. She opened his name and considered blocking him, but couldn't force herself to do it.

Alice believed getting the interview when she did was a sign, and that her finding a new home in a company was going to be a lot easier than she expected. She pictured herself going back into the office. Even daydreamed about running into Perkins and Dustin in a new suit, surprise flashing across their faces, "Alice? Funny running into you here," they would say. "Why we were just talking about you and how we were so wrong to have let you go. We need you desperately. Will you come back? You'll be a partner, obviously, and we'll double your salary."

Alice would relish the opportunity to say, "haven't you heard? I'm a Director now at Black Crow Solar. I'm thrilled to be working with a leadership team full of actual strategic thinkers, not just frat bros." And then she would turn on her heel and haughtily walk away while they watched in shock and awe.

Instead, she was back at square one, maybe even square negative one. And it sucked. Alice skipped her class again. She simply could not face going in today and sharing this news.

Her phone rang in her hand again, this time a picture of Raya flashing on the screen. She quickly declined the call, not feeling up to talking to her friend.

She was not ready to face anyone. Instead, Alice made her way back up to bed. Even though it was just past lunch, she was ready for this day to be done.

* * *

BANG BANG BANG

Alice awoke to the sound of her door. She was extremely confused, not even knowing the time. In fact she didn't even really know what day it was.

The past few days had passed in a blur. She slept pretty much all day, occasionally eating a protein bar because she knew she had too, not because she was hungry. The only evidence of time passing was the piles of tissues around her bed, a red nose and puffy eyes from endless crying sessions and the greasiness of her hair. Plus, all the ignored texts and calls from Raya and Colin. She was waiting until she was in a better place before she spoke with them, not wanting them to see her like this. Raya anyway.

She wasn't sure what she wanted to do about Colin. Though he'd probably run for the hills. She knew now that it wasn't his fault that she bombed her interview. At least she knew that rationally despite the fact that her stomach still tightened in anger every time she thought of him. Which was why she had been avoiding him.

The darkness of those days were reminiscent of the time after her parents died. Where she lost hours at a time and desperately needed to shut everybody out. The world felt like it was off its axis, her emotions a roller coaster of denial that her parents were gone. Begging with God to bring them back and anger at the world for being so cruel to her.

She could feel herself slipping away into the darkness again.

BANG BANG BANG

The door. She wondered if she just ignored it, if whoever was there would eventually leave.

"Alice, open this door!" shouted Raya. "I'm not leaving until you do!"

Alice got up, grabbed her fluffy pink robe, and threw her hair into an oily ponytail. She should wash her face and brush her teeth, but she didn't have it in her. Besides, she was not letting Raya in.

She kept the deadbolt on and opened the door a crack. "Yes?" she asked before taking in who was on her stoop.

Raya *and* Colin.

"Let us in Alice," Raya said firmly.

"Please," Colin said much softer, "we've been worried sick about you."

"I'm not up to visitors at the moment, perhaps in a few days."

"Neither of us has seen you since Monday. What's wrong?" Raya demanded.

"Nothing's wrong, just a reassessment of my priorities and where I should spend my time. Oh, there's my oven timer. The loaf of bread I'm baking must be ready. I really must go," she lied as she closed the door.

"Alice, please," Raya pleaded through the door, "let us in, not just into your house, but your life too. We can help you get through whatever *this* is."

Alice slithered down the closed door, holding back sobs, not wanting them to hear. Not ready to let them in, not ready to lose them completely once they saw the mess she was and realize she wasn't worth the trouble.

"We want to help you Alice," Colin said. "Atticus is a mess without you, I'm a mess..."

"Just leave me alone. Please," Alice begged, her voice cracking.

"Alice," Raya said, her voice thick with emotion.

Alice could hear the two whispering on the other side. Colin saying something in his measured way and Raya hissing back at him. "Let's give her a bit of space Ray, but we'll be back Alice," Colin eventually said through the door.

"You better believe I'll be back, Alice. You're not shutting me out," Raya said sternly.

Alice held her breath as she heard their feet walk off her porch. She then counted to thirty before giving into the sobs. What was *wrong* with her? She was so lonely and was desperate to have someone take care of her. Why then, when two people showed up at her door to help her, did she shoo them away? Why couldn't she let them in?

As Alice sat on the floor, she was transported back in time to those months after her parents died. She shut everyone out. Her friends tried, for a bit at least, they would come visit and sit with her while she was in tears or catatonic. Eventually, she felt too guilty, so she stopped answering the door, their phone calls or texts. She would see them on social media and it was like being kicked in the stomach, that while they seemed to want to help her, they also got to still have a normal life. They went on dates, had parties, and got engaged. Life went on normally for them. Whereas her life would never be the same.

She was almost glad when they finally got the message and stopped trying to reach out and help her. Until she missed them, but didn't know how to reach back out. What would she say? How would she explain? It was easier to just let them go.

Easier still was showing up to work a few months after the accident. White & Dunn had offered her position days before the accident. Her parents never knew. After their disappointment at her even interviewing with them, Alice had been working up to tell them.

Though her father's advice rung through her head on that first day. "Work is work. When you're committed to it, you show up. You give it your all. No matter what's going on in your life, you work." It was advice he gave her when he had broken his leg on their first, and only, ski trip over Christmas Break. The doctor had recommended he take a month off, but he went back to work that very first day despite Alice's teenage protestations that he should stay home.

White & Dunn had committed to her. She was grateful that they pushed her start date once she had told them of her loss. She had committed herself to them and had internalized his advice. Work was work, and it became her life too, so that nothing could ever get in the way of it.

It was that commitment to working hard that had allowed her to claw her way out of the dark hole she had dug herself into. It gave her purpose again. Over the years, she found the harder she worked, the more she could keep her grief at bay.

It was time that Alice followed her father's advice again. It was time to work. Well, to find work. Work was the answer to dealing with her grief before and it could be again. It was time to get serious. It was time to find a new job.

TWENTY-FIVE

It was easier said than done, getting motivated to look for a new job. Alice didn't crack open her laptop or think about her career at all over the weekend. However, she did take a shower, go grocery shopping and clean the house. She figured Monday would be the better way to start this next new chapter, but decided the least she could do was to get herself and the house ready.

It was Monday morning now, a beautiful fall day with a crispness to the air. Alice wanted to get back on the beach, but wasn't ready to see Colin and Atticus. Which was why she set off an hour after the sun showed itself, knowing that they would probably be done and heading home. She threw on her coat and toque and made her way down the street.

As the newly fallen leaves crunched under her feet, a new sense of purpose grew with each step. The excitement of being busy again had allowed her to tamp down her feelings. Exactly how Alice liked it. Once she made it to the beach, she paused to peer around the dunes to make sure it was empty. The sight of a man putting a leash on a dog on the other end startled her, causing her to jump back in alarm, with her heart racing as she feared she had been seen. She peeked again and gasped when she spotted the man look down the beach before stepping off the sand, making it safe for her to approach the water.

The worry of getting caught slipped away as she breathed in the salty air. She took a tentative step, and then picked up the pace until she was almost at a run. A smile lighting her face for the first time since the interview as she jogged down to the water.

The waves were crashing against the sand, sending water droplets her way, coating her face in saltiness that was not from her tears. She stopped at the water's edge and played a game of catch with the waves, laughing as she ran back and forth. This was what she needed. The beauty of the ocean to ground her, to remind her of what she had.

She heard the rumble of the train behind her, and she spun to watch it snake its way down the tracks and away from the beach. The sun shone in the windows, hiding those within it, but she waved anyway. Waved to the people she was confident she would soon join.

❋ ❋ ❋

The bell rang over the door of Happiness Café to announce her arrival. A group of mothers with strollers were settling themselves into the corner and Alice sighed in relief that she had timed her arrival perfectly.

"Alice!" Raya cried when she saw her, "you're here, finally, I've been so worried."

Alice melted a little at Raya's excitement. It was really nice that someone actually wanted to see her.

"Wait a second," Raya said, the tone of her voice turning suspicious. "Did you come here knowing all those moms desperate for their fix of caffeine would be here?"

"No, no, just running late today," Alice responded guiltily.

"Bull Alice, you can't avoid me forever. You're going to have to tell me what's going on. Colin is blaming himself and is miserable, and honestly, I am, too. I thought we were friends."

While Alice felt bad, her shackles still rose. Raya did not understand what it was like to be her. "We are friends. I just need some space, okay?"

Alice saw Raya's face fall, but the sound of the moms interrupted them, chatting as they lined up behind Alice, "Raya, Alice!" said Kelsey. "I'm so excited for the book club coming up. I'm hosting it, right? I think my best friend, Bex, will be in town visiting. Can she join us?"

"Of course, she can," Raya replied while performing her special kind of magic, making Alice's normal order while carrying on the conversation. "Now are you sure you're up for hosting Kels? Baby Bennet is only six months old. I can have it here again?"

"I miss hosting! If Benny is having a rough go of it, I'll take you up on the offer, but otherwise I'm looking forward to using all my event management and party throwing skills again." Kelsey was an event manager with quite a large social media following. She had clients all over the State, but had taken the year off as maternity leave.

"Well, I love when you host so let's stick to the plan. I really need to finish the book, honestly it hasn't been that interesting," Raya said as she expertly created a foam rose on Alice's drink.

"Have you read it Alice?" she asked her friend while handing her the coffee.

"I finished it. It gets better by the end. I'm not sure if I can make the meeting though. I've been pretty busy, so I'll have to let you know, Kelsey."

Raya's head snapped to Alice, her smile vanishing as she threw her friend a look that said, *we'll talk about this later.*

"That's too bad, but I hope you can come. It's nice to have some more younger people in the group!"

"I better be off. It was nice seeing you all," Alice said to the group and Raya, turning to leave. It wasn't until she was out of the café that she realized she had been holding her breath. She quickly picked up her pace and sped walked her way to the safety of her home.

❊ ❊ ❊

Once at home, Alice took her coffee up to her office and set herself for a day of work at her computer. She opened her laptop to check her emails. Nothing but spam. The sting of an empty inbox still smarted. Then sat there confused, not knowing what to do.

Where does one even find jobs? What does she do once she sees a job posting? She tried to remember her job search from ten years ago when she first graduated.

Resume. She had a resume; it was even updated. She opened it up and cringed as she read it. *Was I drunk when I wrote this?* She asked herself and then remembered that she had drank almost an entire bottle of wine when she had updated the document. She knew it needed to be overhauled but did not know on how to do that. Alice struggled to think about how to condense a decade of experience into a few words on a page. She googled it. Unfortunately, "how to write a resume" brought up over two million results.

Alice was an accomplished woman. She spent years researching, gathering data and information, then analyzing it all to come up with a solution or recommendation. So why did she feel like such an idiot going through this information? There was much more to think about now than back when she first looked for a job. There was technology that read your resume that you had to worry about now. No one could agree on anything. Apparently, there was a lot of controversy over how many pages, what font to use, and how you format it. She could not make sense of it. She desperately needed someone to ask.

"Claire!" she exclaimed aloud. Claire was an expert, and the class was tomorrow. Unfortunately, just thinking of Claire and the missed classes left Alice with a lead balloon in her stomach, but she refused to let her guilt and shame stop her from asking for help. She would go early and talk to Claire before class about accommodating her new direction. Alice leaned back in her chair, coffee cup in hand, a smile on her face. *It's all coming together.*

TWENTY-SIX

"**A**lice, I was worried about you," Claire said as Alice walked into the classroom twenty minutes early. She was worried that the others would be there but was pleasantly surprised to find the room empty but for Claire.

"Sorry, it's been a rollercoaster of a few weeks."

"Tell me about it," Claire said, gesturing to a chair.

Alice gave her the cliff's notes version, the increasingly desperate need to find the job, the fear of losing her edge, the disastrous interview and forthcoming rejection, and ending with the confusing resume information.

"Wow, what an eventful time you've had," Claire said. "Okay, let's break this all down. First, what you're feeling–that desperate need to find a job ASAP– is normal, but just because it's normal doesn't mean it's right. Honestly, that's showing us a confidence problem–you don't trust yourself to find something better, you don't believe it's possible for you, and you feel that it's all out of your control." She paused. "What goes through your head when I say that?"

Alice paused. Her initial reaction was defensiveness, that Claire didn't know her or her situation. Her situation wasn't normal. Though there was a little voice that whispered *she's right*, but she quickly shushed it, "I can see how you would come to that conclusion, but it's different for me,"

"How is it different for you?"

Alice listed through all the reasons in her head. In all sense of the word, she was an orphan. She was a highly successful person; she had a mortgage to pay, and she *needed* to work. "It just is," was her response instead, not really wanting to go into it.

"When you're ready to share more about how it's different, I would love to help you through it. Now, how long do you think it'll take you to actually see a decline in your abilities?"

"It's already happening. My clothes don't fit me right. I spent all day on my computer and my whole body hurt, and then the interview-

"Yes, the interview. What do you think happened there?"

Alice did not want to get into it. She was already sick of thinking about all of this and certainly did not want to talk about it anymore.

"I've lost my edge, that's what happened. I bumbled my way through my answers. I didn't know how to talk about White & Dunn and why I'm no longer working there. What I really need is to figure out how to answer that question. Then I think I'll be good."

"Okay, how do you want to answer it?"

Alice's skin prickled in annoyance with all the personal questions. "That's what I'm asking you. How should I answer it!?"

"In my experience, the truth told in a short and sweet manner works best, as it doesn't raise any red flags on the interviewer's end."

Alice sat back in her chair. "Like, Solar Corp was bought by Farley and it was during that acquisition process that the difficult decision was made to let go myself and several key individuals on my team."

"Exactly! That wasn't too hard now, was it?"

Alice smiled for the first time since she walked in the room. "No, that feels good, actually. It's true. But wait a second, he asked why they didn't find me another team or client to work on. I fumbled big time on that."

"He may have only asked that because red flags had been raised with your answer, so they may not probe anymore, but it is good to be prepared just in case. What could you say? How did they explain it to you?"

"They said something about it being a conflict of interest. They laid off all the individuals who were most invested in Solar Corp and their products. We were a concern to Farley as they want to dismantle the company and its products. I don't know how much of that I can go into, though. Honestly, I think I said too much during the interview."

"Hmmm, okay. What about saying something like, unfortunately, some details surrounding the acquisition made it impossible for a transfer, but I can't discuss it more than that because of confidentiality. I'm sure you understand."

"Yes, that sounds great. I can say that. It's all true. They won't think it's weird?"

"It may raise a little red flag, but with confidentiality being so important, it's good to show your ability to stay tight-lipped about certain things. It also shows commitment and loyalty to an organization that laid you off."

"This is what I need, exact answers. This is so good. What about my resume?"

"We actually will start on resumes next week. Many of the others have spent the past week completing their picks of jobs and careers."

"Next week? I can't wait that long. I'm already behind."

"Behind how Alice?"

"It's been more than a month since I was laid off. With that interview, I think I'm even further behind than I was on day one. I'm sure my performance in that interview will get around. I need to show my face *now* to get ahead of it."

"At the end of class today, I can tell you more about the process and you can write the resume this week instead of next."

"I don't know. It seems to move slowly. Remind me again how the classes will work?"   "Next week is teaching how to write Resumes, Cover Letters & LinkedIn. The week after that is feedback and critiques of the documents. Then we'll move into increasing your visibility and uncovering job opportunities. Over three weeks, we'll discuss job boards and networking.

Then we'll be diving into interviews for the last sessions."

"That's five weeks away! It's way too long."

"The course is designed to have you slow down so that you find a job and career you love, not just anything. When you started this, Alice, you wanted to explore something different for your next step. Remember something that was more centered on people?"

"I will do that. Once I have a job." Alice was agitated and desperate to get started immediately. Her leg was shaking, ready to propel her out of her chair and get to work. "I want to get back to work. No, I need to get back to work. I know at the beginning of the course I said I wanted to explore something different, and maybe I do, but I miss working. I don't like having too much time with nothing to do."

Claire watched Alice thoughtfully. "You feel like you need to go back to work to avoid too much free time?"

"Exactly!"

"Why?"

Alice was getting frustrated with these questions. Why does everything have to be more than what it is? "I just do, that's why."

"Alice, the sense I'm getting is that this time off has resurfaced something that you're struggling with, that you want to avoid. Work allowed you to avoid it and that's why you're rushing back. Is that true?"

How dare she. Alice thought. Though she knew Claire was right, too many memories of her parents had been swirling through her head these past weeks. Why wouldn't she want to avoid them? They made her feel horrible. Alice didn't see what was so wrong about that.

Claire was an expert and Alice would really love her advice, but at what cost? If she stayed in the course, it was only going to slow her down and leave her open to more questions like this. Alice scrapped her chair back, coming to a stand while collecting her stuff.

"I don't think this is going to work out. The thing is, I want a job as soon as possible and I understand your process is more drawn out. I think it would be a mistake for me to stay in the course. Don't worry about a refund, but I'm going to stop coming."

"I'm so sorry to hear that, Alice," Claire rushed in, standing to face her. "I'm sorry if my line of questioning made you feel uncomfortable. Your future has so much potential and I have to admit I'm concerned you're giving up on that so quickly..."

Alice went to interrupt her, but Claire raised her hand, stopping her. "I understand why you feel so strongly that you have to take a job as soon as possible, and I would love to support you in that if you were still open. I want you to be happy at work. That's really it."

"Thank you, but honestly, I think it's best for me to continue on my own."

Claire looked regretfully at the woman. "Well, I wish you luck. And remember, I'm here for you whenever you need me."

❊ ❊ ❊

She was so lost in her irritation that she ran into someone without noticing and dropped all of her stuff on the floor. "I'm so sorry. I was lost in thought," she apologized, quickly bending to pick up her stuff, when a hand grabbed hers.

"Alice," Colin whispered.

Alice sat back on the floor in shock. She looked at him, kneeling on the floor in front of her. His normally relaxed face was tense, his cheekbones popping and his strong jaw clenched. His eyes were full of concern and hurt.

"Here, let me help you." He grabbed her arm to pull her up.

The jolt that travelled up her arm when he touched her startled Alice, but she quickly shook him off. "It's fine. I don't need your help."   Alice stood up on her own, grabbing her papers from him. They stood there looking at each other, neither knowing what to do.

A vision of their past and future flashed through her mind. A past where she was so happy to run into him. A future vision of her seeing him here with two kids, all running to her with their arms open wide. She shook the thoughts from her head.

It had been a week since their argument, but it had felt like years. Colin had called, texted and showed up a couple of more times at her house, but Alice had avoided him. While she knew it wasn't entirely his fault that she bombed the interview, she also believed that if she hadn't been distracted by him and their fight that she would've done better. Alice was afraid that seeing him would have her throwing down her walls again and she couldn't afford that.

"You have your course today?" Colin asked. Alice looked at him fully, trying to muster the courage to deny her feelings for him. He looked tired and worried. His hair looked as if he'd been pulling at it, his clothes a little wrinkly.

Immediately, her heart ached for him. She caused this and her arms longed to wrap around him and tell him they'll be okay. Alice fought those feelings as she admitted, "I do, well, I did. I actually dropped out." Alice wanted him to challenge her decision so she could prove how wrong he was for her.

"Well, you know what's best for you," he said instead, echoing her own words from the beach. He was trying to show her he understood and would support her no matter what her decision was.

"You're right. I do." Slathering some plaster on the brick wall, she was desperately trying to build between her head and her heart.

The hurt in his eyes deepened and his shoulders slumped in defeat. Alice watched as Colin tried to lighten the mood, his mouth turning up in a small smile as he told her, "we've missed you on our morning walk, I would say I miss you more but Atticus sits there every morning while we wait, whining away so I've got tough competition."

Alice changed tactics because she couldn't handle anymore of his pain. "I need to get some momentum going before I have any more distractions. Honestly, my life is a mess right now, Colin. While I loved spending all that time with you, it took me away from what matters most: my career."

"Oh, I see," Colin said, looking down at the ground.

"You're a great guy, Colin, but…"

He quickly looked back at her, his eyes narrowed slightly, causing her to trail off. "Hey, you don't have to give me that speech, Alice. We weren't together long. In fact, we hadn't even had *the* conversation about what we were. You don't owe me any explanations."

Alice didn't know whether to feel relieved or disappointed at those words. "Okay then, I'll see you around." She turned to leave, but Colin tugged on her hand.

"One last thing, just because you don't want anything serious to happen between us, I would love it if we could be friends. It's been great having you in my life these last few weeks, and if friendship is how I can keep you, then friendship it is."

Alice could tell that this was a practiced speech, something that Colin had been working on saying these past few days. She immediately wanted to shout yes, but knew that was a slippery slope. Though she also didn't want to tell him no. Ultimately, she decided on a middle-ground. "I'll have to think about that, but I enjoyed spending time with you too, so maybe you'll see me at the beach one morning."

Colin's face broke out into a wide grin, his eyes sparkling like the sun hitting the ocean water. Alice could feel her eyes well up in sadness as she said a quiet goodbye to her dreams of waking up to that face every morning for the rest of her life. She walked away before he could see the emotional effect he was having on her and darted into the woman's bathroom to collect herself.

She waited in there for longer than necessary, hoping when she went back out that he would be gone. He was.

Thomas was there instead, doing his rounds to make sure everything was going smoothly. Alice was shocked at his appearance. It hadn't been long since she had last seen him, but his normally vibrant dark black skin had a grey tinge and was dull. He'd lost a chunk of weight too, so his clothes were hanging off of him. He noticed Alice and gave a tired smile and wave.

"Alice, how lovely to see you! Please come sit with me," he requested.

They settled themselves on a few of the chairs that dotted the atrium area of the community center. "Thomas, are you okay?" Alice couldn't stop herself from asking.

"I'm fine, my dear. Just a little rundown with a virus is all, nothing contagious but a nuisance, nonetheless."

"Can I send you over some meals or something?" Her Italian side coming out, wanting to fatten him up with some good old-fashioned Italian cooking.

"No, no, dear. That's okay," he said, chuckling, "though that's very kind of you to offer."

They sat in silence for a few moments, as a small

group of toddlers came inside from the outdoor park, "Hiya Mr. Thomas," said small voice after small voice as they walked past.

"It must be incredible running this place."

Thomas looked around, a wistful look on his face. "It's been the joy of my life creating this place. When I moved here, it was rundown and decrepit. The town council wanted to shut it all down. I gave up my partnership and law career to take it on. Not only did we save it but we've done this," he said warmly, waving his arms around.

"That must've been really challenging, though."

"Nothing I love more than a good challenge. I think you and I are alike in that way."

Alice laughed, "that's for sure."

"It's everything I ever wanted in a career, standing up for a cause, leading teams, the ability to wear many hats, and that no single day is the same. All of that is amazing, but nothing beats seeing the payoff for all my hard work. The smiles on those kids' faces who get to have daycare in this wonderful space. The laughter of all the old biddies who use the pool to exercise and then the seating area to socialize. The teens who play basketball instead of getting into trouble. The bookworms leaving with so many books they can barely carry them. I get to experience it right along with them. What a gift."

"That's sounds magical. If only we could all be so lucky."

"Speaking of magical careers, isn't Claire's course on

right now? Why are you out here with me and not in there?"

Alice was embarrassed. She didn't want to let Thomas down. Although she hardly knew him, she wanted his approval so badly.

"I dropped out today," she replied sheepishly.

"Oh, dear."

"I thought I could handle the time off work, but it hasn't been easy. It's bringing up a lot of things from my past."

"Oh?"

Alice surprised herself by opening up to Thomas. "My parents died in a car accident, and not working has brought up all these memories and feelings that I'm not ready to feel. I don't think a life with too much time on my hands is good for me." She had so many thoughts and feelings swirling around her head that she felt like she would go crazy if she didn't let them all out. She just knew that Thomas was someone she could trust.

"Feelings aren't something we should run away from dear because when we do, we often end up living a life we don't really want."

"It's more than that though. Work is the only place where I feel like I belong. It feels like home to me."

"Did you want to know something about belonging?"

"What's that?"

"We often think belonging is a fact. That it isn't really up to us, that other people or certain circumstances determine where we belong."

"That is true, though."

"No, it isn't. Belonging is a feeling that you feel in here," he said emphatically while placing his hand over his heart. "That means you decide where and who you belong to."

"For years you chose to belong to White & Dunn, just like I chose to belong to my law firm," Thomas continued, "but *you* get to decide if you want to keep belonging to a company. Or if it's time for you to belong to someone else, to a community, or anything really."

"Why does it have to be either or?"

"Why does it?"

"It doesn't. I was trying to tell Colin this. Just because I get another job in the city doesn't mean that no one will ever see me."

"It must be nice to have people who would miss you," Thomas said, seemingly changing the subject.

"Nice. And scary. I have had no one in my life that would miss me or care for me since my parents died." Alice's eyes welled up and she blinked furiously, trying to keep those tears from falling. She looked down at her hands and steeled herself against the onslaught of emotion threatening to overtake her. "Its why work is vital. It's better for me than all this leisure time."

Thomas looked at her, a questioning look in his eyes as he obviously considered what he wanted to say. He sighed as he reached his hand across to rest it on top of hers and finished their conversation with these parting words, "just remember you can feel you belong, that you're home no matter what, it's all up to you."

TWENTY-SEVEN

Alice was taking a well-deserved break, sitting on her couch watching Netflix. All that talking with Claire, Thomas, and Colin had exhausted her. She had also rewritten her resume and while she was positive it wasn't good enough yet, it still felt so good to have it done. She even quickly applied to five jobs and hoped to get an interview soon.

Just as she was about to start a movie, a heavy banging on the door accompanied by someone yelling, "Alice Miller, let me in!" interrupted her.

Alice groaned. She had had enough heavy exchanges for the day.

"I'm not leaving. I got my mom to watch Annie, so I'm here until you finally talk to me," Raya asserted.

Though Alice desperately wanted to ignore Raya, she knew deep down that it was time to talk with her. While she wasn't ready for a relationship with Colin, she was ready for a friendship with Raya and knew pushing her away much longer would put it at risk.

So, she got herself up off the couch and made her way to the door, all while Raya continued banging and shouting at her. Alice opened the door and, with a wobbly smile and tears in her eyes, let her friend in.

"I know we haven't been friends long, and maybe I'm reading more into our friendship than you are, but we're *friends* in my mind. You know what I mean? Like forever friends, best friends forever, all those inane things we'd write when we were like ten? The way we clicked, I could just immediately picture ourselves as two old ladies sitting on the beach, laughing and talking the days away. Being there for each other for everything, the highs and lows of life. Celebrating and cheerleading. Supporting and caring for each other. So even if you don't feel the same way, please just let me support you and care for you right now."

Raya ended her long rambling monologue with a big shaky breath before finally sitting down on the couch across from Alice.

"Okay, needed to get that off my chest before I forgot about it. I've been working on that for ages. Honestly, it didn't come out as polished and smoothly as I hoped," she continued.

Alice sat looking at Raya, a little shocked. She knew Raya told her time and time again that they were friends, but she was so friendly with everybody that she sometimes worried that it was just something she said to people.

"I feel the same way," Alice got out as a tear snaked its way down her cheek, "but I'm afraid. This is embarrassing to admit, but I have had no real friends in a really long time. I'm used to taking care of myself."

"Oh honey, me too!"

"That's a lie. You have the entire community here.

You are so beloved by everyone."

"Okay, I have a lot of friends, but I don't have a lot of really close friends. The ones you call when you are at your lowest. That person you're desperate to call with the best of news. Or even just to share the most boring of small daily stories. A friend that you share your whole life with."

Raya sat there so earnestly, trusting Alice with her heart that she felt her own heart tighten with fear. "What if you leave me?" she whispered, baring her insecurities completely.

Raya pulled Alice toward her, enveloping her in a giant hug. "Let it out. I'm here for you. I'm not going anywhere," Raya said soothingly as Alice did as she was told and sobbed into her friend's shoulder.

They sat there, Raya rubbing Alice's back until at last all of her tears ran dry.

Alice moved back to her corner of the couch, a little embarrassed at her display of emotion. "Thanks, I guess I needed that," she said as she wiped her face with her hands. She slowly brought her eyes to Raya's face, which was filled with so much love and tenderness that Alice almost lost it again.

No one had looked at her like that in years, but immediately her body reacted in opposing ways. A massive sigh of relief that she wasn't alone with equal parts of needing to run, to shut Raya out.

"What's going on Alice?"

Alice opened her mouth, not sure what to say, before finally just letting it all out. Her insecurities about not working, the horrible interview, her fight with Colin, quitting the course, and her confusing conversation with Thomas. Everything but her parents' passing.

Raya just sat and listened. She didn't interject with advice, or try to change Alice's mind on things or even admonish her for putting herself down. She asked questions, listened patiently and simply held Alice's hand throughout it all.

"Sorry, that was a lot, wasn't it? I didn't mean to unleash it all on you like that." Alice touched Raya's sweater. "And I ruined another sweater of yours!"

"You *have* been bottling that shit up for too long. I'm just glad it's out. Next time, don't push me out and then I can be there for you for everything as it's happening, okay?"

"Okay."

"Promise?"

Alice smiled at her friend, still a little overwhelmed by Raya's steadfast commitment to their very new friendship. She knew she had to decide. Let Raya in completely or shut her out and go it alone. It was an easy choice.

"Promise."

* * *

"I need a man," Raya moaned to Alice as the credits for the last episode of Bridgerton rolled. It was late into the night and gone was a bottle of wine and a frozen pizza as they watched an entire season of the steamy show.

Alice turned towards her friend to reassure her, "come on, you're doing amazing. Anya's great, the café is great, your whole life is great."

Raya leaned her head on the back of the couch in exasperation. "But I'm lonely at night, and it's a lot to take care of. A daughter, a house, a business. My mom is right, life would be easier with a man."

Alice understood. The glimpses she had of what her life could look like with Colin were magical.

"Plus, I'm horny as hell, and my vibrator just isn't doing it for me anymore," Raya said seriously.

Alice barked out a laugh, caught off guard.

"What?" she asked defensively. "Don't tell me you would say no to Colin climbing into bed with you?"

Alice didn't know how to respond to that. She definitely wouldn't want to say no to Colin taking her to bed, in fact just the thought sent a shiver down her spine. But her and Colin were done, so it was a waste of time to even think about it.

But she ignored that question and instead agreed with her friend. "I definitely miss sex. It's been ages."

The two sat in silence, gazing out the window.

"I've got it!" Raya shouted. "A singles night. I saw something on Facebook. Let me..."

Alice's eyes bulged, staring at her friend in wide-eyed horror as Raya scrolled through her phone, terrified about what she was about to suggest.

"Here it is. Next town over, this Saturday night

at 8:00pm. 'Calling All Singles', a cocktail hour at the Anchor Bar. It's not too far, I think the train even goes there. I'll need to find a sitter for Annie…"

"You should go, Ray. It'll be good for you. I'll take care of Anya for you"

"Me? Alone? No way. You're coming with me too. I'm not the only one who's single."

"No. I don't want a relationship, remember? I would be with Colin if I did."

"Who said anything about a relationship? I just need a good roll in the hay, a good old-fashioned screw me senseless, a…"

"Raya," Alice rushed in to interrupt her, "I don't know about this."

"How's your list of adventures coming along?" Raya suddenly changed tactics.

"What does that even have to do with anything?" she challenged.

"Answer me." Raya narrowed her eyes at Alice.

"Fine, it hasn't been coming along at all," she admitted.

"Perfect. We'll put this on the bucket list and that way you'll have something to check off!"

Guilt gnawed at Alice. She had been ignoring the bucket list. She really wanted to become a bigger part of this community. This might be an easy checkmark for her and may motivate her to tackle some of the other things on the list.

"If, and it is still a big if, I go, it'll be to help you find someone."

A wide grin broke across Raya's face as she pumped her fist in the air triumphantly. "Okay, you can come and be my wingman. Wingwoman? Whatever you would be called. Help me get laid. I'm going crazy over here. Plus," she said as she wrapped her arms around Alice. "I'll love you forever."

Alice sighed, she knew she had lost. "Fine. I'll go."

TWENTY-EIGHT

"This is not what I was expecting," whispered Raya to Alice as the two friends walked into the poorly lit bar. The ambiance was brown. Brown wooden walls, brown bar and tables with brown chairs. Most of the light came from illuminated beer signs that hung around the place. In one corner, there were two pool tables, commandeered by the smattering of men who were in attendance.

"It's like we're back at a middle school dance," Alice whispered back. "Boys on one side and girls on the other."

Despite being jampacked, the women formed groups by the bar, away from the men, but occasionally sneaked inquiring glances towards them.

"Maybe we should just go," Raya said back. "There are hardly any men here at all."

"Nope, we're staying," Alice insisted, grabbing nametags and writing their names down in sharpie. "We're out. You look amazing and I'm going to be the best wingwoman there is. It won't matter that there's three women to each man."

"Hello, hello, hello!" said a high chipper voice. "Welcome to 'Calling All Singles'!"

The two friends turned to find a petite woman dressed all in pastels with her platinum blond hair pulled back into a tight ponytail with a pink drink in her hands.

"I'm Sonia, the owner of Single in the City, your one stop shop for all things dating in your thirties, forties and beyond!"

"Hi Sonia, I'm Alice and this is my friend Raya. It's our first event."

"Even better! You'll love it. And if you don't find your match, we've got speed dating, a ton of other singles events, matchmaking services, and even dating coaching if you need more help with it all."

"Wow," Raya for once was rendered speechless and instead just stared at Sonia with an astounded look on her face.

"I know it's incredible, isn't it? Gone are the days of having to go it alone. Single All the Way is with you at every turn. Go have a blast!"

Raya turned to look at Alice, her face still a picture of bewilderment. "I'm sorry Alice. What the hell was I thinking? I don't know if I'm that desperate."

"Hey, we're here. There are some handsome men in attendance. I'm sure one of them will be happy to spend at least one night with you," Alice teased. "Let's get a drink. Worst-case scenario? You and I have a night out together."

The two of them elbowed their way through the hordes of other single women to the bar to order a glass of wine and then made their way over to an empty wooden booth.

As the singles drank more, they intermingled. Small groups formed, usually a man with a couple of women eagerly vying for their attention. Sonia made her way through the crowd, obviously pleased with the turnout.

Alice and Raya watched a man in tight pale blue pants with an even tighter pinstriped button down walk confidently through the crowds of women. He had perfectly styled dark brown hair and a broody look on his face.

"That's Jared Walker, Haven Cove's very own heartthrob."

"Damn, he's..."

"Hot, no other way to say it. He knows it too."

They continued to watch in awe as Jared made his way through the crowd, seemingly unaware of the glares the men were sending his way but all too aware of the adoring looks the women were sending him. Looks that he acknowledged with the odd wink or nod of his head. He looked over at their booth and his face broke into a wide grin.

"Raya Gupta! I never thought I'd see *you* out at one of these events."

"I should say the same of you. Wouldn't think you would need a singles event to meet women."

"Oh, I don't, trust me," he said, winking at the two of them. "I'm here as a wingman for my friend Michael, just waiting for him to show up. May I join you two lovely ladies?"

He slid into the booth before waiting for their response, and turned his whole body towards Alice, his chocolate eyes boring into hers. Alice could feel her body lean into his, almost as if it was magnetized. His lips twitched in a smile and he said smoothly, "why hello there. I don't believe you and I have had the pleasure of meeting."

Alice couldn't help the giggle that escaped her. "Alice, I'm Alice. Raya's friend, I'm here as her wingwoman."

Jared gave her a little pout. "Does that mean you aren't looking for a match?"

"Jared Walker, leave her alone," Raya playfully pushed him back in the seat. "She's as good as taken."

"I figured. I think I've seen you around town with Colin. Really nice and a little awkward, but a great catch. Someone you want to settle down with. I'm someone you only want for the night."

"Like I told her already, you're our resident casanova."

"And proud of it," Jared sat back with a gratified smile on his face. Suddenly, he threw his hand up in a wave and shouted across the bar, "hey Michael, over here!"

An obviously nervous man turned towards them, a relieved smile on his face. "Thank God, I was afraid you weren't here yet, and I'd be left to fend for myself."

Michael was the opposite of Jared with his blond curly hair, light green eyes and jeans and a shirt that didn't fit quite right. He stood there, obviously very uncomfortable in this setting.

Alice looked at Raya to find her looking tenderly up at Michael, a sparkle in her eyes that Alice had never seen before. She shifted over to make room for Michael. "Here, come sit. Jared will go get us this next round."

Michael looked appreciatively at Raya and took the seat beside her. "Thanks, it's not quite what I thought."

"Me too. By the way, I'm Raya and this is my friend Alice. I'm just getting back to dating after being divorced to the father of my twelve-year-old daughter for almost ten years. I figured that this singles night would be an easy way to jump back in. It's so different from what I expected."

"It felt so easy back in the day, didn't it? You met at some school event. That's where I met my ex, at university. It didn't work out though, like you, divorced with two kids."

"Honestly, I've never even really dated except for my husband and our parents arranged our meeting so old school doesn't even cover it."

Alice watched her friend and Michael with a smile. Though Raya was only looking for a one-night stand, it was quite obvious that Michael had the potential to be much more than a hookup.

Jared dropped off the drinks but didn't sit down. "It looks like my work here is done and there are a couple of drop dead gorgeous women begging for my attention. Are you okay if I leave you alone, Alice?"

"That's nice of you, but of course. Go get 'em, tiger," she said before grimacing in embarrassment at her choice of words. Jared just laughed and made his way over to a small group of women who looked like they won the lottery when he showed up.

Alice sat in silence, Raya and Michael obviously in

their own little world, happy to see her friend hitting it off with someone.

"Alice Miller?" a voice said, startling her from her reverie. Alice looked up to see a man in an impeccably tailored charcoal suit. "It is you!"

"Scott Mason? What a small world!" Scott Mason was a Senior Partner at Blue Wave Consulting, White & Dunn's primary competition in the renewable energy sector. "Here, sit down," she said, shifting over to make room for him.

"Thanks. I'm surprised to see you here. Do you live around here? I thought you lived in the city?"

"I did, but a couple of years ago I moved out to Haven Cove. I'm here with my friend Raya, she wanted to start dating again."

"Looks like it's been a success."

Raya and Michael had gotten so close that you would struggle to slide a piece of paper between them. Their glasses were empty, but they didn't seem to care. They were talking and giggling, clearly having an amazing time together.

"I would say so. Do you live around here?"

"No, still in the city, but I want to move out here. Most of the women I've dated in the city want to stay there, so I figured I may as well try some singles events out here. If you're here for her, I'm assuming you're not looking for a match?"

"No, things are a little too up in the air right now, plus there is someone I'm..." Alice trailed off, not too sure how to describe her relationship with Colin.

"That's too bad," Scott remarked as he took a swig from his pint glass. "I heard about what happened to you."

"With White & Dunn? It was pretty shocking, to be honest. The acquisition all the way to getting laid off. I was not expecting it at all."

"All of us at Blue Wave were absolutely shocked. Not at the acquisition, Farley had been sniffing around some of our clients as well, apparently looking for the company that had a product that would impact their business so that they could put an end to it. What was surprising was that they let a talent like you go."

"Really?"

"A lot of other firms felt the same way as us. You have one of the strongest reputations in renewable energy. We all think Perkins is an idiot for getting rid of you."

Shocked, Alice couldn't believe that anyone even really noticed her work. She closed her mouth, realizing that she was sitting there like a fish. "I had no idea."

"It's true. I've been waiting for you. Hoping you would reach out to me or send me a resume. Are you looking?"

"I took some time when it first happened. Honestly, I just started looking this week. I interviewed with Black Crow Solar, but it didn't go too well." Alice didn't want to even mention it, but didn't want to look like she was hiding something in case he had heard about her disastrous interview.

"You dodged a bullet there. I've not heard good

things about them. Besides, someone like you would get bored internally. It would be like chaining an eagle. Okay, that was a weird analogy, but you get what I'm saying."

Alice laughed. "I never thought of it like that. You're right, though, we usually have more freedom than them. This is amazing, running into you here and having this conversation. It's more helpful than you know."

"To be honest, I have my reasons. I want to hire you. We've been wanting to hire you for years, but I wasn't able to approach you because of legalities and all that, but now that you're on the market, I can. I need you to initiate it, though. It's why I've been waiting for you. I can't email or call you because of some stupid non-solicitation agreement between our companies. So, Monday morning, send me your resume and we'll set up an interview next week. The job will obviously be yours, but I still have to follow the process."

"Do you have an opening on your team?"

"Nope, but as soon as I heard you got let go, I immediately got the ball rolling to create a role for you. The board has already agreed to it. Partner, what you should've gotten at White & Dunn."

"What?! You're kidding, right?" Alice was in such a state of disbelief. Not only was she not the laughing stock of the industry, she was highly sought after?

"Not at all. I know other firms want you too, which is why we've created the partnership role for you. We've never created one for an external candidate before, but we don't want to lose our chance at you. It's also a significant pay increase, more than you would've made even at Partner level at White."

With a promise to send her resume first thing on Monday morning, Scott left Alice to meet a potential love match. Alice sat back in the booth and reflected on the insane conversation she just had. It was like a kaleidoscope of butterflies had just been let loose in her stomach; the nerves overtaking her whole body. It was all happening, everything she ever wanted. The ball was firmly in her court.

TWENTY-NINE

The next few days flew by. Alice sent her resume and Scott quickly scheduled a day of interviews for Thursday, wanting to get all of them done in one day. A quick call with him also prepared her for all the different people she would meet and exactly what they would be looking for.

Alice was confident that these interviews would go nothing like the other one. Especially after the massive confidence boost Scott had given her at the single's night. She was excited about this new future that was coming her way, so much so that she found she was finally ready to make her way back to the beach to resume her morning walks with Colin and Atticus.

Though she was ready to see Colin and Atticus again, it didn't stop the jitters from coming as she made her way down to the beach. It was still mostly dark, the sun a mere hint of light in the sky. She wanted to get there early to meet them, as she was certain that by now Colin had given up waiting.

She stood at their meeting spot, listening to the waves crash into the beach, tasting the salt in the air, and feeling the wind on her face. Then she heard barking and looked up to see the silhouette of a dog pulling a man behind him.

"Alice!" Colin said, his face a picture of happiness. His eyes crinkled as his mouth opened into an enormous grin. "You're here, waiting for us."

Alice kneeled down to give Atticus a loving pat and snuggle, the dog licked her face and panted in glee. "I missed our walks together and decided it was about time I came back."

Alice stood up, unsure of what to do with Colin. Should she hug him? Colin didn't leave it up to her. He put his arms out with a questioning look in his eyes, and she fell into his arms. They stood there hugging until Atticus took matters into his own hands, pulling the leash completely out of Colin's hand and taking off down the beach.

"I love this beach so much," Alice said after they had chased Atticus down and given him his freedom. "It's like a daily reset, you know?"

"Agreed. Though it's better sharing it with you, we missed you so much. *I* missed you so much."

Alice could feel the blush spread all the way through to her toes. "Me too. This is embarrassing, but I didn't really stop coming. I just came later in the morning. I needed it, but you're right, it isn't the same as walking it together."

They watched as Atticus chased after a small crab, laughing as he just missed the shellfish.

"I'm so sorry Alice. You were right. I was letting my baggage get in the way of being a proper friend to you. If you want to go back to a job in the city, I'll do whatever I can do to support you. Your career is obviously very important to you, and since your friendship is important to me, then your career is too."

"Hey, I'm sorry too. I totally overreacted. And then I bombed that interview and I didn't know how to deal with it, so I just shut you and Raya out. I'm not used to having people in my life who are there during tough times."

"Well, I'm here for you. 100%."

"Thanks Colin."

"How is the search? Update me."

"Actually, you won't believe this, but I met up with a Senior Partner from another consulting firm at a singles night this past weekend."

"A singles night?" Colin asked, his voice dripping in confusion and hurt.

"It wasn't for me." She put her hands up in defense. "I went to support Raya. Apparently, she's ready to get back to dating. Anyway, I was sitting there by myself watching Raya hit it off with this guy when the Senior Partner came over. He apparently has been wanting to hire me for years and has been waiting for me to reach out to him ever since I got laid off. For some legal reason or something, he couldn't start contact."

"That's amazing. Though not surprising. I'm sure they all want to hire you."

"That's what he said. And get this, they've created a partnership role for me, which is practically unheard of. I'm interviewing with everybody, but the job is essentially mine."

"That's great Alice, I'm so happy for you," Colin said sincerely. "I can't wait to celebrate with you."

* * *

Alice took her seat on the train back to Haven Cove, exhausted but exhilarated after a day full of interviews. She had five separate interviews; Human Resources, Scott, the Senior Partnership team, her potential team and the Board of Directors, since it was such a unique situation. They all went remarkably well. The dynamic was completely different from at White & Dunn. A good half of the Leadership at all levels were women and people of color. They seemed to be much more collaborative and respectful of each other. All the clients she would work with and overseeing were dream companies to deal with.

The only downside was the conversation she had with Scott around work/life balance and impact. The partners put long hours in, with most of them happening in the office. Plus, the job actually came with more travel than she had before, as she would now oversee multiple clients across the globe, instead of just being the lead on one.

While there was more human interaction, she would spend a lot of time with the leadership teams at the client sites, which meant that this position was further removed from the impact they would be having. It was a niggling concern. She couldn't help but think about what Claire told her about what would make her happy. A collaborative environment where she could 'feel' the impact she was having. Witness it, be part of it, and experience it right along with those she was impacting.

She would figure it out when it came to it, she promised herself. Right now, she was going to bask in the glory of an amazing day of interviews.

She took out her phone and turned off the 'do not disturb' and noticed a flurry of texts and missed calls from Raya and Colin. A smiled played at her lips as she assumed they were reaching out to find out about the interviews. She opened the texts from Raya first.

"Call me ASAP," the latest one said.

Assuming Raya was just too excited to hear about the interview, Alice immediately called her back. "You have nothing to worry about, it went great," Alice said as soon as her friend picked up.

"That's not it," Raya sobbed into the phone. It was noisy in the background, but not the noise of happiness or busyness but the noise of alarm, concern and sadness. Alice was immediately on alert, her whole-body tense. She could feel her body freeze, afraid of finding out more, but needing to just the same.

"What is it Raya? What happened?" She could hear the panic in her voice and tried to rein it in. "Is Annie okay, Colin? What's going on?"

"It's Thomas," Raya said. "He passed away this morning."

Alice was ashamed to admit it, but her first thought was *phew*, that it wasn't a person she was closest to. Then her mind went into overdrive, flitting back and forth between memories of a similar call ten years ago and the present call.

"He collapsed this morning at the community center,"

"This is Officer Michael Riley."

"Apparently, he was diagnosed with pancreatic cancer a month ago."

"There's been an accident."

"They rushed him to the hospital."

"I think you should come to the hospital."

Alice's head was spinning. She was faint, confused at what was happening. Fighting back the inevitable tears of loss and grief, she said. "Stop Raya, stop. I'm on the train. Let me come back to you first. It's too much for me to take in right now."

Without waiting for Raya's response, she hung up. Confusion washed over her at her reaction. She barely knew Thomas, after all. She was relieved at first, for goodness' sake. What was happening? The train passed the community center, the heart of the town. The heart because Thomas was the heart. Alice couldn't fight the tears anymore, unleashing them to stream down her face.

Colin was waiting for her when her train came in, not saying a word, just enveloping her in a bear hug, rubbing her back, holding her as she cried. As they began walking to her house, Alice couldn't help but ask, "why did you come get me? Shouldn't you be with Raya, the others? I barely even knew Thomas."

"I thought this might bring up memories for you. And, I don't know, I just felt I needed to be there for you. Is that okay?"

Alice's heart exploded in her chest. He was worried about her and thought of her needs before she even realized she had them. It was such a simple act of love and devotion, but one that she hadn't experienced since her parents were alive, when they anticipated her needs and took care of her without even needing to be asked.

"It's more than okay," she choked out. "You're so good to me, Colin."

They walked the rest of the way in silence, holding hands.

THIRTY

The day of the funeral was a gorgeous sunny day. Thomas' partner decided to do it outside, in the open field behind the community center. He'd made the decision for a variety of reasons. Obviously, Thomas loved the center, but it was also logistical because none of the town's churches could accommodate everybody who would be in attendance.

For it was truly everybody. The entire town and many of the people from the surrounding towns were there, too. Thomas' impact went far and wide.

Alice sat sandwiched in between an inconsolable Raya and Colin. It was a difficult but also incredibly inspiring day. There were lots of tears, of course, but also stories upon stories of the difference Thomas had on peoples' lives and the community.

Once the service was over, many of the people went into the community center for the reception, but a select group of individuals followed the hearse to the local cemetery. Alice wasn't going to go, but Thomas' partner insisted.

"He thought so highly of you dear, he would really want you to be included," he said, making Alice's eyes smart with tears.

She joined the group as they drove in a long line of cars towards the cemetery. The plot was beautiful, overlooking the ocean, right beside a large oak tree. They listened as the pastor said the final readings,

"Ashes to Ashes..."

Alice was present physically, but her mind was not. Memories of the day she buried her parents were desperately trying to come to the forefront of her mind, but Alice was fighting them off. *Not yet*, she kept telling them, desperately trying to keep them at bay. She did not want to fall apart here.

Her hands were shaking as she took a flower and laid it on the coffin. She couldn't take it any longer. She had to leave. She whispered to Colin that she was going, insisting that he stay and go to the reception. And then she left.

She walked to the beach, a tsunami of emotions threatening to pull her under. She made it to the water's edge just as they crashed.

The day of her parents' funeral was nothing like today. Instead, it was rainy and windy. After she left the hospital, she was in a fugue state. She could barely remember that time, just snippets of the nightmare crashing over her again and again as the realization that her parents were dead kept hitting her continuously. It was like being caught in a riptide that she couldn't swim free from.

She struggled to remember the funeral service at all, but the memories from the graveyard were etched on her soul. It was pouring rain. The funeral home had provided everyone with black umbrellas, but she was too weak to hold one up and too distraught to even

SARACURTO

stand by anyone. She almost welcomed the rain pelting her skin, the wind whipping at her hair, because at least she felt something. The world crumbled around her as she looked at the two coffins holding the people she loved most in the world.

She had stood there, swallowing the anguish, and trying to listen to the words of the priest. He motioned for her to lay a rose on each of the coffins, which she did, and then fell to her knees in the mud, crying out in pain. Her friends rushed to her side, trying to help her, but she shrugged them off. It was too much to let them in to help her.

Eventually, everyone left. It was just her standing in the rain, letting it disguise her own tears, desperate for a new phone call. One where Officer Michael Reilly was calling to say it was all a case of mistaken identity, that she wasn't alone anymore, that her parents were, in fact, alive. A phone call that would never come.

The beach came back into focus. Alice was wracked with sorrow, desperate to change everything. The anguish of losing her parents overcame her again, as if it had just happened. She wondered why was she experiencing this again when she had spent so long trying to push it all down. It was too much.

She curled into herself on the beach, sobbing to herself.

✱ ✱ ✱

Alice didn't know how much time had passed before

247

her tears finally stopped. The sun was getting lower in the sky but hadn't set yet. She heard footsteps behind her, so she quickly wiped her face; she didn't want anyone to see her like this.

"Hey, it's just me," said the loving voice of Raya. "Can I sit?"

The tears Alice assumed were all dried up, returned as she nodded.

Raya sat down close, placing her arm around Alice's shoulders, leaning her face on her own knees, mirroring Alice's position. "Are you okay?"

Alice gave a little shake of her head. "Today brought up a lot of shitty memories. Of my parents' funeral. Memories that I've avoided for ten long years, that seemed to have caught up to me today."

"Oh honey, that must be so hard. You lost them at the same time?"

"Yeah, to a drunk driver."

Raya's mouth opened in shock, but not a sound escaped.

"I try not to think of it, of them. It's too hard," she wept. "The problem is that I'm realizing I've lived a half life for all these years because of it. For ten years, I refused to slow down, terrified that if I did, I would get glimpses of the memories of my life before. Like a kiss on the forehead from my father, or my mother rubbing my back while I was sick, or meandering through museums with them."

Alice paused, turning to look away from the intensity of Raya's eyes and out into the endless water of the ocean. "Memories that caused my heart to literally ache, like it does today. I miss them so much Ray, so so much."

"Of course you do," Raya said as she moved her hand to Alice's back, rubbing it just like her mother had when she was younger.

"The sad thing is, though? I'm realizing today, as I relive it is that trying to avoid those memories didn't actually stop my heart from aching. It just shifted the why."

A flock of pelicans flew over the water, one separating from the pack to dip down to the water to catch a fish.

"Instead of my heart aching for my parents, it ached with loneliness and longing to belong to somebody again, multiple somebodies. But I've been terrified of letting people in because if I did, then they could leave me too, just like my parents. I've spent years avoiding a feeling by feeling it anyway."

Alice was overcome with emotion again, putting her head in between her knees to cry as Raya continued to stroke her back lovingly.

"When I lost my parents, I lost my two biggest cheerleaders. And I'm seeing that I stopped living a life they would be proud of. Because I didn't miss them when I had wins at work because I knew they would've known it wasn't the career for me."

"I stopped doing anything they would have been proud of. Meeting a new friend, dating someone I liked, not because they were convenient and going after my dreams of having a real impact on people."

"Because if I didn't do any of those things, then I

wouldn't have to miss out on them not being there to cheer me on. And if I didn't let anyone new into my life, then I wouldn't be reminded that my parents would never get to meet them."

"I'm sick of it though, this living half alive. If my heart is going to ache anyway, I may as well live a full life, one where I'm actually happy. One where I let others in. Like you, Raya."

"Letting you bulldoze your way into my life has been one of the best decisions I've ever made, even though you didn't give me much choice."

"I'm not one for holding back," Raya laughed through her own tears. "I just wish I knew all this, not that I'm blaming you for not telling me. That's not it at all, more blaming myself for not inviting you to share your story."

"Oh gosh, this is not your fault. I don't tell anyone anything about me. In fact, I've opened up more to you than I normally do."

"I'm so sorry I told you about Thomas while you were on the train. What a crappy place to hear the news. I was just in such a state of shock and needed my best friend."

"Thomas is the first person I know that has passed away since my parents died, no matter what, the whole thing would have been jarring. I'm so glad that I have you and Colin to help me through it though, even though you're experiencing your own grief."

"I know we talked about his appearance, and it seemed like he was sick, but I never thought that this would happen, that he would go so quickly. He was such a vital part of Haven Cove, it's hard to believe he's gone."

"He was the heart of it."

"Have I ever told you about the time Anya played hide and seek in the community center without telling anyone?"

The two friends stayed entwined on the beach as the sky darkened, sharing stories of Thomas and Alice's parents. "Thanks for not giving up on me," Alice whispered as the last hint of the sun dipped below the surface of the horizon.

"Thanks for coming home to me," Raya whispered back.

THIRTY-ONE

A lice had turned off her phone on the train ride back after the interview in order to shut out the world. Once the funeral was done though, it was like a bubble had burst and Alice remembered that a life was there to live.

Her phone had died, so she plugged it in to charge while she checked her email. In her inbox was a message from Scott, the Senior Partner from Blue Wave Consulting. Her potential new boss.

Alice,

I've left a couple of messages. I hope you're still interested in the job. Maybe you're just playing hard to get?!

Anyway, call me as soon as you see this. Let the negotiation begin.

Scott

Alice had almost forgotten about the interview. It had only been a few days since she met with Scott and the team, but it was as if a lifetime had passed. She had been so excited about the role, but she felt like a different person now, which left her confused.

She decided to at least call Scott. She didn't even know what they had decided.

"Alice Miller, as I live and breathe, I thought you

were ghosting me there for a second," Scott said confidently when he answered the phone.

"Hi Scott, sorry about that. There was a death in the community that needed my attention."

"Oh well, I'm assuming I have your attention now?"

Alice was a little put off by the way Scott brushed aside her news, but also knew that it was normal in the consulting world to brush most things aside in favor of business.

"You do."

"Excellent. Well, I have tremendous news. We would like to offer the position of Partner, overseeing the solar energy division, which we'll be creating just for you."

"Wow, that is great news." Alice waited for the rush of happiness and excitement, but the feelings didn't come.

"I'll send over the written offer right after this. It's everything we talked about already, so you shouldn't be surprised or need anything."

One thing Alice had decided over the last few days was that she wanted to spend more time here in town. Ideally still have a few morning walks and coffees with her friends. She had mentioned it briefly in the interview, but knew now was the time to show Scott that this was important to her.

"There is one more thing Scott, I would like to work from home as often as possible."

"Work from home? That's quite impossible. We really like to promote an environment of teamwork and collaboration and it's a little hard if we're not in person, right?"

"Well, in some ways, yes, but I also think allowing people more flexibility would actually promote innovation and collaboration. Doesn't this role require quite a bit of travel? I would be out of office for those trips, so wouldn't it make sense that I could work from home too?"

"It's not to say that you can never work from home. Maybe in a year or two, once you've gotten this new division fully established, then we can potentially revisit this conversation. It's going to take a lot of hours to get this division up and running and fully profitable. You'll be on the road a good three weeks of the month the first year at least, so that last week we'll need to see you in the office. We're taking a big chance on you, Alice, but we're positive you're worth it."

Alice's heart sank when she heard this, despite the compliments.

"Can I tell the team you're a yes?" Scott asked.

This was everything that Alice wanted, all the sacrifices she made and the extra hours worked. It was all for this. A partnership in a leading consulting firm. She should be an immediate yes, but she couldn't make herself say it. Her heart was shouting *no*, but she couldn't get those words out either. Instead, she stalled. "You know I need to see the written offer before I say yes, Scott," she said in a voice that sounded more confident than she felt.

Alice immediately turned off her computer, fired off a text, and then did the same with her phone. She needed to think, and did not want to be interrupted by

Scott or the offer letter.

* * *

Alice was making her way to Happiness Café, but instead of taking her normal way along the beach, she instead made her way to the community center. The air had turned colder, hinting that Fall was in full swing. Alice was glad she grabbed a toque and mittens to keep her warm.

Alice walked through the doors of the community center, the atrium still full of all the flowers from Thomas' celebration of life. It looked like it was just any other day, people going about their business, but it was muted, and empty somehow. The smiles not quite reaching eyes, laughter only halfhearted, and even the children weren't as boisterous as normal.

Alice made her way to the couches she and Thomas sat on the last time she saw him. She chose the seat he was in, hoping that some of his wisdom lay in the cushions. She didn't know him for long, but during the time she did, she saw him as someone to advise and help and she ached for him now that she had such a massive decision to make.

A group of teenagers walked into the community center with their sports bags flung on their shoulders and basketballs under their arms. They were joking and teasing each other, but quieted down as they entered, almost in reverence to the grief the center was experiencing. They stopped at a table of octogenarians to say hello, surprising Alice yet again at the power of this place to bring people together.

She recalled that last talk she had with Thomas and his insistence that she got to choose who and what she belonged to. While she didn't completely believe that belonging was completely up to her, she could see now that she got a say in the matter.

Haven Cove was definitely a place she wanted to belong to. She'd gotten a taste of life here with the walks on the beach, the friendships and, well, everything and she didn't want to give it all up. In theory, she wouldn't have to if she took this job, but in reality, it would be like what Scott said. Long hours. Travelling three weeks a month. Commuting.

Even though she knew she used work as a distraction from her grief, Alice had believed White & Dunn was the only place she belonged because it was easier to tie herself to a company instead of people. She was certain that she wouldn't do that again, at least on purpose, but she was not naïve enough to think that her intent would be enough. It was easy-to-use work as a distraction because there was just so much of it, and it sounded like there would be even more at Blue Wave.

Which meant it was a choice that was up to her. Did she continue to make Haven Cove her home or did she make Blue Wave it?

Her head was telling her she had to take the job, that it was everything she worked for at White & Dunn, and it was being handed to her on a silver platter. Didn't she owe it to herself to not make those ten years a waste of time by at least trying it out? She'd be crazy to turn it down.

The message from her heart? Completely different.

She'd be crazy to take the job. The more she tried to picture herself doing the work, the more she saw she didn't actually want to do that type of work anymore. Yes, it would make a difference, but was it the difference she actually wanted to make? She couldn't get Claire's words, "you need to *feel* the impact", out of her mind. Her heart reminded her of the lack of time and energy she had for a life, that taking the job would mean barely seeing Raya, not being able to walk on the beach with Colin, and not being a part of this community.

It was exhausting being in her head with the dueling opinions fighting to make themselves heard, she needed to talk it out.

✳ ✳ ✳

"Here she is," Raya said with a wide grin as Alice walked through the door of Happiness Café, coming around the counter to give her a hug. "You go sit. I'll bring over your drink and some goodies."

Alice was thankful for the afternoon slump in here, as she sank into the plush leather chair by the fire, warming her bones on this cold day. The café was empty until the bell dinged over the door to announce the next customer.

"You came," she smiled.

"Of course, your wish is my command," Colin said jokingly as he bowed before he sat down on the couch across from her.

Raya brought over a tray of drinks and a variety of mouthwatering pastries that the three friends quickly devoured. Crumbs flew as they chatted and ate, laughing at each other's mess.

"So, Alice, you texted..." Raya prompted.

"Yes, I did, and thank you for showing up like this. I'm not used to reaching out for help, but I didn't even think twice, to be honest. I just texted knowing you would be here, but it still surprises me you both came, so thank you," Alice rambled, a little uncomfortable being in the limelight and needing their help.

"Yeah yeah yeah," Raya said. "Blah alone blah don't enjoy asking for help blah blah. Get on with it, woman!"

"I think what Raya is trying to say is that we're both so happy to hear that you immediately thought of us and invited us in instead of shutting us out. It means a lot to us. You're welcome, but also thank you for trusting us," Colin said more eloquently.

"Okay, show-off," Raya laughed. "I just want to know what's going on!"

Alice took a deep breath and gathered herself, not sure the emotion she wanted to convey with the news. "Well, I got the job."

Raya and Colin looked at each other.

"Yay?" Colin said questioningly.

"Shit," Raya said honestly.

Alice laughed, "that's exactly what I was thinking. I should be excited, but it feels more like 'shit', and now I have to decide."

Alice walked them through the good news of the

offer, that they're creating not just a role but an entire division just for her. That the money was mind-blowing amazing. That this was everything she worked for and more.

"That's my best friend," Raya announced to the empty café. "Super intelligent and amazing. Everyone is desperate to hire her."

"That's incredible Alice, congratulations." Colin reached across the table to squeeze her knee.

"Here's the bad news of the offer, no work from home, travel three weeks a month and super long hours," Alice said in a rush.

Raya and Colin both deflated like popped balloons. Raya leaned back in her chair, shock on her face. Colin hid his face in his hands.

Alice watched them quietly, her reaction to the bad news mirrored theirs.

Raya was the first to break the silence. "Okay, well, things are different now, right? You taking this job doesn't mean it'll go back to what it was like before, right? We'll still see each other. Besides, you barely know me. You can't make a decision about this thinking about us."

Colin added, "I'll miss our walks so much, but it could be like a movie where we have a moment. You pass on the train and we wave at each other?"

Raya rolled her eyes while Colin and Alice acted out waving to each other while pouting.

"I know I used to use work to avoid my grief and while I won't be perfect, I know I won't do that here."

"That's good, right?" Raya asked.

"Yeah, it's great," Alice paused.

"But," Colin prodded.

"But I don't think that will matter. There is so much work here, ten-to-twelve-hour days will be normal, working weekends too. Add in commuting, and it's right back to a life leaving before you wake up and arriving after you go to sleep. Never mind all the travel. I'll be handing over my life to them."

The three pictured going back to being practical strangers,

"Shit," Raya said again. "I know you worked so incredibly hard for this, and believe me, I'm no stranger to hard work. I rarely take days off and work ten-hour days, too. But I love this café. I get to stay connected with everybody. I can work in a place where Annie can relax and do her homework, and I'm never bored. I'm happy."

Raya grabbed one of Alice's hands. "I always dreamed of owning a place like this, and while it's been so much hard work, I haven't had to give up my life and it's been exactly what I want. You've dreamed of this for years..."

"I did," Alice interrupted. "It was everything I wanted. It was the reason I sacrificed so much. But I don't think I actually wanted it because of some noble purpose to do the work. I think I really only wanted it because it was something to want. Something to focus on so that I could ignore my grief and the loneliness of losing not just my parents but also my friends."

Alice picked up her coffee cup, cradling it in her

hands as she took a fortifying sip. "I don't want to do that anymore. I think it's time I actually grieved my parents, as scary as that sounds. Plus, I'm not lonely anymore. I have you two, and all these amazing people in Haven Cove who have accepted me with open arms. You get to do your dream job AND live your life. If I take this job, I won't get to do either."

"Don't take it then," Raya said decisively.

"I don't really want to take it, if I'm completely honest. It's just, these past ten years, how can I turn it down considering it is what I thought I wanted? Wouldn't that just mean I wasted an entire decade of my life on something I didn't even want?"

"Maybe," Colin supplied. "You could probably come up with some 'lessons learned' about that time to make yourself feel better, but maybe it was just wasted and that's okay."

"Don't hold back or anything, Colin," Raya said, defending Alice.

Colin nervously looked at Alice, checking her reaction. She looked thoughtfully at him and then nodded her permission to continue. "The way I see it? If you take this job just so you can feel better about the last ten years, then you're potentially wasting even more time. If this is not the road you want to be on, eventually you just have to get off of it, no matter how shitty it feels, to realize all that time was pointless. Wouldn't you rather face that crap now rather than in a couple of years?"

"That's some wise words there," Raya said with a smile. "You can tell you're a writer."

"You actually sound like Thomas and Claire, imparting some mic drop wisdom," Alice agreed.

Colin laughed, uncomfortable with the praise, "besides, this Scott guy told you that a bunch of other consulting firms wanted you too, they just couldn't reach out to you for some unknown legal reason. It sounds like you know exactly how you want your work/life to look like, but just need to figure out what actual work you want to do. You can always begin reaching out to them while you figure it out. If this is the work you want to do, I'm sure one of them will be more open to how you want to work."

"Genius!" shouted Raya.

Alice looked at Colin appreciatively, "wow, that is genius. Okay, decision is made. I'm turning down the offer."

"Okay," Raya said giddily. "Wait, now that you've made that declaration, how do you feel?"

"Like I wish we had some champagne to pop."

"Oh girl, you're in luck. I got some because I knew no matter what, we would be celebrating."

That's exactly what the three of them did. Popped the champagne and toasted to Alice's future and their friendship.

THIRTY-TWO

"You are my sunshine…" Alice had slipped into her recurring dream that no longer felt like a nightmare. Her mother coming to visit her in bed, stroking her hair while she sang to her.

"Am I making you proud, Mama?" Alice whispered to her mother.

"Always, my little girl," she whispered back.

"Am I making the right choice?"

"You're finally letting your heart guide you, my little ray of sunshine. It's going to take you home, to where you belong."

Alice rolled over, a soft smile on her face as she fell back to sleep.

✳ ✳ ✳

"Scott was *not* impressed," Alice said to Colin as they walked down the beach the following morning, Atticus up ahead, digging in the sand, looking for some sort of buried treasure.

Popping the champagne was exactly what Alice

needed to let the idea of a partnership go. Once their first glasses were poured, they immediately toasted Alice saying no to the job. Then they tearily toasted Thomas and jokingly toasted Raya for dating again. The café stayed open, which meant that customers still came in and an increasingly giggly Raya had to serve them. It was the sort of fun, spontaneous afternoon that reminded Alice of how much she now had to lose if she took a role like the one at Blue Wave Consulting. It gave her the courage to go home and call Scott to let him down.

Strolling down the beach, Alice sighed at how glorious it was. The sand shifting under their feet and the sun warming their skin from the cool air. With the weather turning colder, they now had to pile on more layers. Alice was struck by how adorable Colin looked with his navy wool hat that made his eyes somehow pop even more than normal.

"I bet. I'd be pretty pissed at losing out on you too," Colin said. His eyes widened as he realized what he had said. He fumbled trying to recover, "for the job, not for something else, you know because he talked about wanting you so badly. Again, for the job. Oh, you know what I mean."

Alice's cheeks warmed, and she hoped her pink hat didn't make her blushing even more noticeable than normal. "In his defense, calling him after we finished that bottle of champagne probably wasn't the smartest move. At first, he tried to say he could get me more money. When I told him it had nothing to do with the money and everything to do with the work/life balance, he grew really confused."

Alice continued, sarcasm dripping from her voice, "then he got really generous and said that I'd could travel two weeks a month–maybe. And after a year, they could explore the potential of letting me work from home a day or two *a month*."

"Sounds like you dodged a bullet." Atticus ran up to Colin and dropped a slobbery stick at his feet.

Alice bent to pick it up and then tossed it to the retriever. "Especially when I turned that down and Scott became nasty, accusing me of using their offer to leverage a better one. For not being dedicated enough and for being inconsiderate. Did I not understand how far he stuck out his neck for me, and how he was going to be a laughingstock?"

"What a piece of work," Colin said as he took his turn tossing the stick.

"By the end, he was almost pleading with me. I actually felt bad for the guy."

"You're a nicer person than me. I certainly don't feel bad for him. After you hung up, did you have any regret?"

"Not at all. I felt light and hopeful. In fact, I had this dream," Alice paused, unsure if she wanted to continue. She'd never told anyone about the dream before, worried that they would think it was weird that she kept having this recurring dream about her mother.

Colin looked at her, understanding crossed his face and he patiently continued to walk, giving Alice the space to decide what to do. Atticus had abandoned the stick and was now chasing seagulls up ahead.

She studied Colin, the way he strolled beside her

with his hands buried in his pockets. The brown hair peeking out from his hat was shimmering in the sunlight, his jaw cut sharply in juxtaposition to his soft lips. Quietly supporting her, always supporting her.

"It's a recurring dream," Alice began. "Whenever I was sick, my mom would lie in bed with me singing the song, 'You Are My Sunshine.' Do you know that song?"

Colin nodded. "Sure. Everyone does. Great song."

"I know it's a kids song but I still love it. So, in the dream, I'm in bed and the sun is shining through the window, the room is ethereal with the way it glows. My mom is laying beside me singing while stroking my hair. Then she whispers, 'I'm here, my sweet girl, always and forever'."

Alice sighed as she remembered how this beautiful dream terrified her for so long. "I know it sounds so peaceful and tranquil, but it honestly felt like a nightmare for so many years. I would wake up in a state of panic right at that point, gasping for air and crying. It was like a gut punch, always bringing on the pain of the loss. I avoided thinking about my parents because it was simply too much for me to handle."

Alice paused in her story and in her walking. She turned towards the water and plopped down on the cold sand. She needed to feel the waves' grounding presence before she continued. Her heart raced, telling Colin about the dream was more nerve-wracking than she'd expected. Colin dropped right down beside her without a second hesitation. Atticus ran over, thinking it was a game, licking Alice's face while she laughed before climbing into her lap. This was quite a feat since Atticus was so big.

"Atticus!" Colin tried to pull the dog off her.

"Actually, leave him. It's really nice. He's helping." Alice buried her face in Atticus's fur to collect herself.

She then took a deep breath in and continued. "Recently, the dreams have gotten longer, and I stopped waking up in sobs. It's become a dream now where I wake up feeling safe and peaceful. It's been really nice."

"Especially last night. I asked her if I made the right choice, and my mother said…"Alice paused, fighting back tears. "She said I'm finally making choices with my heart and that it's good. That my heart will lead me home."

Alice's tears broke free, streaming down her face as she hugged Atticus. She glanced over at Colin, whose own eyes shined. "It may sound silly, but it's just so nice to see her, even if it's only in my dreams."

Colin embraced her, pulling her in tight. Atticus stretched to lie across both of their laps. Colin leaned his forehead against her head and softly whispered, "it doesn't sound silly. It sounds lovely."

They continued to sit on the damp sand as they watched the waves. Alice laid her head on Colin's shoulder, and he leaned over to kiss her forehead. Atticus panted happily as his two favorite people patted him.

"I think I'm going to see Dr. Anita. My grief terrifies me, it's why I've done everything in my power to avoid it but I think it's time to face it. It will not be easy, and I know I'll need her help to process it all."

"I think that's a great idea. You're so brave for facing all of this head-on."

"Brave? Yeah right. I've been a coward for ten years, burying myself in work to avoid it all."

"Which makes it harder to face it now, but you're doing it. That's brave, Alice."

"It's easier when I have people like you standing in my corner."

"You're an easy person to support."

Alice laughed at that. "Okay, that's not true, but thank you."

"Anytime. All the time. Always," Colin said.

THIRTY-THREE

"Well, I better get to work," Colin said, a hint of regret in his voice.

The two were standing in Raya's shop. Atticus tied up outside with a pile of dog biscuits to keep him happy. They had just gotten their coffees and were about to part ways for the day.

"It was a great walk today," Alice said.

Colin smiled, bumping his boot against hers, "I think most days are great walks."

Alice tilted her face down to hide her blush.

"Okay, well, same place tomorrow?"

"Wouldn't miss it."

"I think it's going to rain."

"That's okay, I've got rain gear. We've been so lucky. I guess it's about time we had some crappy weather."

"I've also got a massive golf umbrella that I can bring. It'll fit both of us under it, no problem."

Alice grew silent and got lost daydreaming about walking close together, feeling Colin's arm brushing hers. She snapped to attention, embarrassed, to see Colin looking around the room shyly, their eyes met before she quickly looked down at her boots.

It was time to part, but neither of them was ready to say goodbye for the day.

Colin's cell phone ringing interrupted them. "Shoot, I'm late. One second. Hey Matt? I'm almost home. I'll call you back in fifteen." He looked at Alice regretfully. "Okay, I really have to go."

"Have a great day at work," Alice said, with forced cheerfulness.

"You have a great day too," he paused, looking at Alice before shaking his head. "Right then, okay, bye."

Alice watched him walk to the door and flushed as she caught herself appreciating how his jeans worked like magic on him, as if they were designed solely to make his butt look irresistibly perfect. As the bell rang above him, Colin turned around raising his hand in a wave, "bye Alice."

"Bye Colin."

Through the window, she continued to watch as he untied Atticus and then, with one more glance in and a wave; he left.

She turned towards Raya, who was standing there, mouth agape. "What?" she asked her friend.

Raya patted the stools at the coffee bar. "You sit there so we can talk."

Alice watched as Raya bustled around the café during the morning rush until finally the last customer left, signaling a slight break before the mid-morning rush happened.

"When are you going to tell him?" Raya demanded.

"Tell him what." Alice knew exactly which *him* Raya

was alluding to.

"That you love him."

"Okay, well, love is a strong word. I barely know him."

"Bull, you know him plenty. And it's obvious the two of you are absolutely crazy about each other. You're all awkward teenager, googly eyed and blushing messes."

When she was honest with herself, Alice knew she just might be in love with him, though it terrified her to think too much about it. The thing was, he was constantly on her mind. When she cooked, she wondered if he would like it. When she laughed at a show, she wished he was laughing beside her. She loved his laugh. At night, she fell asleep to the memory of his lips on hers. The walk down to the beach every morning was torturous anticipation and when she saw him standing there or striding towards her, her racing heart calmed.

"See, you're thinking about him right now, aren't you? You have this loved up look in your eyes and your face is beet red."

"Okay, okay. I do like him. A lot," Alice gave in, and then dropping her voice down to just barely above a breath, "maybe even love him."

"I knew it," Raya said in excitement, slapping a tea towel against the bar. "Tell him!"

"It's not that easy, first my life is still a mess. And I've already put an end to any potential with us. I've probably scared him off me."

"Trust me, you haven't."

"The thing is, Stephanie did a number on him, deciding to go back to the city instead of starting a life here with him. What if while I'm figuring things out, I realize I want a job in the city? You didn't see how he reacted when I got that first interview. I don't want to hurt him."

"You're a better person than me. I would be all over that. Well, not him exactly, ew, no offence or anything, but any potential love match…"

"Speaking of, what's going on with Michael? Have you rescheduled the date?"

"Not yet. He's great, really nice and kind. Exactly the type of guy I'd want after experiencing life with my ex."

"I'm sensing a but here."

"He's moving really slow. I think he's confused. While I've been divorced for years now, he's pretty fresh. It's only been about a year. His wife left him for her personal trainer. They actually took off to California. She wants to become an actress."

"Whoa that's intense. Didn't they have kids?"

"Two, she left all three of them. He has two girls, five and seven, so you can imagine how overwhelming it must be. He wants to be there for them, but it means he's not as available for me right now."

"That sucks Raya. What are you going to do?"

"Wait. He's worth it, Alice, I can just tell. Besides, I'm not technically in any rush. Just my libido, but I guess I can work on that in-house if you catch what I mean," she winked at Alice suggestively.

Alice chuckled, "loud and clear. I guess we're both in

a waiting game for love right now."

"Hey girl, at least we've got each other right," Raya reached her arm across the bar to grasp Alice's hand in hers.

✳ ✳ ✳

"Welcome, come in out of this cold!" Kelsey said with open arms. It was book club night, a little delayed because of Thomas' sudden death. "Can you believe Halloween is a few days away? On the one hand, the fall is flying by and how is it this cold and it isn't even November?!"

Alice gave her coat over to the hostess and took in the giant foyer as Kelsey continued to talk while she hung up her coat. The house was in a newer section of Haven Cove, a small subdivision with humongous houses. Alice's whole main floor of her house could fit into this foyer with the large chandelier and the stairs curving to the upper floor. Alice followed Kelsey through to the great room, which lived up to its name. She could see the other members of the book club mingling in the kitchen and seating area.

Kelsey led Alice to the kitchen island, where a woman she didn't know was putting some appetizers on plates. "Alice, this is my best friend Rebecca, or Bex as I like to call her, who I made sure came up for the club. I'm trying to convince her to move here once she becomes a doctor. Tell her how amazing it is while I get the door."

Alice turned to Kelsey's friend. "You're in medical school?"

Rebecca was the opposite of Kelsey in every way. Kelsey was tall and lanky, her hair a shiny chestnut brown that fell in perfectly styled waves over her perfectly styled and trendy outfit. Rebecca was shorter and curvier, with wild blonde curls wearing a t-shirt with a typewriter on it overtop of plain jeans. Even their voices were different, Kelsey confident and flashy to Rebecca's gentle and quiet.

"Not that impressive, really. It's just a Ph.D. in English Literature, nothing too important," she said self-deprecatingly.

"Stop putting yourself down Bex. A Ph.D. means you're a doctor. It's still quite impressive," Kelsey said as she walked by them to grab a bottle of wine to fill up some glasses.

"It really is," Alice agreed. "I couldn't imagine all those extra years and work you must've put in. Are you almost done?"

"I defend my thesis in December."

"Wow, and then what?"

"I have no clue. Spencer, my fiancé, will finish his Post-Doctorate in Applied Physics around the same time." Alice found it weird that Rebecca seemed more confident talking about her partner than she did herself. "He'll start on the tenure track to being a professor, so where we end up will depend on where he gets a job."

"What will you do?"

"I'll probably just wait and see until after that. He

has more job prospects than me. There are only a few people in the country with advanced schooling in Applied Physics, whereas I'm more dime a dozen, plus the work he'll do will be more important."

Alice's heart was slowly breaking for Rebecca. She barely knew her, but had a feeling that the relationship she was in was horrible. Her confidence seemed to be so low and it hurt to see someone so accomplished putting themselves down. She wanted to give this woman a hug and tell her how amazing she was, but was interrupted by Dottie and Raya striding into the room, their hands clasped together above their head, shouting, "we're here, the party can start now!"

* * *

Book club was riotous, a much-needed relaxed night out after the stressful and emotional few weeks they've all had. Talk of the book only lasted thirty minutes before the women started telling their own stories. The group laughed hysterically at Dottie's latest breakup and how she met a fine gentleman at Thomas' funeral.

"You're shameless," Cat, the knitter said, this time in a wool sweater with a monkey on it. "It was a day of reverence, not a day to pick up men."

Dottie shushed her. "When you're my age and facing your own death, you'll find that funerals are actually the perfect place to meet new men, or women, whatever your preference is. There's nothing like a good funeral to leave one feeling like you should live each day like it's your last. And let me tell you, this fella really is a phenom in between the sheets."

The women guffawed, Rebecca spluttering on her wine in shock. A contemplative silence fell over the crowd, as none of them could stop themselves from thinking about Thomas.

"It seems empty without him," Cat said sorrowfully.

Raya's face fell. "How are they going to replace him? He's left such big shoes to fill!"

"Martin's really worried about that, actually," Mary spoke up. "As chair of the Recreation Committee, they're in charge of finding a replacement."

"Won't it go to Hana? She's been Thomas' right-hand woman for years now." Anita questioned.

"She doesn't want it," Raya answered, causing sounds of surprise to ripple through the room. "She came to the café the other day, and I shamelessly asked her."

Mary continued, "with two young kids and living a couple towns away, the role would be too much for her. Martin said that there's been some grumbling from the town council that has him worried."

"Worried about what?" Alice asked.

"Wouldn't say much more than that. All I know is this volunteer position has become a full-time job for him. He tosses and turns at night too."

The group sat in stunned silence. They all depend on that center. The news that it could change somehow terrified them. It seemed like the future of the community center was just like Alice's. Undecided.

THIRTY-FOUR

Alice was about to run out the door for her morning walk with Colin when her phone rang. Assuming it was Colin wondering where she was, Alice picked up without noticing the name on the screen.

"Hiya," she said. "I'm almost ready!"

"Alice Miller?" a voice asked.

Stupefied, Alice looked at the screen and noticed the name Helios. Her heart picked up. Helios Consulting was *the* leading solar consulting company in the country. They were mostly in the Southern States and had little presence in the Northeast. "Sorry, yes. This is Alice Miller."

"Alice, this is Amanda Levine. I'm the cofounder of Helios Consulting."

Amanda Levine was Alice's idol. A rockstar in the sustainable and renewable energy space who launched Helios a few years ago and was an immediate success story. She was featured on the covers of multiple magazines, and Perkins *hated* her.

"Amanda, hi. I'm Alice Miller." Alice paused as her cheeks flushed. "You know that. You're calling me. Unbelievably. How can I help you?"

Amanda chuckled, "believe it Alice. The word on the street is that White & Dunn were the idiots I always suspected they were and let you go. And then you turned down Blue Wave and their incredible offer because you wanted work/life balance. As soon as I heard that, I knew I had to talk to you."

Alice's eyes widened at hearing that she was important enough to warrant gossip, especially all the way in Atlanta.

Before Alice could say anything, Amanda jumped in. "Let me cut to the chase here, Alice. I want to launch a Northeast division. I had planned on finding someone in New York City, but after I heard that you're available, I want you. I'll match Blue Wave's offer plus 10%. You can work from home and while there will be travel and expectations, I'll let you set your own hours."

Alice dropped to her bed. Amanda was offering everything she could ever want, plus she would get the chance to work with Helios and be mentored by her idol. "Wow..." she trailed off, speechless.

"I know I have probably come out of left field here, so take a few days to think it through. I'll have my assistant send you over the package for your review and please reach out with any questions. We'll talk in a couple of days. How does that sound?"

"That sounds like a great plan. Thanks Amanda, I'm completely shocked over here."

Amanda chuckled again, "hopefully a good shocked. Have a nice day, Alice."

And as quickly as the conversation started, it ended.

In a daze, Alice finished getting ready and sent

off a text to Colin saying she was running late. As she walked down the street and saw him and Atticus standing there waiting for her, Alice made a snap decision not to say anything yet. This checked all of her boxes. It was even a dream come true. *But is it?* She couldn't help but think to herself.

She only felt confused and couldn't put her thoughts and feelings into words. Until she could, she didn't want to worry Colin by even mentioning it.

❋ ❋ ❋

Colin and Alice walked into Happiness Café, Alice still feeling shell-shocked from the call that morning, before noticing the air sizzling with electricity, a stark contrast to its normal calm and peaceful morning vibes. The café was much busier than normal, with crowds of people talking anxiously.

Alice could feel her heart spike, *did someone else die?* There were no tears streaming down faces, just shock and dismay.

"They're going to close the community center," Raya blurted out once she saw them through the people.

Someone may as well have died.

Colin instantly said what Alice thought, "how?"

Mary spoke up, "last night they called an emergency town council meeting to discuss it. Those sleazy bastards blindsided Martin and the Recreation Committee. It was lucky that he was even home to get the call."

"They told us that unless we could find a replacement by the end of November that they'll have no choice but to close it down. December has too many events to run with no one overseeing it." Martin rubbed a weathered hand over his face. "I don't know what to do. We'll post the job, but one month isn't long."

The sounds of shock and alarm rippled through the crowd. The community center couldn't close. It was too vital to this community. What would become of Haven Cove without it?

"We're there every day," one mother said, "with dance, creative writing, swimming and volleyball. Where will all those extracurriculars go? Will the pool even stay open?"

"What about the library? We're there constantly getting more books. They can't close that down too, can they?" said another community member.

"I didn't even think about that," Raya said. "I assumed they would stay open, but you're right, who knows?"

The bell above the door jingled to signal a new arrival. Everyone paused and looked at the newcomer. The cacophony increased as they all noticed Thomas' assistant, Hana, walking through the door.

Mary immediately went over to the woman, giving her a hug. "How are you, dear?"

"I'm in disbelief, really. How can the community center close? What am I going to do? What are we all going to do?" Hana's voice trembled as she spoke.

"It's just heartless," Raya angrily said.

SARACURTO

"We're already grieving, Thomas," Hana held back a sob. "And now we have to grieve this, too. It's all too much for me to handle."

Mary put her hand on Hana's shoulder to comfort her. "You're phenomenal Hana, you're handling everything so well. Martin is always saying how wonderful you are."

"I am," Martin agreed. "The place would fall apart without you."

"Thomas built such a great team. We work really well together. He had a vision for the community center, a vision we all shared. I feel guilty, really," Hana dropped her head.

"Guilty," Raya demanded. "Why would *you* feel guilty?"

"Maybe if I was ready for the job, then maybe, just maybe, this wouldn't be happening. It's too big of a job for me though. I live too far and with Keith travelling so much and the girls still so young, I just can't. Besides, I don't think I could do half of the stuff Thomas did."

"Pish," Raya said. "You have nothing to feel guilty for."

People nodded around the room, making sounds of agreement. Alice watched as everyone crowded around Hana to lend their support, her heart contracting as she felt so proud to call these townspeople her friends. She wanted to show them she was one of them, that this was something worth making a stand for.

Alice took a deep breath in, found her own voice and spoke up, "it's not your fault, it's the town's fault. I understand the need for someone to take it over but to only give it a month? That's crazy. It takes months to find good people."

"Truthfully," Hana dropped her voice, causing everyone to lean in closer. "I think there's something fishy going on. Thomas had been saying a property developer had been sniffing around the last few years and that this property with the fields and everything would go for a pretty penny. The last two years, they've given us large budget cuts, but Thomas was able to secure some grants and funding to make up the difference. Obviously, someone on the council wants this place to close to make it really easy to then sell the land."

"Those bastards," Raya and Alice gasped at once.

"It's true," Martin stated. "Thomas and I have believed something was up ever since the last election. There is someone on this council that is throwing this town under the bus. I'm determined to figure out exactly who it is."

"What about Halloween? Is that still happening?" a parent asked, causing a look of alarm to pass amongst everyone.

Hana put up her hands to calm everyone down. "Don't worry, it is. The planning for that is completed way in advance, so we're all set for Friday."

"Thank goodness," Raya sighed. "This morning, I paid Cat to rush order a squid costume for Annie since she had a last-minute costume change."

Everyone chuckled half-heartedly, still too lost in their worry. Slowly, the townspeople left, many with a look of despair on their face while others attempted at hope. "They could find someone. Maybe a director from another community center will want to live here," she heard Dr. Anita declare on her way out.

The news left the three friends speechless, still trying to process it. Then Raya's face lit up. Obviously, a brilliant idea had come to her. "You!" was all she said as she pointed her finger at Alice.

Alice looked behind her, then back at her friend. "Me what?"

"You!" was all she said, just in a louder voice as she danced in place.

Alice looked at Colin, who shrugged, looking as confused as she felt.

"You should take over!" Raya finally blurted out. "I can't believe I didn't think of this before. You would be perfect, and it would be perfect for you."

"Um, no. Are you crazy?" Alice immediately rejected the idea. There was no way that would happen. She wasn't qualified. She did not know how you would even go about running a community center. If she would even want the job.

I would want it, she thought to herself, remembering that moment with Thomas, in the atrium, him describing why he loved the job so much, and her heart bursting with desire for it.

She quickly ignored that. *It was only a passing fancy,* she insisted to herself. A quick look at Colin surprised her. She expected he would be just as shocked, but no, his head was slowly nodding in agreement.

Alice knew she had to put a stop to this at once. "Okay, you two, that's enough. Yes, the job would be pretty cool. And if I'm being honest, I did daydream about having Thomas' job but I'm not qualified *at all*, I would be in way over my head. Plus, I got a phone call this morning about another job."

Raya went rigid. "Already?"

"Already. But it's nothing like Blue Wave. This is with my idol in sustainable energy and her consulting company. She wants me to launch a northeast division. I'll work remotely and get to set my own hours. It'll still be hard work, but I'll have time to be mentored by her and have more flexibility."

"Sounds perfect," Colin said.   Alice leaned back in her chair and sighed. "It is."

"Then why aren't you floating on cloud nine?" Raya asked.

"I know, right? I should be, but I don't know." Alice rubbed her face with her hands in frustration. "I'm so confused. I should be jumping for joy and an immediate yes, but I'm not and I don't know why."

"Maybe it's because you want the Executive Director job?" Raya said pointedly.

Alice rolled her eyes at her friend even when she felt a pang of longing in her chest for that role.

"Fine, I'll stop," grumbled Raya. "It just seemed like the perfect solution."

"I think you need to talk to Claire about this," Colin said, ever the sensible one of this group.

"I quit her course! She won't want to help me."

"Give her a chance, Al," he continued. "What's the worst that can happen?"

"She slams the door in my face? She tells me I'm a hopeless case?"

Alice watched as her two friends rolled their eyes at her this time.

"Fine. I'll go," Alice conceded and then, desperate to change the subject, asked, "fill me in on Halloween. I saw a flyer but have never been here for the treat or treating. What exactly goes on?"

"It's mind-blowing." Colin got the message and helped lighten the mood. "Haven Cove really goes all out for it. Right Raya?"

Raya sighed, realizing she had lost. "It's pizza night at the center before everyone goes off trick or treating. Honestly, as a parent, it's amazing to not have to worry about dinner and it's fun to go off in groups. The kids love it and the parents do too. Especially because it becomes like a Halloween parade. There's a route we follow through town, so you don't have to hang out at home all night. You just need to be there while everyone is in your area."

"And is everyone invited?" Alice asked. "Even non-parents?" Alice asked.

"The whole town," Colin answered. "It's really a lot of fun."

Raya got really excited. "Come. We can dress up together. Wilma and Betty? Romy and Michelle? Dionne and Cher? The options are endless!"

THIRTY-FIVE

Alice was ready to swallow her pride. Raya and Colin were right. She needed Claire's help. It meant a bit of embarrassment considering their last conversation, but Alice was sure it would be worth it. Okay, she hoped it would be worth it.

While Alice was hopeful, she was still nervous, which was why she was loitering in the Atrium of the community center. She was reading a Bulletin Board that announced many of the upcoming events, including the Halloween Pizza Party. Never mind all the events happening around Thanksgiving and during the holidays. There was even a Polar Plunge on News Year's Eve. Alice shivered just thinking about it.

She glanced over at the welcome desk to see the workers huddled and talking anxiously together. Alice grew more concerned about Mary's worry about the future of the community center. She was sure that they would find an Executive Director. After all, it sounded like the perfect job. There must be a line of people who would be happy to take the job.

"Alice!" Claire exclaimed, cutting in on Alice's thoughts. She turned to see the coach, who had an enormous smile on her face. "How are you? We've missed you in class. Tell me all the things!"

Alice had been waiting for Claire outside of the classroom and was pleasantly surprised at how happy Claire was to see her. The two of them walked into the classroom and sat down at a table, Alice telling Claire all about the ups and downs she'd experienced in the last couple of weeks except for the Helios job.

"Can we just pause here?" Claire broke in, stopping Alice before she told her why she had come. "I want to take a moment to celebrate the shit out of you, pardon my French. You leveraged a night out into an interview. You had an organization not only to create a role for you but an entire new team. They offered you everything you wanted except for the thing that mattered most. And you *turned it down*! The Alice of a few months ago would *not* have done that. You've grown so much. I'm so happy for you."

"I guess when you put it like that, I sound pretty impressive." Alice shook her head in awe. "You're right. I almost can't believe I turned it down. I don't regret it. Especially since my hero reached out asking me to launch a Northeast division of her consulting company, giving me all the freedom and flexibility that Blue Wave would not offer."

"Wow, that's amazing. Are you going to take it?"

"That's the thing. I don't know. I should be thrilled at this, but I'm not." Alice shrugged. "I'm so confused."

"It's okay to be confused, Alice. Let's break it down. I'm going to ask you a question and I want you to tell me the first thought that pops into your head. Okay?"

Alice readied herself, straightening in her chair. "Okay."

"Why are you confused?"

Alice opened her mouth and let the first words come up, "because I don't want the job." A whoosh feeling swept through her. Stunned, she closed her eyes to process this. Claire let her sit in the silence of the room, only the faint sounds of talking from other the other side of the door could be heard.

Immediately Alice's brain tried to talk her out of that statement, rationalizing all the reasons she should want that job. She opened her eyes and found Claire looking at her patiently. "I should want this job, but I don't."

"Why don't you want it?"

Alice thought through everything she had learned about herself over these past few months, starting with that first class on personality types. "Well, I'm realizing that I want to help *people* and not in some roundabout way that working in sustainable energy does. I want the work/life balance and flexibility but actually that matters less than the people aspect of it. I want to do something good, make the lives of people around me better and more enjoyable. And I want to see that I have."

"You want to feel your impact."

"Yes! I want to experience it right along with them." Alice looked out the small window in the door out into the Atrium. She thought back to that day when Colin found her spinning in place, imagining what it would be like to run the community center. To her conversation with Thomas, where her heart yearned for what he had done for this town.

Turning back to Claire, Alice considered telling her about Raya's idea. She knew it was silly and a long-shot but maybe she needed to give it a chance. And she wanted to see what Claire, the career expert, had to say.

"Raya had this crazy, wild idea. It's out there. Pretty impossible, but..." Alice paused, her nerves intensifying. She didn't know what she was more terrified of, Claire thinking it was silly or thinking it was possible? "It's a long shot, really. I probably shouldn't even be thinking about it."

Alice knew she was rambling, but she struggled to get the words to leave her mouth. With a deep breath, she finally said what was on her mind, "okay, here goes nothing. She thinks I should apply for Thomas' job. The job would be amazing, but it would be crazy to apply. I'm not qualified at all and they'll want someone who can jump into the job, actually it seems like that's mandatory since they have said they'll close this place done if they can't find someone by the end of November. Which is a month. I'd never get the job."

"But you want the job?" Claire asked softly.

"Maybe? Yes? I don't know. I think I love the idea of the job but do I really want the day to day of it all? And does it even matter if I want it?"

"It does matter Alice. It matters the most."

"But can I even do the job?"

"That's something you would have to answer for yourself."

"Claire, please just let me know if I'm crazy. Do you think I could do the job?"

"Honestly? I do. The job is complex. It's more than

walking around and making people happy. It's project management, event planning, leading people and then all the administrative and financial pieces. Thomas had to wear many hats since he didn't have a big team. With your work ethic, smarts and your experience, I think you would actually be perfect for it."

Alice let out a breath she didn't realize she had been holding.

"I think you need to decide if this is what you really want to do."

"How do I do that, though?"

"An exercise that has you doing some time-travelling. A future self exercise. Actually, two future self exercises. First, I want you to picture yourself taking that original dream job with your idol. You're a year into the role. Picture your days and ask yourself what do they look like? Walk through a typical day. What is happening in your life? Let's take this to the people, since we know that they're integral to you feeling fulfilled. Who are you interacting with? How are you making their lives easier, different, better? Or what kind of impact are they witnessing you make in the world? Once you're fully there, I want you to ask yourself, what are you thinking, feeling and doing?"

"Then I want you to take a day and do it with the Executive Director job. Ask yourself all the same questions. Then I want you to reflect on what felt the most fulfilling. Typically, a rush of love and gratitude washes over you when you have found it."

"What if neither has me feeling that way?"

"Then we'll still have an answer. That we need to

keep looking."

"And if the future self exercise leads me to one of those two jobs?"

"We get to work landing it."

THIRTY-SIX

Halloween night seemed to come on fast, and for once, Alice was ready for it. Raya took her a couple towns over to buy costumes for themselves, but Raya was dismayed when all the couple costumes were sold out. After picking through what was left, warmth ultimately won out with the pair of them buying adult onesies–Alice a deer and Raya a unicorn. Raya then helped Alice stock up on enough candy to feed the entire state, never mind the town, and get some much-needed decorations for Alice's house.

Alice spent the day decorating. A family of Jack-o'-lanterns, that she carved with Raya and Anya, lined the staircase with fake cobwebs covering the railings. She transformed her door with a set of outdoor stickers of gravestones, bats and the silhouettes of witches flying on their broomsticks.

Standing on her front lawn, Alice admired her work. *Much better than last year*, she thought to herself. With a quick glance at her watch, she realized she wouldn't have time to do the future self exercise for the Executive Director role. In all honesty, she had been putting it off as she was terrified of what would come of it.

Completing it for Helios had been easier. And it was all fine. In it, she was content with the work and her life, but she didn't get that feeling of love and gratitude. She did not know what that meant, though.

Oh well, she said to herself. *Maybe tomorrow.* It was time to get ready.

*   *   *

Perfecting her deer make-up took longer than Alice expected, and she was running late. As quick as she could, she made sure that the bowls of candy were well stocked and close to the door, along with a table she would set up at the bottom of her porch stairs to make sure she could set up really quick before she got inundated with throngs of children.

As she rushed to the community center Alice spotted Cat and her partner, decked out in their elaborate knitted costumes, a purple dragon hood for Carla and a red mushroom hood for Cat.

"Those are...wow. I'm speechless actually, they're outstanding," she said, at a loss for words at the creations.

Cat immediately blushed, while Carla threw her arm around Cat's shoulders proudly. "She's really so talented, isn't she? Next year you'll have to commission her, get something a little better quality than your deer onesie."

"You look great, Alice. She doesn't mean it." Cat said, blushing.

"It's fine, it's fine! I haven't had to think about Halloween for ten years so I kind of forgot about wearing costumes. Next year I'll make sure to be more prepared. Speaking of last-minute costume requests, were you able to come up with something for sweet Anya's weird giant squid request?"

Cat looked pleased with herself. "I did, and not to toot my horn or anything, I'm pretty impressed with it. I don't want to ruin the surprise, so I won't say anymore."

They walked up to the community center front door and opened it to find the atrium filled to the brim with families, the delicious smell of pizza wafting towards them. Alice's stomach grumbled in hunger, so she grabbed some pizza and a bottle of water before even attempting to find her friends.

A giant red oddly shaped hat with two eyes on top and tentacles framing the sides of an adorable little face with a bright smile walked up to her. "Alice!! Or should I call you Bambi?"

"Anya! You look amazing, exactly like a giant squid!"

"I know Ms. Cat is just the very best knitter in the world. She made this for me, and it's perfect. Exactly what I wanted."

"You're one lucky girl, aren't you? Did you already eat?"

"We're over there. I saw you and ran over to get you. Come with me." Anya grabbed Alice's free hand and pulled her towards a table with Raya, the unicorn, and the back of a large bunny rabbit.

"I've got her! Bambi Alice is here. Now can I go see

Abby? She just walked in the door." Without waiting for a yes, the very enthusiastic little girl took off in search of her best friend.

"No fair," a sparkly Raya immediately said as she cleaned off Anya's place at the end of the table to make room for her friend. "You did your makeup all expertly, and I'm going to be shedding glitter until next year."

Alice sat down and noticed for the first time that the rabbit was, in fact, Colin. She burst out laughing and pointed at him. "What are you wearing?"

"Hey, a bunny rabbit can be manly," Colin said in a deeper voice than normal before he himself cracked up. "Well, I loved the idea of the warm onesie, and when I saw the rabbit and remembered you were a deer, I thought Bambi and Thumper. You know, two best friends."

Alice's heart swelled, but then quickly sank. Friends. Alice didn't know much about her future, but she knew that her feelings for Colin still hadn't went away. She had hoped that he would wait patiently while she got her life together, but knew that was too much to ask and obviously he had moved straight to being just friends. She didn't know what to say and was terrified of her voice breaking and giving her away. Luckily, she was saved by Raya, who slapped Colin from across the table.

"Hey, you can't be her best friend. *I'm* her best friend."

As they dove into their pizza, Alice looked around the packed room. She had expected a lot of families but was surprised to see so many others in attendance, too. "Everyone is here," Alice voiced her observation.

"It's a major event here, actually all our events are well attended by the entire community," Colin said.

"Except you, for two years, the bane of our engagement stats," Raya joked.

"No, but seriously, the families you expect, but there's also the people without kids, the retirees, singles. It's like everyone."

"I know you're still getting used to how it works here in Haven Cove, but that's just the sort of community we are. It's what makes us so special," Raya said.

"And why it's going to be so hard on all of us if they shut down the center," Colin said quietly.

They all sat in silence while they continued to watch the crowds. Alice hadn't told her friends that she was even thinking about the Executive Director role. She didn't want to get their hopes up. Eventually, Alice noticed a group of individuals garnering more attention than the rest. "Who are those people with the mayor?"

"That's the town council. You weren't here for the last election, were you?" Raya asked rhetorically. "We vote again next year, and I can't wait to vote out Stuart McNiven, that weaselly looking man over there. He acts like a weasel, too. I bet he's the one Hana was talking about the other day."

Alice looked over to see an overly tanned gentleman with dyed blonde hair and teeth that seemed too big for his face. "I've never seen him either."

"Get this, he doesn't even live here anymore! He moved a couple towns over, one of the more *affluent* ones. The worst is that he was so sneaky too, he did it right after the election. But he kept his house here so he can claim he's still a resident."

"He sounds gross."

A squeak of feedback interrupted their diatribe as Hana stepped up on the bottom stairs of the stairwell with a microphone in her hands. "Sorry about that!" She paused, looking around the room with a proud smile on her face. "Oh my, Haven Cove, you've outdone yourselves this year. It makes me so happy to see you all here, together as a community, to celebrate this fun night. Now I'll hand it over to Mayor Cummings, and he'll officially kick off Halloween!"

The mayor, all dressed up in a tuxedo, resembled the man from Monopoly. Alice couldn't help but wonder if that was intentional or not. He accepted the microphone from Hana. "Hello Haven Cove, are you excited for Halloween?!"

The noise of the children screaming YES was deafening.

"I'll take that as a resounding yes, then! Okay, before I let you loose, a quick reminder of the rules. As a town, we travel street to street. Dear Hana, here will use the handy megaphone to remind the next street, allowing you more than enough time to get back to your house."

Alice could see Hana, now with a little kitty, obviously one of her kids in her arms, hold up the megaphone for all to see.

"Thomas came up with this concept years ago, before my time as your mayor. A way for parents to be with their children while also getting to hand out candy. A way for us as a community to celebrate this spooktacular occasion together. Thomas was a great man and a dedicated leader in this community, one we were so blessed to have had. So tonight kids, make sure you eat a candy for our dear Thomas, he would've loved that." Mayor Cummings winked at the parents at that.

Colin whispered in Alice's ear, "every year Thomas would kick off the event with two requests: have fun and for the kids to eat an extra treat just for him." A shiver shot down Alice's spine, but she didn't know if it was from the words Colin said or the tickling of his breath on her ear and neck.

"With that, I hereby proclaim the beginning of trick and treating! Have fun Haven Cove!"

The crowd, like a tidal wave, slowly moved in tandem towards the front doors. "Has anyone seen Anya?" Raya asked.

"She's coming," Colin said, pointing to a knob of red wool snaking its way amongst the crowd moving in the opposite direction.

"Are you coming Mama? Let's go! Can we walk with Abby and her family? Please please please," she begged.

"Alice, are you going to help Colin hand out candy or come with us?" Colin had to leave as his street was the second to be visited, Alice's the fourth.

"She doesn't have an option. She's helping me and I'm helping her. Otherwise, we might not make it out alive," Colin said as he wrapped his arm around Alice's shoulders, pulling her in close enough that his scent of pine and salt overwhelmed her.

Raya raised her eyebrows at the two of them. "You

two have fun. We're one of the very last streets, so find us after Alice's."

As the two strode towards Colin's street, Alice's head swiveled around as she tried her best to take it all in, the groups of parents behind their skipping children, and the colorful houses all decked out for the occasion. She watched as one house handed out paper cups to the parents.

"What's that?" she asked Colin.

"The cups? That's a little treat for the adults. Each street has one. It's alcoholic, though if you serve alcohol, you must serve a non-alcohol version, or some sort of food. You'll love it."

A look of concern must've flitted over her face as Alice wondered if she'd missed an important memo because Colin reassured her, "don't worry Al, it wouldn't be your turn to serve the adults."

She sighed in relief. "That would've just been too much. My first Halloween and I screwed up already. Wait, are you telling me we'*ll* get treats tonight too?"

"Oh yeah, I know the Pearlmans on my street are doing their famous clam chowder," Colin said, rubbing his hands together in anticipation.

Though Alice had just eaten a few slices of pizza, her stomach, embarrassingly, grumbled at the thought.

Colin must've heard as he agreed, "me too. Oh look, they're actually all ready to serve. Let's grab one before we set up."

Once they were ready, the two of them sat on the porch of Colin's navy house with their cups of soup. Alice admired Colin's lawn with its sunken ship themed display. "This must've taken you all day," Alice remarked with awe.

One side of his lawn had a small dinghy rowed by a pirate skeleton and a treasure box in the back while the other side had a slew of skeleton bones and gold coins lying around. Some skeletons were crawling towards the dinghy, and some had hands reaching out.

"Where did you even get all this stuff?"

"I borrowed the dinghy from the Pearlmans. He's a fisherman, hence the clam chowder being the best you'll ever eat. Honestly, as a street, we share all our decorations so we can change up our themes every year. It's a lot of fun."

Alice shook her head, continually surprised at the way this community worked together. She took her first bite of the chowder and groaned appreciatively, "wow you weren't kidding. This really is the best chowder I've ever eaten."

"It's a perfect way to stay warm, isn't it?"

They watched as the rest of the street got themselves ready. Alice admired all the unique displays. There was an elaborate graveyard, a giant spider and spiderweb, and a house with a lawn full of the twinkling faces of countless jack-o'-lanterns.

Suddenly, Colin jumped up. "Be right back," he said as he took off down the street. Alice noticed a couple of others join him to help an older couple that Alice hadn't met yet, who had just entered the street. She watched as the group helped them set up a table and some chairs.

A few kids turned the corner, and she watched Colin

raced back over. His smile wide and eager, he put his hand to help Alice up. "Are you ready for your first Haven Cove Halloween, Miss Alice Miller?"

She didn't really need his help. She could easily stand up on her own. But as she looked into his crinkly eyes, Alice's heart exploded. *I love this man,* Alice couldn't help but think. Putting her hand in his, her smile was just as big. "You bet I am Colin Delaney."

The next hour flew by in a flash. The previous talk of hordes and throngs of children was, in fact, an understatement. Alice thrust treats into the bags, pumpkin pails and pillowcases belonging to the elaborately costumed children. It was so busy that they were barely even able to notice what the children were wearing.

As they said goodbye to the last family, they quickly cleaned up, him making sure he helped his elderly neighbors again, before they dashed to her house. The set up was quick, but they still were done just in time, and it was another whirlwind of smiles and laughter. A few kids excitedly said that they were happy she was out, while some others were disappointed that her house wasn't in fact haunted as they remembered the dark house from the past few years.

Alice felt a brief pang of regret. She couldn't believe she had missed out on this remarkable event, but even that couldn't dampen the pure joy from finally being a part of it.

❋ ❋ ❋

"This is the best one," Raya said as she took a sip of her grown up hot chocolate.

"You've said that every single time," Alice pointed out, elbowing her friend playfully.

Alice and Colin had finally joined the others, and she was having the time of her life. Getting to see all the little superheroes, witches and princesses run from house to house, occasionally coming back to show off their treasures, with chocolaty smiles from all the taste testing.

Warmth spread through Alice as gulped her hot chocolate laced with Baileys. "Mmm, that is good though," she said appreciatively.

"I don't know," Colin chimed in. "The Rodkeys' mulled apple cider with whiskey was pretty delicious."

"Oh yeah," Raya and Alice agreed.

The number of drinks and food that the adults got to sample blew Alice's mind. They've had chili, mulled wine, beef stew, pulled pork with mini cornbread muffins and so much more. Haven Cove really went all out.

"Honestly though," Alice groaned. "I don't know if I can eat anymore, and I don't want to wake up with a hangover tomorrow. I might need to pass on the next few."

"Amateur," Colin teased.

Raya looked at Alice, affronted. "Nope, not happening. You are joining me in sampling every thing because friends don't let friends miss out on delicious treats."

As they walked on, Alice listened while Raya and Colin reminisced about the adult treats of years past while she took in the sights around her.

Mary and Martin, in their matching costumes that looked antique, Dr. Anita and her doctor husband, dressed a little on the nose, as physicians. Kelsey looking gorgeous, like usual, as Malibu Barbie.

She was surprised to even see Jared, the supposed town flirt, dressed as Spiderman, joking around with the kids as he put gigantic bags of chips in their already overflowing containers.

Haven Cove was truly a special place. It was like happenchance all those months ago when her realtor called her up about the house here, but now? This was where she was meant to live. She had ignored it while she mistakenly believed that White & Dunn was her home, but it patiently waited for her to be ready and, as soon as she was, it welcomed her with open arms.

Thinking of Amanda and Helios, she knew she should be jumping at the chance, but something was holding her back despite it being her dream job. But was it her dream job? The Alice of six months ago? No brainer. Even the Alice before Thomas had passed away would've jumped at this chance.

But now? Thomas' death had forced her to face the grief of losing her parents. She had taken her heart and had forced it into a tiny box, far away from anything that really mattered to her and these past few weeks the box was burst open and destroyed. She didn't feel called to do the work she once did. At all.

That's why the future self exercise she did of working for Helios left her feeling just fine. She simply didn't feel like that was where she belonged anymore.

In fact, she couldn't help but think that the community center and Thomas' job might be where she belonged. People said cliché things like "the heart of a town" all the time, but in Haven Cove, the community center truly was the heart. Watching the crowd move down the street as one for this event put on by the community center hammered that home. Alice couldn't help but picture Thomas moving around the groups of people, but slowly the picture of him faded and was replaced with her. Her sitting in the office coordinating all the employees, instructors, and facility rentals. Standing in boardrooms as she sought grants and presented budgets to the city. Planning, with the team, all the events of the year. And finally, her smile wide as she talked to parents, children, and all the men and women of this town.

Alice stopped in the street. She watched as Anya, Abby and Nolan sang an off-key version of "Under the Sea" at the top of their lungs. Raya and Colin approached Dottie, who was in front of her house showing off her latest beau, while handing out homemade cookies. Alice's eyes smarted as she saw Thomas' husband sharing hugs and doling out high-fives.

Suddenly, she was picturing Thomas in the community center moving around the atrium talking to groups of people but it faded and was instead replaced with her. Her sitting in the office coordinating all the employees, instructors, and facility rentals. Her standing in boardrooms as she sought out grants, and presented budgets to the city. Her planning, with the team, all the events of the year. And finally, her smile wide as she talked to parents, children, and all the men and women of this town.

Then that vision shifted to the community center with a big CLOSED sign on it. It being demolished and replaced with a large condominium, forever changing this wonderful little town.

Alice couldn't let that happen.

A wave of love and gratitude hit her. Her heart expanding, an electric current of confidence and resolve, a settling in her stomach that the Executive Director job was it. It had everything she wanted. The leadership. The wearing of many hats. The greater purpose. And most importantly, the people.

She wondered what it would be like to talk to her parents about this role and instead of wanting to push down the stark feeling of loss that this line of thought normally brought up; she wanted to explore it. She could picture them clapping their hands together in excitement. Her father saying in his calm melodic voice, "that sounds exactly right for you, my girl." Her mother pulling her in for a hug and whispering, "I knew your heart would lead you to where you belong."

Losing her parents had left her feeling completely untethered, like not only did she not belong to anyone but also like she didn't belong anywhere. But Thomas was right all those months ago, no one could make her feel like she belonged. It was her choice to make. And she chose the community center and Haven Cove.

Alice knew she wasn't ready to share this secret, she had to think it through but as she rushed to catch up to her two favorite people surrounded by the most wonderful of townsfolk, her heart swelled with love for this magical place, and for the first time in more than a decade Alice felt like she was home.

THIRTY-SEVEN

Alice woke up tired and groggy after Halloween but she knew she had to talk to Amanda this morning. She sent a text to Colin to say she was going to miss the walk this morning but that she really wanted to talk to him at the café.

It was difficult to let Amanda and the Helios job go, especially as she was incredibly supportive and even excited when Alice told her about her ideal career change.

The one thing that getting laid off had shown her was that some things happened for a reason, and she had a feeling everything that had happened to her these last few months led her to this very realization.

Standing at the door of Happiness Café, Alice watched as Raya walked over to Colin with three mugs of coffee. She couldn't wait to tell them, but her heart beat heavily in her chest, more from nerves than the run over here.

"There you are, sleep in?" Raya asked as Alice stepped through the door.

"Nope, I was up at the crack of dawn. Had to make a call."

"Oh?" Colin asked, his eyebrows shooting up.

"I had to call Amanda from Helios this morning. That's why I'm late."

"To take the job?" Raya asked.

She watched as they arranged their faces into looks of encouragement and happiness, but she could tell that it wasn't the job that they wanted her to take.

"No, to turn it down. Last night I realized I don't want to do that anymore. I want to work here, in Haven Cove. Also that I want to try to get Thomas' job. I'm going to save the community center."

"Yeah, you are!" Colin whooped as he jumped across the couch and swept her into a hug.

"I told you!" Raya had jumped up and was dancing in place. She shouted to all the patrons of the café, "I want it to be known that I gave her the idea!"

The café laughed as they burst into applause and cheers.

Mary and Martin called them over to their table, making room for the larger crowd. "Martin, do you think I'll be good at it?" Alice held her breath. If anyone knew what it would take to fill Thomas' shoes, it was him.

"I think you'll be sensational, truly, Alice. Thomas even said so himself. A few days before he passed, he visited me to tell me he was sick and that he may not have long, though he had hoped for months, not just days," Martin paused, shaking his head at the memory. "But alas, he went sooner than he thought. He came to me to talk about his replacement. He knew it would be you."

Alice could feel the pinpricks of tears threatening to

spill. "You never said," she breathed. Raya squeezed her shoulder as she took her seat at the table.

"No, he didn't want me to. He wanted you to come to it yourself, and he trusted you would. So much so that I trusted you would too. And now that you finally have, we've got a lot of work to do. We'll call Claire and Hana today, see if they can come by the office, and we'll come up with a game plan. With my knowledge of the council, Hana's of the center, Claire's expert career knowledge, and the three of you, we'll come up with a plan that'll knock their socks off."

* * *

The next few weeks were an absolute whirlwind. Claire was a godsend, helping Alice put together her application package, including a resume that made Alice even more confident. She knew she had the transferable skills, but it wasn't until she saw it on paper that she truly believed it to be true. Not only could she do each line of the job posting, but she had plenty of examples to back it up.

Martin was true to his word, and he managed Alice's application process like it was a complex project, for which she was forever grateful for. He set up meetings with each of the four town councilors, though slimy Stuart McNiven did not accept their request.

Alice had never really done any networking before, so Claire walked her through exactly how. Plus, they strategized on who she should talk to before the interview stage, including a brilliant idea of talking with some Executive Directors of other small town community centers.

During the day she was growing more certain that the job was potentially within reach, but it was when the sun went down that the doubts creeped in. She woke up many nights during the darkest hour with her mind racing at all the reasons she was being ridiculous for thinking this role was for her.

After a rough night, Alice was ready to remove herself from the competition, but then Thomas' husband, Patrick, showed up. He tearily called it a "passing on the torch" conversation as he handed over a binder of information that Thomas had prepared for her.

"He wanted to make sure you had what you needed to be successful in the role," he said, watching Alice thumb through the thick binder. She was shocked at all the details. It included the seasonal events, the day-to-day operations and even a breakdown of the most frequent customers.

"This is incredible. Thank you so much." When Alice finally looked up from the manual, she saw Patrick was holding out a letter for her to take. On the front was her name in Thomas' neat writing.

"He also wanted you to read this. Before you do, as I trust you'll want to read it in solitude, I just wanted you to know that Thomas thought highly of you my dear." Patrick gulped before continuing, "getting the diagnosis was devastating. Especially when they didn't give him much more than a few months. I urged him to stop working..."

Alice reached her hand across the table to hold the

grieving man's hand. "He was too committed, wasn't he?"

"Til his dying breath. For the past few years, Thomas had grown concerned about who could take over his role. It was a constant stress as we approached retirement age. The question of his replacement would've made getting such a horrible diagnosis even more heartbreaking. He had just met you though, and he knew almost immediately that he could let go because you would be there to take his place."

Alice had tears running down her face as she shook her head. "I can never take his place. He was so incredible. His shoes will be impossible to fill."

"I'll let you read that letter, my dear. I trust it will help you see that you're the one. That you may not fill his shoes but that you'll forge your own way in your own shoes."

Alice walked him to the door, Patrick turning to envelop her into a hug. "We're all in your corner, Alice."

THIRTY-EIGHT

My Dear Alice,

If you're reading this letter, then you've decided to apply for my position at the Community Center. I am so happy for both you and Haven Cove, as you two are a match made in heaven.

Now I must apologize for not preparing you as I had hoped to prepare you. I really wish we had more time together, as I'm certain this realization would've come to you. I saw the future of the community center in you the very first time we met officially. It was cemented one day when you and I were sitting in the atrium together. You may not remember, but I remember so clearly the flickering of how this position was the one you had been looking for your whole life.

You are fiercely independent, a trait much needed for this role, but one that also had me treading carefully about bringing this up. I knew you had to come to it on your own terms. So please forgive me if that was the wrong decision since I'm not able to be there to mentor you. You'll be thrown to the wolves, but you have survived the lion's den before, so I know you'll survive those individuals who want to close the community center.

You remind me so much of myself. Your intelligence, your warmth, your dynamism, and your optimism. You are so hopeful to find a place to belong to, and I want to welcome you with open arms to our community as we've been waiting to belong to you.

With Love,

Thomas

Alice read the already very tear-stained letter to Raya and Colin, having to make many stops as they all had to dab their eyes with tissues.

"He knew," Raya whispered.

"All those months ago too," Alice replied. "He's right. I do kind of wish he'd just told me then. It would've saved me months of turmoil, plus it would've given me the time to learn from him."

"It makes sense though, what he was saying, you needing to come to it yourself," Colin added.

Alice remembered what she was like when she was freshly laid off. While she was open to exploring, she definitely wasn't open to suggestions. "I'm just glad he wrote this letter. It means so much to me. His vote of confidence has boosted my resolve to get this job."

"How have your networking meetings been going?" Raya asked, "I'm guessing amazing, because Stuart McNiven came in yesterday with his wife, and I'm surprised I survived the daggers he sent my way."

"They've gone really well. Two of the councilors are really excited about me. They really didn't want to close the center, but the way Stuart had gone on, they felt it was a foregone conclusion. They're hopeful I can convince Stuart and Henry Wilkins."

"Henry? I never would have thought," Colin mused.

"According to Mary and Martin, Henry is a little old school and is not sure about a woman running the place."

Raya sat back in her chair, obviously trying to think of something before her face lightened with an idea. "He's had a thing for Dottie for years. We need to get her to convince him otherwise!"

"We are *not* pimping Dottie out for this," Alice demanded.

"Fine, fine. I'll maybe just mention a little something and let her come to her own conclusions," Raya conceded.

"Above board. Don't forget, I'll have to actually be the ED if I get the job. I don't want Henry to feel he was manipulated. It'll make my life that much harder."

Alice could feel the flutter of nerves pick up speed as she thought about the process. "Besides, I haven't heard anything yet. I may not even get an interview."

"You'll get an interview," Colin said confidently. "I'm sure of it."

"We'll I'm glad at least one of us is," Alice muttered.

✳ ✳ ✳

The call came later that afternoon, in fact. Alice was at home, nervously cleaning the already immaculate house when her phone rang, the caller ID showing, "Town of Haven Cove".

"Alice Miller," Alice said professionally as she picked

up.

It was the Town Manager's assistant, Elinor, who was also a member of the book club. "Alice, it's me. This is so exciting! Okay, I have a script I'm supposed to follow." Elinor's tone switched from friendly to serious as she went on, "I'm calling you to set up an interview for the Executive Director of Haven Cove Community Center position. It will be a full day interview. It'll start with a 1:1 with the town manager, Brian Haverman, followed by a town hall style meeting with the staff of the community center, and will conclude with you presenting your three-year vision for the community center and panel style interview with the Town Council, Town Manager and the Recreation Committee Chair, Martin Schmidt."

"That's sounds excellent. Was there a particular day they had in mind?"

"Next Thursday, starting at 10:00am and to conclude by around 5:00pm. Does that work for you?"

"It does."

"Great." Elinor switched back to her friendly tone. "Let me tell you, we got tons of applications, but they're only conducting this one interview. I honestly don't know if that's a good thing or not. Brian is finding the council to be a tough read, though he's pulling for you just like the whole town is!"

Their expectations weighed heavily on Alice. It was a lot to have the future of the community center squarely resting on her, though if she got this position, she had a feeling this was how she would feel every day.

"Thanks Elinor, for everything. I have to admit, I

was getting nervous that I didn't get the interview. Now I'm nervous about the interview itself."

"We're all rooting for you, including the staff of the center. It's just half of the council and the mayor that you'll have to convince. You got this, Alice!"

* * *

Alice certainly did not feel like she had it, which was why she immediately reached out to Claire for extra help on preparing for the day of interviews.

"It's a lot of pressure and it's making me really nervous," Alice confided to the Career Coach.

"You can do things nervously. We already practiced how to handle rambling. You feel good about that?"

"I just stop the ramble, crack a joke about it and bring it back to answering the question. That worked well in my last interview."

"Exactly, my bigger concern with your nerves is the constant ups and downs of your adrenaline firing, so we'll want to make sure you have easy to digest foods to sustain you through the long day of interviews. Perhaps have some bananas, a smoothie and some nuts to munch on between and then bring some juice into the interviews."

"I'm worried about going from interview to interview."

"Here's the thing. You'll feel like you're repeating yourself. More than likely, you aren't, so don't not tell a story because you think they've already heard it.

Instead, if you wanted to make sure you could always ask, 'not sure if I said this story already,' or 'stop me if I've told you this one,' with some humor in your tone."

"That's good." Alice was quickly jotting down the tips.

"I also think you'll want a little reset in between each, even if it's in the bathroom stall, maybe some breathing or a quick meditation. Ideally, you can get outside for a few breaths of fresh air, though. The email said there were fifteen to twenty minutes in between each step so you may even do a quick 5-minute walk, which would be perfect."

"I'm not super worried about Brian or the staff, not that they'll be easy, but I'm confident that I can handle them. I think the staff are just happy that someone is getting interviewed and I've heard that most of them are thrilled that I'm being considered. Hana did also say that she's advocating for me with the staff before then."

"I agree. I think you've got those two interviews in the bag."

"It's the presentation and panel interview that scares me, it's definitely where I can blow it. Not all of them want me to do well. Plus they want a three-year plan? I have no clue on what I would say there."

"Okay, let's break this down. For the panel interview, I really don't want you to only focus on Stuart and Henry."

"What? I was thinking all my focus should go there?"

"I know, that's what you would think, but here's the thing. If you spend all your time trying to convince them, you'll get more nervous, you'll focus purely on their objections, and you'll feel like a used car salesman. Which means not only will you probably not convince them, but you'll also lose the trust and backing of the others."

This advice reminded her of a meeting she and Perkins ran with a potential client. He stood up there trying to convince the few who did not want to hire them, and they just sat there with their arms crossed. She had noticed too that during his part of the presentation that they lost their allies that were in the room. Until she had stepped in and focused on showing all of them the benefits instead of speaking to the objections. They won that client, and she remembered that their biggest objector had told her after the meeting that it was her part of the presentation that saved the pitch.

"I need to show them how the center and the community benefit from having someone like me. Not try to convince them not to close the center or convince them I could fill Thomas' shoes."

"Yes! You go in there and show them your shoes. You know why you're made for this role, and you know how valuable you would be for the center."

"I do," Alice said confidently, before slouching back in her chair. "But what about the three-year plan?"

"Here's my take on it. You can't really present a complete three-year plan, and honestly, you shouldn't. There will be a need for you to take some time to transition into the role before coming up with something like that, even if you came from another community center! I'm sure you have some ideas, though. Your meetings with those other Executive Directors were really helpful, right?"

Alice nodded. "They were so supportive and encouraging. Actually, come to think of it, one of them emailed their five-year plan. He said it would probably come in handy during the interview process and obviously once I got started."

"Well, there you go, but here's the thing: if you present a three-year plan that's detailed and specific, it may tie you to that plan. I was thinking maybe we approach this a little differently, maybe not a three-year plan for the community center but a three-year plan for you."

"Okay, tell me more."

"It's your development plan essentially and we link it to center activities, growth and funding. It's more about you with some sprinkling in of the center plan. I don't know, it just seems more you than the coming up with a plan you don't even know will completely work."

Alice pictured standing in front of these people who knew way more about the ins and outs of the Haven Cove Community Center, heck she didn't even know what happens there in the winter and summer, never mind years from now. It would feel disingenuous to stand up there presenting something she wasn't one hundred percent confident in.

"It would be genuine. It's something I've already been thinking about, more for me and my stress about taking on an opportunity of this magnitude, besides it would show them my openness to input and learning. Also, how serious I am about my commitment to the success of the center."

Claire added, "and bonus, you could address some of those objections, but in a way that feels authentic and not salesy."

Alice could feel the surge of ideas hitting her brain as she leaned forward in her chair to get them all down before they flitted away. She knew this was perfect for her and was now excited to show the rest of the town, too.

* * *

"It's 6:00pm, she should be done by now," Raya said nervously, wringing her hands from her seat in the Atrium of the Haven Cove Community Center. She looked up at Colin, who was too agitated to sit.

He stopped mid-pace, turning to the group of women. "It must be a good sign, right?"

"I sure hope so," Mary chimed in.

Dottie patted Raya's knee reassuringly. "If it was horrible, it would've ended quicker."

The double doors to one of the larger rooms opened. A broadly grinning Martin let an equally happy Alice out. "Thank you, Alice, for coming in and regaling us with your story and presentation. We will discuss and get back to you shortly." With a wink at Mary, he made his way back into the room.

The small group rushed to Alice's side, frantically asking questions.

"Whoa, Whoa, one at a time. Actually, can we go to the Happiness Café? I need a coffee and a pastry the size of my head."

The others sat on the edges of their seat trying to wait patiently while Alice took her first sip and ate half of the croissant.

She brushed the crumbs off her lap and leaned back with her coffee in her hands, and with a gigantic sigh said, "it went amazing. The meeting with Brian was really more of a conversation, him and Martin are the two I actually work the closest with and he even told me he could see us working really well together and that I had his vote."

"Phew," Raya sighed.

Alice was so pleased at how welcoming the employees of the center were to her. They were smiling and laughing, and really hopeful that she would get the position. "The town hall was more like a party," she giggled. "They had treated it more like a reception than an interview. They had drinks, non-alcoholic since it was the workday, and snacks and we just chatted."

"We knew that interview would go amazing," Mary said. "You were all anyone could talk about at the center this week! How did the council like you? More importantly, the Mayor, Stuart and Henry."

Dottie interjected, "Henry shouldn't have been a problem. I had a little talking with him the other day."

"Dottie! How did you know?" Alice asked, then looked at Raya accusingly. "Raya, I thought we agreed?"

"Pish, leave Raya out of it. I've known Henry for years and know what he's like. I spoke to him because I wanted to."

"Well, the panel was good, actually. Though Stuart

stewed the entire time, pun intended." Alice leaned against the back of the couch, the exhaustion of the day beginning to catch up to her. "The interview part went well. I could answer all their questions, not perfectly, but I hope good enough. Most of them loved the presentation, actually. Claire was right on the money with the approach. Martin said that they were nervous I would come to the table with a highly detailed three-year plan. He said it would show them I was a little too overconfident."

Colin squeezed her tight to his side and Alice lost herself to the feel of his arm on her shoulder. "You worked so hard, I'm so proud of you, no matter what comes of this."

"Why were you in there forever?" Raya asked.

"They wanted to read me something," Alice paused, gulping back some tears, "I wasn't the only person Thomas wrote to his last few days."

The others gasped.

"I know, I couldn't believe it," she replied, her expression showing her shock. "The things he said about me in those letters," she could feel some tears break free as she shook her head and bit her lips to control her emotions, "they were just so kind and well, he saw something in me and now I really want to live up to it you know?"

"Stuart must've loved that," Raya clapped her hands, gloating.

"All of us got teary in there, Stuart included, actually."

The group sat there together as they pictured

a scenario where heartless Stuart McNiven actually showed his heart.

"Nah, I don't believe you," Mary broke the reverie.

Their laughing was interrupted by the tinkle of the bell above the door. Alice's eyes widened when she saw Brian Haverman, Dean Cummings, and Martin walk through the door.

"Ah," the mayor exclaimed, "we were hoping you would be here! May we join you?"

The confused group made room for the newcomers. "Now I know we said we would get back to you next week," Martin started, "but a decision has been made and we thought, why wait?"

Brian continued, "I debriefed the employees about the town hall and it was actually unanimous that we should hire you. Let me tell you, they're a hard bunch to get to all agree!"

"Now I wish I could say the panel was unanimous, but alas, it wasn't," Dean said.

Alice's heart leapt into her throat. Colin and Raya moved in beside her, both grabbing her hands. She looked at the two of them and gave their hands a squeeze while taking a deep breath in. No matter what she heard, she had them by her side. She could get through this.

"For the hiring of you, Alice Miller, for the Executive Director role for the Haven Cove Community Center which also extends to the keeping open of the community center, the votes were: one nay and six yays," Dean said thrusting his hand over the coffee table. "Welcome to the team!"

The group cheered, tears streaming down their faces. Raya and Colin sandwiched Alice between the two of them as she shook her head and laughed.

"I'll leave you all to celebrate. I'll call you on Monday Alice to officially offer you the job and to negotiate salary and all that jazz. We just didn't want you to wait." They watched as the mayor strode through the door with Brian at his side. Martin stayed back and hugged his wife in relief.

"This calls for champagne," shouted Raya as she hurried over to the fridge, pulling out two bottles of expensive bubbly. "Alice, do the honors."

Alice grabbed one bottle and popped it open to cheers, and began filling up mugs. Once everyone had a drink, she cleared her throat. She had something she wanted to say.

"I've been alone since the day my parents died. Their death rattled me to the core, and I did everything I could to ignore it. I cut everyone out and I threw myself into work. I missed this though," she said, her voice cracking as she gestured around to the small group. "People to support and help you. Like Martin, Mary and Dottie."

"People to push you. Like Raya, pushing yourself into my life and then pushing me to go for what I really wanted." She reached her hand to Raya, who squeezed it, tears sparkling in their eyes.

"People to be there for you and take care of you." She looked at Colin, wanting to say more, but afraid she would say too much. She knew she was ready to confess her love for him but wanted to do it just the two of them, on their beach with the sun rising at their backs.

"People and a place that you can call home. Haven Cove saved me from a life that I would've regretted and now I get to show my gratitude by taking over the Community Center. Thank you so much for all your help. I truly couldn't have done it without you."

They all raised their glasses, clinking them in cheers. "To Alice and Haven Cove."

THIRTY-NINE

S tanding on the beach the next morning, Alice watched the glimmer of dawn change the dark blue sky to purple. She was here early despite being tired as she struggled to sleep last night in anticipation of telling Colin how she really felt about him. The celebrations had wrapped up early the night before; she had been exhausted from her long day of interviews and wanted to go to bed. But sleep eluded her as she relentlessly practiced what she wanted to say this morning.

The nerves were overwhelming her, and she knew she simply had to get out of the house. Which was why she was at the beach in the dark, waiting for the man she loved. Who may not love her back.

She had considered not telling him at all, but she knew her Halloween night realization was something that she couldn't keep hidden from him. He liked her once and while she had screwed it all up; she was hoping there were still some lingering feelings underneath his friendliness.

A bark woke her from her reverie, and Atticus was suddenly there in front of her, begging for a pat.

"Well, good morning, Ms. Executive Director. How does it feel to be the one saving our community center?" Colin said to her as he released Atticus from his leash.

Alice looked at him and sighed. The darkness couldn't hide how gorgeous he was. His blue eyes trained on her and a flash of concern shot through them.

"Hey," he said, his voice dropping to a whisper as he gently touched her arm. "Is everything okay? Are you regretting it already? We can figure this out if you are."

"No, it's not that. I don't regret it." Alice followed Atticus down the beach. This was much harder than she had expected.

Alice looked to the train track, just as her old morning train appeared on the tracks, and for the first time in a long time, Alice truly knew that she would never join their ranks again. A realization that made her giddy with excitement. And gave her the courage to tell Colin her truth.

"I used to watch you," she gestured to the train, "I know I've kind of mentioned it, but every morning I would look for you and Atticus. Watching you walk down the beach. My full body yearning to be right here with you. Not just on the beach, but with *you*. Then I met you, and you took my breath away."

Colin went to say something, but Alice held up her hand to stop him. "I need to get all of this out. My heart races just thinking about you. I get goosebumps whenever I see you. You're the person who is on my mind an embarrassing amount of time. Kissing you was magic, being held by you ignited a fire in me while also making feel so safe. I feel like I'm home whenever I'm with you. And I know I screwed everything up by pushing you away, and I may be too late, but I needed you to know that I love you, Colin Delaney. I love you with every fiber of my being. Atticus too, I love him so much."

Alice had tears running down her face as she watched Colin, a shocked look on his face. And then he smiled, and her heart burst open. "I used to watch you too, Alice Miller. I would see you walking around town like a baby foal getting her legs, cute as can be. That first day you showed up here on the beach, you took *my* breath away. I was so awkward and did not know what to say to the dazzling and way smarter than me woman. I see you and it's like the lights come on. You're the sun lighting my life. And you didn't ruin it, I did."

He took a step towards her, an orange glow popping out of the horizon behind him, awakening the sky. "I love you. We love you. I've known it for ages, but I was waiting for you. You said you wanted to get your life together. I didn't care how messy your life was, but I knew it was important to you. I know you belong with me and I belong with you."

He stroked her cheek, Alice matching the move, feeling his rough cheek under the pad of her thumb as he touched his forehead to hers, looking deep into her eyes, before biting her lower lip. "I love you," she whispered as she pushed her lips to his, bringing her hands around his neck. The kiss was hungry, the two trying to make up for lost time.

As they kissed, the sun fully rose over the water, shining its warm light on the two of them entangled in each other. Atticus came over to investigate but quickly grew bored with his barks being ignored, so he took off to the water, figuring he would take advantage of his distracted owner.

Walking hand in hand with Colin down the beach, laughing as they predicted Raya's reaction, Alice felt that love and gratitude wash over her again. Just a few months ago, she was miserable. She was in a job she didn't really like, though she wouldn't admit it to herself. She wouldn't admit anything to herself really, so afraid of feeling anything good or bad because she was too terrified to let her grief in.

Losing her parents so suddenly sent shockwaves she hid from for years. It made her feel untethered. Like she had nowhere or no one to call hers. She pretended to herself that she belonged at White & Dunn, because it was the easy thing to do. She didn't have to feel anything but stressed there.

Alice had assumed that getting laid off was the worst thing to happen to her career. Now though? She had friends who stood in her corner. Had this new career to look forward to, one that was so right for her. She had Colin, who she loved but also who she trusted to open her heart to. Most importantly, though, she had Haven Cove. A place to call home.

EPILOGUE

"**W**hat the hell were we thinking?" Raya said through chattering teeth, rubbing her exposed arms.

"I honestly blame you and your list," Alice responded as she jumped from foot to foot, trying to stay warm.

"My list? It's called Alice's List of Adventures, not Raya's. In fact, I should blame you and your list," Raya teased.

"You know it isn't mandatory that you do this, right?" Colin grabbed Alice and brought her back into his chest to warm her up.

It was New Year's Eve, which meant it was time for Haven Cove's annual Polar Plunge. Another one of Thomas' incredible initiatives that Alice had gotten to plan since she started in her new role as Executive Director.

It had now been six weeks since she started and she had already overseen one of the busiest seasons with Christmas and the Holidays. It seemed as if they hosted events daily, which meant that she was really thrown right into the deep end of the pool.

Though she wouldn't have had it any other way. Her team was amazing. Hana was a gift sent from above who seemed to anticipate all of Alice's millions of questions. The training binder that Thomas created for her made it easy to just follow his plan.

That first day she felt weird trying to settle into his, well, her, office. She still had changed nothing, though she had plans to do so in the New Year. Thomas had died so suddenly that his stuff had all been there, so one teary afternoon she, Hana and Patrick, Thomas' husband, went through it all together. As Hana was going through the desk, she discovered an envelope with her name scrawled on it in Thomas' handwriting. Alice opened it and read shakily,

Dear Alice,

Congratulations! I knew you'd get the job. I'm so proud of you and am glad to know that the Community Center is in safe hands. As you may have noticed from the Training Manual I developed, that you have everything you need to run the Center for the next year. I encourage you to follow it, as it will make your life easier.

However, come next Fall, I want you to file the manual away. I want you to forge your own path here and I don't want you to feel that you have to preserve my memory by doing everything exactly the same way I did. This is your community center now.

Best Wishes,

Thomas

"How thoughtful of Thomas," Patrick said after he read it. "I agree. Make this your own."

"He's lucky you got this job," Hana laughed. "How awkward would it have been if someone else had gotten it and found that letter?"

Alice had taken his advice to heart, following his lead and his plan, but making notes on things she may want to do a little differently the next year. Though many of the big events she would want to keep the same. Like this Polar Plunge.

Most towns do the polar plunge on New Year's Day to start the year off. Thomas believed that plunging into the ocean in the dead of winter was a cleansing ritual, so he came up with the idea to host one on the last day of the year as he believed it more appropriate. The town obviously agreed, as they all seemed to turn up.

"I know I don't have to do this," Alice said, snuggling into Colin. "But it seems like the best way for me to end the year. Swim in the Ocean is the only box I haven't checked on my list yet." Since starting her job she had been able to check a few boxes. She had a party, well her definition of party, as she hosted the holiday book club, so she had checked that off.

In fact, she had even added to the list. Like going to the cemetery to visit her parent's graves. She was ashamed to admit it, but she had never gone back after their funeral. Her therapy sessions with Dr. Anita really helped her unpack her repressed grief. It hadn't been painless. Many times she wished she could stuff it all back down again, but it was easy to remember how much changed for her once she allowed herself to mourn their loss. In fact, Dr. Anita suggested the trip to their graves. Raya and Colin both offered to come and while she was tempted to take them up on the offer, she wanted that first time to be just her.

She drove the few hours with a small potted

Christmas Tree and sat on the cold, hard ground updating them on her life. It was therapeutic in a way that she never thought possible. Colin had since come with her so he could "meet the parents." She still dreamt of her mother and no longer dreaded it, but looked forward to the overwhelming sense of peace when she woke up from the dream.

"Stop being such a bunch of wusses," a voice rang out from behind them. They knew the owner of that voice and were not surprised to see Dottie being supported by her granddaughter, Poppy, who was chuckling alongside of her.

"Maybe we wouldn't be so cold if we were as hot as you, Dottie," Raya joked. Dottie was sporting an old-fashioned hot pink one piece under a fuzzy white robe and white swim cap with raised flowers on it. "That's not what you normally wear to Aquafit."

Dottie sashayed from side to side, letting them admire her outfit. "To Aquafit, I wear my pool swim outfit. This is my Polar Plunge outfit. Need to keep the boys on their toes," she said, winking at the group while doing a finger wave to a couple of older gentlemen who were there just to watch the event.

"Oh, there's Mary and Martin!" Alice exclaimed, calling the couple over. They were standing with two towering gentlemen, a nephew, Alice believed, and their son.

"It's a good turnout, isn't it?" Martin asked as he strode over. "Is the mayor starting the event?"

Alice looked at her watch. "He should be. It's supposed to start in a couple of minutes. I got him all set up before I got myself ready. Maybe I should check with him. We don't want anyone to come down with hypothermia."

"Nonsense, you stay here. I'll go," Mary volunteered. "I'm not plunging, anyway. You're all crazy!"

Alice smiled as she watched her walk off as Martin and Dottie argued over the best way to get in the water. She was so grateful to have these people in her life. Dottie knew how to lighten the mood and was an example of living the life you want to the fullest. Mary and Martin's generosity to not just her but also the community was never-ending. Mary was the Chair of the Holiday Events Committee, a volunteer position, and worked alongside the community center team tirelessly to ensure that the season was magical in every way. Martin was always available to talk through a problem and regularly stopped by the community center to check in with her.

If you had told Alice a year ago that three of the most important people in her life would be a retired couple and a horny elderly woman, she would have laughed, but she was so glad that they took her in.

"Haven Cove!" The voice of the Mayor, Dean Cummings, boomed over the megaphone. "Are you ready for the News Year's Eve Polar Plunge?!"

The crowd whooped and cheered.

"Okay, drop your robes."

Alice dropped hers while Colin and Raya did the same on either side of her.

"Ready..."

Alice grabbed Raya's hand on her left and Colin's on her right.

"Set..."

She turned to look at each of them. Raya's face filled with anticipation. Colin turned to face her with a smile. Atticus at his side, ready to go in with them.

"GO!"

The three friends dashed into the water, and immediately shouted, "cold, cold, cold." The water was like ice. Alice wanted to turn around but kept jogging in deeper. Her breath caught in her throat as her skin stung from the frigid water.

Raya quickly ducked in and then ripped her hand from Alice's grasp and rushed back to shore, dodging the people still making their way in. She yelled over her shoulder as she retreated, "I can't do anymore."

Atticus jumped around Alice and Colin's feet as they kept going deeper. "Oh my, oh my," Alice kept repeating as her skin developed goosebumps on top of goosebumps.

Jared darted ahead of them, diving under the water before coming up for air yelling "yes!" As he ran back to shore, he high-fived them and everyone he passed.

Colin squeezed her hand tighter. "You good?"

"Just a bit farther," she got out through her rattling teeth, "that okay?"

He answered by pulling her forward faster until they were past the crowd. They were up to their shoulders now and somehow her body had somewhat acclimatized. The water still stung, but she was no longer in full body shivers.

It was just the three of them. She turned to look at

him, the sun spotlighting his beautiful face glistening with droplets of water. He was hers. She was his. They belonged together. He closed the distance between the two of them, his thumb rubbing her cheek as he leaned in to kiss her. She could taste the saltiness of the ocean as she nibbled his bottom lip and embraced him.

"You ready?" he breathed into her mouth.

She nodded in response as the two of them, mouths locked, ducked under the water.

* * *

As soon as they were back on dry sand, all wrapped up in their robes, they made their way over to one of the bonfires to grab one of Raya's specialty hot chocolates to warm up.

Not a day went by that Alice didn't thank Raya for pushing her way into her life. Alice never had a friend who was so unwavering in her love and support. Who was there with the largest of smiles to celebrate any win, big or small, or with a shoulder to lean on when Alice was overwhelmed. Raya's zest for living life to the fullest was infectious, and she was constantly compelling Alice to do new things with her. Raya showed her that living the life she wanted, being the person she wanted to be and that finding a new family was her choice to make. She pulled her from waiting on the sidelines and thrusted her in to being in control of her own life.

Now she watched as Raya stood at another bonfire

with a dry Anya, Michael and his two children. For once, Raya was taking things slowly, giving Michael the space he needed. It was his first Christmas without the children, so he joined the friends in their small celebration. He calmed Alice's best friend in a way that actually made her shine even brighter and it warmed her heart that Raya was finding her own love story.

"I still can't believe that was your first-time swimming here," Colin said, shaking his head. They were sitting on a log warming up by the fire, their hands curled around their hot drinks, trying to absorb as much heat as possible. Atticus was dozing in the sand at their feet.

"It's embarrassing, actually. Was I even a resident of Haven Cove because I hadn't?" She rested her head on his shoulder, his arm enfolding her close to him.

"Better late than never," he said.

It was interesting starting a relationship and a job as demanding the Executive Director at the same time. She had never fought with anyone before and it took a while for her to realize that an argument wasn't the end of them.

"We're fighting for our future," Colin had told her one time when she had panicked that he was going to leave her. He had pulled her down into his lap and caressed her back to help calm her down. He stroked her hair as he said, "I'm not going anywhere. I want it all with you. Marriage, kids, old age. The good, the bad and the ugly. The kind of life where we fight, we love, and we take care of each other."

She wanted it all with him too and though she had struggled with letting him in completely, she was slowly learning that he wasn't going anywhere.

While she worked almost as many hours as she did at White & Dunn, she could still have a life. Every morning Colin, Atticus and she walked the beach before they headed to Raya's for a coffee. With Colin's schedule being flexible, he would bring her lunch or sometimes even bring his work to the Community Center.

The two were homebodies by nature, which had them alternating nights at each other's house. Some women at Book Club joked about how they went straight to an old married couple, but it was exactly what Alice craved. They were already talking about moving in together and were just figuring out whose house.

Colin and Alice, now fully dressed, helped the team of the community center clean up and put out the fires so they could restore the beach to its calm haven for the town. The two had decided to not attend any of the dinners or parties going on, instead wanted to get an early start on an actual vacation as tomorrow the two had an extra long weekend. Now that the busy season was done, Alice was about to have her weekends back and she was actually excited for them.

She loved weekends now. She had social plans with friends and the start of a new chosen family to see and spend time with. Weekends were now a reminder of how full her life was, how she had a home where she fully belonged.

Alice saw the train round the corner and happily sighed. If you had told her three months ago what her life would look like now, she knew that the old her would have struggled to believe it to be true. Now she raised her hand to wave goodbye. Not just to the train but also her old life.

"Ready?" Colin asked, putting his hand out to her, Atticus already back on his leash.

She grabbed his outstretched hand and squeezed. "Let's go home."

Alice's List of Adventures:

✓ Sign up for Course at the Community Center
✓ Kiss Someone
✓ Make my house look like a home
✓ Read a book a week
✓ Join a Bookclub
✓ Go for drinks
✓ Dance with someone at Harvest Dance
✓ Take an exercise class
✓ Have a party
✓ Swim in the ocean

✓ Get a real Christmas tree
✓ Go to a holiday party
✓ Visit cemetery

Loved This Book?

I would love it if you left a review on goodreads or amazon so that other readers can fall in love with Alice, Colin and Haven Cove.

Alice's story may have come to a close, but the adventures in Haven Cove are far from over.

First, I invite you to start receiving your own Love Notes from Haven Cove. A monthly newsletter to inspire your own story of reinvention plus updates on my upcoming novels, exclusive content and my monthly reading recommendations.

Take another trip with me to Haven Cove in the 2nd book of the series. We'll follow the journey of Becca (or Bex as Kelsey like to call her) as she navigates life, love and new beginnings in Haven Cove with her enemy and town heartthrob, Jared Walker.

To get updates and to receive the Love Note please sign up here: www.saracurto.ca/author.
Thank you for being part of this journey,
Sara Curto

ACKNOWLEDGEMENTS

Writing this book has been one of the best experiences of my life, getting to know Haven Cove and everyone living there is truly a gift.

But all of this couldn't have been done without the support and encouragement of many wonderful people.

First, to my husband Justin for encouraging me to take this seriously and sign up for a writing course and for putting up with all my book and series talk! Your patience, love and support mean everything to me. For my kids, Nolan and Abby (yes they made a cameo!) whose imaginations are wonderous and who inspire me to keep creating stories.

To my parents, Paul and Karen Reardon who have also believed me capable to do whatever I put my mind to. For my aunt Sheila Kay who imparted so much advice. Thank you for being my cheerleaders.

Thank you to my Enjoying Creative Writing class (taught by the incomparable Brian Henry), my Beta Readers and anyone who provided some insight and advice. Special thanks to Lisa Bailey and Robyn Soules for your detailed analysis of the book that really shaped it for the better.

A huge thank you to my friends who have been there for me throughout this process. Your encouragement and unwavering belief in me means the world to me.

I also want to thank all of my Career Coaching Clients – helping you prioritize your happiness in your career definitely inspired me to walk the walk and add the "author" hyphen to my name.

Lastly, to my readers—thank you for taking a chance on my story. I hope it resonates with you and brings you as much joy as it did for me to write. Love stories made me rethink my career, I hope that a spark of something ignited by reading this book.

I'll see you soon for the 2nd book in the Haven Cove series where we're exploring Jared's and Becca's love story.

ABOUT THE AUTHOR

Sara Curto

Sara Curto is a career coach who found her true passion through romance novels and now helps clients discover their dream jobs. Now, Sara has embraced her own dream of becoming a romance author.

Sara lives with her high-school sweetheart husband and two kids in Burlington, Ontario where she enjoys running, reading and spending time in the woods.

This is her debut novel. Connect with her on www.saracurto.ca/author or on instagram at @saracurtoauthor

Manufactured by Amazon.ca
Bolton, ON

40831224R00206